DARK ECSTASY

He lit oil lamps for the last and most important part of the ceremony. Their warm glowing smell would blend with the other sweet, heavy odors. The flames flickered, tiny red tongues of fire in the inky blackness. From his niche, the god Anubis gazed down benignly.

"Open your eternal gates, ye gods," he prayed. "And take my beloved. May her beauty shine and be reborn like the sun."

She was a perfect work of art. The best he'd done thus far. Simply gazing upon her gave him intense, erotic pleasure. His heart palpitated, his blood raced.

He touched her face, traced the lines of her cheekbones, leaned over to kiss her lips through the thick fabric. The taste was salty and satisfying. Oh, ecstasy!

Harper
Monogram

Pretty Birds of Passage

ROSLYNN GRIFFITH

HarperPaperbacks
A Division of HarperCollinsPublishers

HarperPaperbacks   *A Division of* HarperCollins*Publishers*
                    10 East 53rd Street, New York, N.Y. 10022

Cover illustration by Jim Griffin

First printing: September 1993

Printed in the United States of America

HarperPaperbacks, HarperMonogram, and colophon are
trademarks of HarperCollins*Publishers*

❖ 10 9 8 7 6 5 4 3 2 1

To our editor, Katie Tso, who
took a chance on something different.

And thanks to Edward Majeski
for his valuable research.

Come, pretty birds of passage.
Wing your way from beyond the lands
of the Great Green.
Come to my nets, lovely ones.
Lie as offerings on my altar of gold.
—Anonymous
Egypt, 1200 B.C.

AUTHORS' NOTES:

Birds of Passage was the name Egyptians gave to the sweetly scented birds who migrated through their land to the Mediterranean or Great Green. Regarded as culinary delights, the birds were caught in the Egyptians' fields with nets.

The poems in this book have been extrapolated from translations of ancient Egyptian writings.

Prologue

Candles flickered against the dark, windowless walls and picked up the sparkle of gold in the niches where he had placed his most priceless treasures—a lapis necklace, a bronze mirror, a small statue of a jackal-headed god. The rich aromas of incense, fresh flowers, and ripe fruit permeated the air. The place could very well be an ancient tomb.

At least he liked to think so. He could easily imagine other, more glorious days as he went about his own sacred task.

The girl seated beside him stirred. She adjusted her crown of delicate flowers, complaining, "Why's it have to be so terrible dark in here?"

He murmured soothingly, "To add to the ambience, dear." He was very careful about creating the correct atmosphere. Pouring more wine into the shallow chalice before her, he smiled benignly. "Now be a good girl and drink this."

She finished the contents of the cup as he wiped a dribble of red from his starched white cuff. They had already partaken liberally of roast goose, fruit, and fresh bread. The time was at hand.

Inspired, he recited some of his favorite lines from an ancient manuscript, "'The shrill of the wild bird unable to resist the temptation of my bait./ While I, in a tangle of love, unable to break free, must watch the bird carry away my nets . . .'"

She frowned. "Birds? What're you talkin' about?"

"I'm quoting poetry."

She shrugged, undoubtedly incapable of appreciating literature of any sort, he decided. No matter.

"I'm feelin' sleepy."

"Good. You shall be wanting to take a long nap soon." He'd laced the wine liberally with his special laudanum mixture.

"I'm to take a nap?"

Her large black eyes widened. Actually, her eyes were her loveliest feature, he decided. Her rather full face and pouting lips were pretty enough, but would likely coarsen with age.

How lucky she was that he would make sure that never happened.

He quoted more poetry, "'When they find me empty-handed, what shall I say?/ That I myself was caught in *your* net?'"

"I know what you're doing," she announced suddenly. And with a hiccup, she leaned unsteadily across the table, a strand of dark hair falling across her forehead along with a stray flower petal. "You're tryin' to get me drunk so's you can take advantage of me, ain't you?"

He laughed, amused, though he could understand her faulty logic. "Certainly not. I have already told you that you are much too good for that. In fact, you are blessed among women."

"Like the Virgin Mary?"

He laughed again. "More like Hathor . . . or a very great queen."

"Ha-ather-r?" Her voice slurred. "Never heard of anybody named that. You sure are an odd gentl'man."

Which he knew she would never have the fortitude to say in the usual servant-master situation. When her elbow wobbled, nearly sending her facedown on her plate, he realized the moment had come for him to take action.

"Let me help you, dear." He rose and half lifted her from the chair.

She leaned against him as he walked her toward the chaise and dais at the other end of the room. The warmth of her flesh crept through the thin tunic he had given her to wear in place of her frowsy dress and cheap petticoats. She moaned when he lowered her into a reclining position on the dais.

"There, there." He allowed himself one hasty caress, his hand gliding over her hair, her soft cheek, her breast. His heart leapt with excitement; the room burned with energy. "You shall soon feel much better, my beautiful little dove." There would be only two tiny pinpricks of pain.

"Do you really think I'm beautiful?"

"Indeed, extraordinarily lovely."

Tonight she would be mistress, he but a lowly worshipper.

"'I bow before you,'" he intoned, as he knelt beside the dais that served as her pedestal. "'You are a star coming over the skyline at new year.'" And he assured her, "I shall make certain your beauty is preserved forever."

1

The World's Columbian Exposition, Chicago, 1893

"*For the sentimentalist* again exclaims: 'Would you have woman step down from her pedestal in order to enter practical life?' Yes! A thousand times, yes!" cried Chicago's redoubtable Mrs. Potter Palmer, who was assuredly encouraged by the sight of so many eager female faces before her.

At least five thousand had crowded into the World's Columbian Exposition Woman's Building for the formal opening. And like most of her surrounding companions, Aurelia Kincaid applauded. When she glanced at her aunt Phaedra, who was seated next to her, the two women exchanged smiles.

And as soon as the clapping died down, Mrs. Palmer continued. "If we can really find, after a careful search, any women mounted upon pedestals, we should willingly ask them to step down in order that they may meet and help to uplift their sisters. Freedom and justice for all are infinitely more to be desired than pedestals for a few."

Again, Aurelia and Phaedra joined the crowd's applause.

Mrs. Palmer beamed, resplendent in a gold-shot dress trimmed with jet and ostrich feathers that contrasted becomingly with her pale hair. At forty-odd, she was an attractive if forceful woman and, in Aurelia's opinion, very enlightened for a society belle.

"Women have no desire to be helpless and dependent," Bertha Palmer continued. "Having the full use of their faculties, they rejoice in exercising them. . . ."

Sentiments with which Aurelia entirely agreed— women should not be judged solely on their relationship to men, to be labeled beauties, helpmates, spinsters, or harlots. Unfortunately, society was not as forward-thinking as Mrs. Palmer, her aunt Phaedra, or she herself.

When the ceremony ended, Aurelia and Phaedra made their way through the crowd and out of the newly constructed Woman's Building, a pastel paean to the charming jumble of archaic ornamentation and traditions that was called Beaux Arts style. Sculpted angels spread their wings atop the roof's pedestals, and caryatids supported architectural columns, though the ancient figures did not promise eternity.

Like most of the other sprawling structures erected on the fairgrounds near Lake Michigan, the Woman's Building was an iron-and-timber shed overlaid with staff, a lightweight mixture of plaster, cement, and jute fibers. After the exposition was over, all would disappear like a fleeting dream.

Though, by that time, Aurelia hoped she would find something equally fascinating to help her remain content on her return to the city of her childhood.

Phaedra interrupted Aurelia's musings. "What did you think of Mrs. Palmer's speech?"

Aurelia noticed that her aunt gazed at her closely, as if she wanted to ask another sort of question entirely, and she hurriedly expressed her opinion. "Very inspiring. Mrs. Palmer is an impressive president of the Board of Lady Managers. And the opening went well, considering the problems you wrote me about."

Phaedra laughed heartily, her sensual mouth curving beneath her sharp, witchy little nose. A woman who'd once been banned from its more conservative circles, she enjoyed juicy gossip involving Chicago's upper class and had passed it on via letters to Aurelia over the past two years.

"The Isabella Society was a particular thorn in Bertha Palmer's side," Phaedra said. "But if the Spanish queen had been given credit for discovering America instead of Christopher Columbus, the name of the exposition itself would have been different."

"Not to mention certain details of Isabella's history that have been conveniently forgotten. I believe she funded the Inquisition with as much enthusiasm as she did exploration."

Phaedra laughed again, attracting the attention of two passing gentlemen in sober suits and derbies. To strangers' eyes, forty-nine-year-old aunt and twenty-five-year-old niece appeared the same age. Phaedra's diminutive stature and girlish figure, as well as her animated personality made her seem far younger. Only up close did one notice the silver threads twining through her frizzy brown hair or the tiny lines around her bright hazel eyes.

The two women strolled along, passing the Horticulture Building and skirting the fair's lagoon where a mythological sculpture seemed to be pointing toward the wooded island in the center. Aurelia adjusted her straw boater and the high collar of her lacy blouse. The day was growing warmer.

"I fear the Isabella Society will have to make do with the queen's statue erected in the California Pavilion." Again, Phaedra peered closely at her niece, raising her eyes, since Aurelia was at least half a head taller. "But enough talk of silly disputes. I cannot help but note that something has been bothering you these last few days. You do not fool me. You are dissatisfied with your position at O'Rourke and O'Rourke, aren't you?"

Aurelia sighed. Her aunt had always been very insightful, even when she played caretaker.

"Is it the company's classical approach to architecture?" asked Phaedra. "Or is it that you have had to take a step backward?"

"A bit of both, I suppose."

Aurelia wouldn't confide her more personal reasons for sometimes feeling out of sorts. Not that Phaedra wouldn't be understanding—a staunch suffragette, her aunt had been somewhat notorious before inheriting sixteen-year-old Aurelia after Phaedra's brother died.

But Aurelia wasn't yet ready to talk about the disastrous mistake she'd made in Rome. Keeping the secret made it seem less shameful . . . and frightening.

"Don't worry, Aunt Phaedra," she told the older

woman. "I'm sure I shan't be doing architectural renderings forever."

A fully qualified architect, she had nevertheless expected to serve another apprenticeship, even though she had recently reached the design level in a progressive firm in Rome. The fact that she had *had* to leave her position in Italy, that there'd been the debacle with Rosario, was what really troubled her.

"I don't know why Sean didn't give you more responsibility," Phaedra groused, frowning.

"He thinks every architect he hires should start at the bottom." And Aurelia assumed Sean's absent partner, his son Liam, felt the same.

"I shall have to speak with Sean again."

"Please don't." Aurelia already felt uncomfortable about her aunt pulling strings to obtain the job in the first place. "I have only been there a few weeks and am lucky to have obtained an architectural position of any kind on such short notice." She added, "Especially since I'm female. I'm content to prove myself at O'Rourke's."

Phaedra shook her head in disgust. "One would think a woman would have an easier path to tread in these enlightened times. I have worked toward that goal for thirty years—"

"And without your example," Aurelia interrupted, "I would never have pursued and obtained such education and training. I am certainly in a different position than most women in our society." Because of Phaedra, Aurelia was not only free-thinking and single, but also self-supporting. "You are my inspiration."

Phaedra's face softened. "Oh, dear one." She paused to hug her niece. "You say such sweet things."

"But they are quite true."

"You have given meaning to my life, too," asserted Phaedra, who had had to change her ways immensely when she became guardian to a minor. "And your situation is indeed better than most of our gender." She drew away and glanced back toward the Woman's Building. "Though we have failed to gain the vote, the average woman's life has improved greatly, even since my younger years. I often tend to forget exactly how much."

"That's because you are always looking toward tomorrow."

Phaedra nodded. "A modern world."

Where, hopefully, a woman could pursue a profession as well as find an open-minded man with whom to share her life. Though she'd had a bad experience with love and was wary of the bonds conventional marriage placed on a woman, Aurelia hadn't given up hope on finding a mate. Liberal in her views, she would nonetheless prefer avoiding the notoriety of her aunt, who'd had a string of lovers in her youth.

"Speaking of modern, shall we take a look at the inventions displayed in the Electricity Building?" Phaedra asked.

Aurelia glanced at the watch pinned to her blouse. "I have an hour or so."

"Only an hour?"

"I promised Mariel I would drop by the house to see her," Aurelia said, referring to her older sister. "Would you like to accompany me?" Phaedra seemed to consider for a moment. "Thank you, no." And then the older woman complained, "Now there's a woman whose life is barely up to the standards of the nineteenth century, never mind the twentieth."

"Only because you dislike her husband."

Wesley Sheridan was a conservative banker, who was equally disapproving of Phaedra, Aurelia knew.

"He is too demanding of Mariel and treats her with condescension."

"Really?" Aurelia had had little contact with Mariel since her recent return to Chicago, and Wesley had seemed polite enough in the past. "Perhaps it only seems that way."

"You will be of a different mind as you get to know Mr. Sheridan better," warned her aunt.

Aurelia nodded politely, though she hoped Phaedra was wrong. Mariel was as intelligent as she was musically talented and Aurelia wanted the best for her sister.

Just as she wanted the best for herself.

With that, Aurelia resolved to forget about Italy and look to her own future.

Chicago, the Queen of the West, was the perfect place for an aspiring architect. The great fire of 1871 had destroyed vast acres of buildings. The raw, new metropolis looked gray but was far more solid in comparison to the pale, ephemeral White City, as the fair was whimsically called. Chicago's winds might carry the stench of stockyards and tanneries, its streets might teem with poor immigrants, but its professional population was future-oriented and brimming with potential and excitement.

Having spent several years in Europe surrounded by age-old refinement and culture, Aurelia could still appreciate Chicago's "skyscrapers," those unusual, modernistic structures being erected by such companies as Adler and Sullivan.

The new challenges she faced could eventually give her satisfaction and even bring fame and fortune. Aurelia had only to remain alert, to look carefully for her opportunities and to tread her own path.

Who was the exotic-looking young woman with Phaedra Kincaid?

Strangely excited, heart palpitating, he literally gaped before regaining his senses enough to step behind the corner of a building.

When he peered out again, Phaedra's companion could be observed in profile. And such a profile— straight nose, long-lidded eyes beneath winged dark brows, finely-drawn lips turned up at the corners. If her near-black hair were to be set in an antique style and her slim figure clothed in a more simple garment, she would closely resemble a tomb painting come to life.

Unfortunately, for his purposes, she might as well be a tomb painting, rather than a creature of flesh and blood. From the clothing she *was* wearing, as well as the companionship she kept, he knew she was not at all his sort.

Regretfully, he heaved a deep sigh, though he could not bring himself to turn away. If nothing else, since he knew Phaedra, he intended to arrange an introduction.

Look but do not touch, he told himself.

That rule would have to be kept, no matter how frustrating.

*   *   *

Her aunt agreed to hire a horse and cab, so Aurelia took their driver and carriage north to the Prairie Avenue neighborhood where both her aunt and her two sisters lived, the latter with their respective spouses and families.

Alighting from the carriage on the beautiful tree-lined street, Aurelia mounted the steps of the Sheridans' three-story graystone and rang the bell. Even before the butler ushered her inside, she heard Mozart being played on the piano. The elegant, lilting notes rose and fell, wafting through the air from the back parlor Mariel used as a music room.

Asking that the butler not announce her, Aurelia made her way down the carpeted hallway and stopped at the doorway to watch her sister.

Her lovely face intent, Mariel sat at the keyboard, her long fingers coaxing intricate music from the instrument as easily as the wind created waves on water. The light filtering through the lace curtains opposite added to the stunning effect, illuminating Mariel's ivory flesh and setting her red-brown hair afire.

Taking a deep breath, Aurelia entered the room quietly and slid onto a green velvet settee. The movement caught Mariel's eye and she stopped to glance up.

"Aura, there you are," she said, using her pet name for her sister.

"Please don't allow me to interrupt," Aurelia urged. "I'm enjoying the performance."

"I didn't invite you here to play music for you." Mariel smiled and rose from the piano bench to embrace Aurelia and sit down beside her. "It has been so long since we've talked or been alone together for more than a few minutes. You haven't even told me about Rome."

Only three years separated the sisters and they had been very close as young girls.

"I fear that telling you about my Italian adventures would take longer than the little time we have."

Aurelia and the Sheridans along with hundreds of others had been asked to attend the buffet and reception at the Palmer House hotel that evening.

"Are you comfortable in the old house?" Mariel asked. "Do you and Aunt Phaedra still get along?"

"Yes to both questions. I am living in my old rooms." The same suite that had belonged to her when she was a girl, since Phaedra had inherited her brother's house when she'd gotten custody of his daughter. "I plan to make the sitting room into a studio of sorts."

"And you like your new employment?"

"I am content," Aurelia hedged.

Mariel shook her auburn head. "Employed—you are working. Mother must be turning over in her grave. She wanted all of us to marry well and keep grand houses."

"Luckily, we had a more liberal father to offset her views." Mariel smiled, though Aurelia knew her sister was thinking she ought to have a husband by now. Not that the middle Kincaid sister would say so openly. Unlike Fiona, the eldest of the three girls, Mariel had a sweet and even temperament, a personality nearly as melodious as her singing voice.

"Mother was right in calling Fiona her swan and you her nightingale," said Aurelia, certain Mariel could perform as well in a concert hall as she could at family social events.

"But mother wasn't correct in calling you her blackbird." Mariel affectionately traced a line down Aurelia's jaw. "You are much lovelier now that you've matured."

"I believe handsome is as far as one could truthfully go."

Aurelia knew she was too tall, too olive in complexion, too broad-shouldered for current fashion. Blonde, swan-necked Fiona was the real beauty, while Mariel came in a close second.

"Now, Aura, you must have more confidence in yourself."

"I have confidence. I simply prefer to direct my faith toward my achievements rather than my appearance."

"You can excel in both," Mariel insisted, then reached for the servants' bell. "And this conversation is growing far too serious, don't you think? Let's have some tea and cake."

For the next hour or so, the sisters shared confidences, Aurelia asking questions about Mariel's children, Peter and Ruth, Mariel inquiring about Aurelia's two years in Rome. Aurelia discreetly avoided mentioning the name of any gentleman other than her employer. Mariel would not understand about Rosario.

In return, Mariel said little about her husband, except for indirectly remarking that Wesley expected considerable attention from his wife. The sisters also discussed Fiona and her husband. A railroad baron, Upton Price made a great deal of money and had settled

Fiona and their three daughters in a new mansion on Millionaire's Row, as South Michigan Avenue had been dubbed.

"Fiona's whirl of society events keeps her busy while her husband travels for months at a time," said Mariel, taking a sip of tea. "But I wouldn't like that. When Upton is so far away, don't you think he could be tempted by other women?"

Feeling a slight chill of guilt, Aurelia stared at a huge fern on its nearby pedestal.

"Aura? Is something wrong?"

"What?" Aurelia focused on her companion again. "I'm sorry, my mind was wandering. I don't think you should entertain such ideas about Upton. If a man and woman love each other, why should they not be true to each other?" And she thought Fiona and Upton did care deeply. "I am certain our parents were true, even when Father was traveling to set up the Lake Michigan Shipping Company."

Mariel sighed. "Well, perhaps I am only reacting to the gossip of old biddies. That harpy of a Mrs. Snodgrass implied that Upton had a woman in every railroad town, you know."

"Don't listen to people who have nothing better to do than spread rumors." Glancing at her watch, Aurelia realized she should be leaving. "It's getting late. Could you play again, Mariel? Finish that lovely Mozart piece before I go?"

Acquiescing gracefully, Mariel rose and crossed to the piano. She had only played a few bars, however, before Wesley Sheridan suddenly strode into the room and Mariel's fingers froze over the keys.

"What is this, Mariel? Have you been playing the

piano all day once again?" Wesley asked his wife in an accusatory tone, his dark mustache and his eyebrows bristling. "I swear I shall get rid of that infernal instrument!" Then he noticed Aurelia on the settee and cleared his throat. Nodding in her direction, he said, "Good afternoon, Aurelia."

"Good afternoon." She was taken aback by the man's aggressive behavior. His manner had been as unobtrusive as his banker's dark sack coat when they'd met on other occasions.

Wesley gazed from woman to woman, then again addressed his wife, "I have been at home some fifteen minutes now. I went to the nursery, thinking you were there. Then I looked in the front parlor, assuming you had received visitors. The servants are nowhere to be seen."

"I am sure the butler is helping cook in the kitchen," Mariel cut in, her face bright pink. "And I have been talking to Aurelia."

"I requested that she play for me," Aurelia added.

Wesley cleared his throat a second time as if he were hesitant. Obviously in a snit, however, he soon returned to berating his spouse. "Nevertheless, Mariel, a wife should be ready to welcome her husband home."

"I'm sorry, Wesley," murmured Mariel.

"I won't have you neglecting my needs, or the children's."

Aurelia raised her brows, wondering what on earth the man was complaining about. He'd only been home for minutes and his six-year-old son and four-year-old daughter had a live-in nanny.

Wesley went on, "You should be overseeing the

children's dinner menu and preparing for our outing tonight."

"Cook is preparing their food, darling," Mariel said in a soothing voice. "And I've decided on the green Redfern gown."

"You know I despise green."

"Then I'll wear the blue Worth."

"And what is that bird doing in the nursery?"

"Bird?" Mariel looked confused. "You mean the children's parrot? They've had Polly for several months. She's a pet."

"I don't care whether it's a he or a she," Wesley said. "I want the filthy thing removed immediately."

"But Ruth loves Polly . . ."

"I *said* the bird will go."

No wonder Phaedra didn't like Wesley. Afraid that if she stayed a moment longer, she would say something unpleasant herself, Aurelia got to her feet.

"I shall be going now." She spoke directly to her sister, for the moment ignoring Mariel's husband. "I need to prepare for tonight's celebration."

"I'm glad you stopped by," Mariel said softly. She remained in the music room with Wesley as Aurelia left.

Seething, her heart going out to her sensitive sister, Aurelia wondered if Wesley would throw the piano out with the parrot. He obviously believed he was living in the Middle Ages instead of modern times. She thought back to Bertha Palmer's speech. If most men wanted their women on pedestals, Wesley Sheridan obviously preferred his under his feet.

On the way home, Aurelia wondered how the sweet Nightingale had ended up with such an ogre. Fiona, the strong-willed and temperamental Swan, was married to a devoted if sometimes absent man who seemed to delight in granting her every wish. At least she was happy enough, if not in a situation that would be to Aurelia's own liking.

Aurelia determined once again that she herself would tolerate nothing less in a companion than intelligence, generosity, humor, loyalty, and kind-heartedness. Not to mention the courage to go against convention and accept a woman who was an architect.

To her everlasting shame, she had thought Rosario such a man.

Aurelia only hoped she had learned her lesson well enough to avoid an equally unpleasant entanglement in the future.

2

It looked as if this celebration of the Exposition's opening was a sucess. The Palmer House was crawling with people. The new structure, built on the same site at Monroe and State streets where the old one had been burned in the great fire, boasted seven hundred rooms and more bricks and iron than any two hotels on the continent. Potter Palmer, a merchant prince for a quarter of a century now, had made certain his hotel's interior was lavish.

Liam O'Rourke examined the details with an architect's eye as he shouldered the crowd in the rotunda. Walls and floor featured only two of the thirty-four varieties of marble in this building of columns with gilded capitals, Florentine mosaic mirrors, satin and velvet upholstery, and specially woven Axminster carpets. Illuminating all were giant gaslight chandeliers, as well as the electric sconces that had been installed in the public rooms the year before.

Liam had aborted his East Coast business trip, which had kept him from Chicago nearly two weeks longer than he'd expected. He'd arrived that very morning only to have the gala day start out with a horrific argument. His father had hired another architect during his absence—a decision that required both partners' approval. Irritated anew simply thinking about the matter, Liam gazed about in search of Sean, who'd told him to go to Hades before stalking out of the office.

His gaze fell on one of their architectural clients, a bearded thick-set man in the requisite evening dress.

"Good evening, Mr. Drummond." Liam nodded to the man's wife. "Mrs. Drummond."

The attractive society matron blinked coquettishly. "So nice to see you, Mr. O'Rourke." Diamonds dripped from her ears and glittered about her wrists and throat. She smoothed the bell-shaped skirts of her deep magenta satin gown as if to draw attention to her tightly corseted waist. "Are you attending tonight's festivities alone?"

"I'm meeting my father and several associates," Liam was quick to answer. A thirty-two-year-old bachelor, he did not wish to be earmarked as a potential lover for Charlotta Drummond, which was likely if the wealthy woman were given an opening. "I'm sorry, but you'll have to excuse me. I see a member of my party waving from the other side of the rotunda."

Even as he moved away, Mrs. Drummond purred, "I am sure we shall have more time to talk later in the evening."

Not if he could help it. O'Rourke and O'Rourke needed the Drummonds' business, but that didn't mean Liam had to service the rapacious wife. Charlotta Drummond had quite a reputation. Like a spoiled pretty bird, she flitted from interest to interest until she got bored. Liam hadn't forgotten the days when women like her had stared down their noses at him, the son of a poor Irish immigrant. Only after he'd combined his architectural talents with his builder father's to form a profitable firm had he been deemed worthy of such ladies' attentions.

Across the crowd, Liam spotted Prentice Rossiter, M.D., a studious bespectacled surgeon who was a fellow member of the Society for the Study of Ancient Mediterranean Cultures. He waved to Rossiter, but wasn't in the mood to approach him.

Though a discussion of archaeology would stimulate Liam, tonight it would reinforce his regrets, as well. This was one of those times when tramping through wilderness in the quest for ancient history seemed far more attractive than scrambling after the dollar and seeking a higher position within civilization. If he didn't feel a certain responsibility to his father, he knew which choice he'd make.

Already tiring of the loud murmur from hundreds of voices echoing off the marble walls, Liam headed for the parlor's expanse of thick carpet, then exited another door on the opposite side. Beyond lay the great dining room being set up for the buffet. The numerous waiters paid Liam no mind as he leaned against a column and watched them arrange silver tureens and platters among the fresh flowers and candelabras on long linen-covered tables. Although the hot foods were only just now arriving from the hotel's kitchen—a smaller detached building in the courtyard outside—a selection of pies and cakes already sat on the dessert table.

In the middle of the sugary array was a marzipan rendition of the White City itself, cleverly sculpted buildings with tiny statues, meandering walkways, and reflecting lagoons.

As Liam's eyes glided over the small wonder, a lovely young woman stepped out from behind another column nearby. Dressed in a simply cut cream-colored gown, her rich black hair upswept into a Psyche knot, she resembled a Mediterranean goddess. Seemingly unaware of Liam, she leaned over and started rearranging the little fair buildings.

A waiter stopped in his task of placing candles in a candelabra and stared.

"They have reversed the location of the Horticulture Building and the Transportation Building," she explained, pointing. "And the Electricity Building is in the wrong place entirely. You want to be accurate, don't you?"

"Er, yes, miss," said the waiter, probably wondering if she were someone important.

Liam found her interesting if only because she seemed knowledgeable about the layout of the exposition buildings and because she was bold enough to step in and rearrange the buffet table. Furthermore, her simple, elegant dress, in direct contrast to the fussy fashions of the day, announced her as an individualist. Perhaps she, like Liam, respected integrity more than social convention and had entered the dining room seeking privacy.

"Good evening," he said, appreciating her wide-spaced dark eyes and straight chiseled nose when she turned in surprise. "Those diminutive buildings are nicely done, aren't they?"

She nodded. "They add the perfect touch." Very attractive, albeit unusual looking, she was tall, only a few inches shorter than he.

Smiling, he switched his gaze from her to the dessert table, then back again. "Shall we examine this scene thoroughly to see what other inaccuracies are being presented?"

She seemed embarrassed. "I was only trying to be helpful."

"I'm sure." He explained, "I have nothing to do with the hotel. I'm merely a guest like yourself."

Then she smiled as well, her voluptuous mouth softening. "Thank goodness, I thought I had been caught doing something untoward."

"It would take a bit more than rearranging a dessert table to shock me," he said, amused. "Actually, the most untoward deed you could perform here is to ingest a few of these charming structures. The Transportation Building appears quite inviting."

She laughed softly. "A good idea, though I'd rather save the marzipan for the end of the meal."

Liam wanted to know more about this woman who seemed to possess a refreshing straightforwardness. Outspoken himself, he wondered what else they had in common.

"We needn't remain strangers, you know. Shall we introduce ourselves?"

She held out her hand. "Aurelia . . ."

"Lovely. Both you and the title," Liam said, covering her hand with both of his. "I believe Aurelia means golden or goddess of the dawn, if I remember my Latin correctly."

"And the last name is Kincaid."

He clasped her hand a little too long, enjoying the softness of her skin . . . until the name sank in.

"Kincaid?" It couldn't be. "Are you perhaps related to an architect?"

"I *am* an architect."

Aurelia Kincaid. Oh, Lord. It *was*. His smile froze.

"And you are?" she inquired pointedly.

The crowd was now swarming into the room but he ignored everyone but her.

"I am an architect, as well." He watched carefully for her reaction. "Liam O'Rourke." He explained, "My father, Sean, hired you."

"Yes." Now she looked uncomfortable.

Liam decided to be honest. "I wasn't pleased he did so without my approval."

Not to mention that he feared Sean had hired the woman purely to impress her unusual, if charming, aunt. That was no way to make a business decision as he had informed his father that morning. Sean's ire had not been long in following, and as stubborn as his father was, Liam wasn't certain the older man would be coaxed out of his black mood for days.

"You weren't pleased?" Aurelia asked tightly, obviously now on the defensive. "Well, there shouldn't be any problem. I am quite qualified."

"Yes, I've seen your credentials. I know you studied in this country and apprenticed with Solini in Rome."

"And that is not good enough?"

"Your skills aren't in question." He pointed out,

"Simply put, my father finds your aunt very engaging. I believe she used that knowledge to influence my father unduly."

"My aunt?" Aurelia's eyebrows sprang up like dark wings over her piercing eyes. "Oh, I see. You're not only prejudiced against female architects. You do not like women in general."

If Liam weren't so aggravated over the reminder of the source of his and his father's disagreement, he might laugh at such an accusation. And perhaps perversely, he was finding Aurelia's spirit as attractive as her beauty.

"On the contrary, I like many women a great deal. I would simply prefer that an architect, male or female, be hired in a more businesslike fashion." Not to mention at a time when another employee was actually needed by the firm. "Both partners should review the application from a practical standpoint. Had I been given the opportunity, I might have agreed to hire you myself."

Though Liam wasn't certain that was the truth. He'd never before worked with a professional woman and couldn't conceive of dealing with one so attractive.

"I shall be happy to give you my resignation if you desire."

Liam's temper flared—that would widen the rift between him and his father. "I made no such suggestion." He stepped closer and narrowed his gaze, noting the slight flicker of panic behind her eyes as she stepped back. "Besides, the damage has already been done, hasn't it?"

She was afraid of him—he could see it in her pale

face—and yet she straightened her spine and demanded, "What damage?"

Having specifically meant the argument between himself and his father, Liam was not about to share that information with a stranger who also happened to be an employee. "Now, look —"

"Think carefully about retaining my services, Mr. O'Rourke," she interrupted. "Despite my less than favorable impression of you, I do not wish to ruin your business."

Then, before he could retort, she turned and walked away.

As Liam watched her retreating back, he felt challenged, irritated . . . and also disappointed.

Why did Aurelia Kincaid have to be the bone of contention between him and his father?

And even if she were excellent at her work, she was lovely enough to disrupt the men's attention at the office. Worse, she could disrupt his own thinking. Not that she'd seemed inclined to act the part of the seductress. Still, trying to rationalize his own burning anger at the impossible situation, Liam determined that beautiful Aurelia Kincaid would have to prove herself. He wouldn't have an employee on the payroll taking a free ride.

Aurelia's talent had best match her impeccable credentials or she would soon be looking for another position.

Although the buffet tables groaned with food, Aurelia was too agitated to eat. Wending her way among guests who were helping themselves to brisket of beef, red snapper in wine sauce, broiled quail, Parisian potatoes, and a variety of vegetables, she had to use all her willpower to stop herself from cursing aloud.

Liam O'Rourke was an absolutely dreadful man! Obviously aggressive and fierce in temperament, he'd reminded her of Rosario during those last terrible months in Italy.

And, despite his disclaimers, the younger O'Rourke obviously believed women should be confined to bedrooms and kitchens. Why else would he have suddenly turned cold when she told him who she was? How dare he insinuate she had no skill as an architect. She had not expected to start at the top but she expected to be treated decently. How dare he insult her Aunt Phaedra! Too bad he hadn't been present the day his father had interviewed her. Then she wouldn't have wasted even one hour in a firm where she wasn't wanted.

And to think she had been impressed with the handsome green-eyed, auburn-haired man! At least she had recognized his true character as soon as he opened his mouth. Relieved that she didn't see Liam anywhere nearby, she picked up a plate and took some lobster and chicory salad. She was helping herself to a small slice of melon mango when she almost backed into Bertha Palmer.

"Oh, dear." Bertha balanced her plate, then laughed. "We almost had a collision."

"My fault. I wasn't looking where I was going," Aurelia said. "Let me congratulate you on such a wonderful reception. And even more, I want you to know how much I admired your speech at the Woman's Building this afternoon."

Bertha beamed. "Why, thank you, dear." A whisper of a Kentucky accent was apparent in her cultured speech. "You are Phaedra Kincaid's niece, aren't you? The architect?"

"An architect?" The older woman accompanying Bertha Palmer stared at Aurelia through small wire-rimmed spectacles. Her white hair was swept back in an old-fashioned style. She smiled at Aurelia and held out her hand. "I am honored to meet a woman with ambition. I am Susan Anthony."

"Susan B. Anthony?" Aurelia shook hands. "It is *my* honor to meet you."

Bertha Palmer said, "Miss Anthony has been shaking hands all day. She must be exhausted by the exercise."

"I'm inspired," said Miss Anthony with a laugh. "I felt tired thirty years ago when I stood alone with no hands to shake at all."

And the hand-shaking was far from over. As soon as they recognized Mrs. Palmer's companion, more women approached and Aurelia stepped back. Susan B. Anthony had many admirers, though her views were considered radical by most of her contemporaries. The gentle schoolteacher had been a champion for women's emancipation for decades. What was left of Aurelia's own anger completely dissipated at the thought of all Susan had done. Musing over the lot of the modern woman, she found an open spot near a small alcove but had barely taken a few bites of food when her older sisters found her.

"Aura," gushed Mariel. "We've been looking for you."

Aurelia smiled as she hugged Mariel, and noticed

Wesley wasn't at her sister's elbow. "Where's your husband?"

"He's here and about."

"Upton's talking business," Fiona added, raising one brow. "And where have you been all evening, Aurelia?" Then with an edge to her voice, she asked, "More importantly, where's *your* escort?"

"I don't have an escort."

"No escort?" repeated Fiona.

Aurelia was aware that she was a spinster in her oldest sister's eyes. Fiona's golden hair was piled artfully, and she wore a silvery low-cut mousseline gown that made her look like a fairy-book princess.

"I hope you didn't come here completely alone, Aurelia," Fiona complained. "That simply isn't done. Phaedra should have accompanied you."

"Aunt Phaedra is here. And her friend Theodore Mansfield accompanied us both to this gathering. So you see, I am not in disgrace, after all."

"Nevertheless, a personal escort is more in order," Fiona said decisively. "I could have introduced you to DeWitt Carlton this evening if he hadn't had to take his ailing mother home."

Though she didn't care one whit about some eligible bachelor, Aurelia softened her sarcasm. "How unfortunate."

Fiona frowned. "DeWitt is a true gentleman."

"A widower," Mariel put in enthusiastically. "He has perfect manners, is heir to the Carlton Department Stores, and is very nice-looking."

"Then pray let us hasten to put me on the auction block." Aurelia didn't bother to hide the satire this time.

Fiona's eyes narrowed in anger. "You will forever be an old maid with an attitude like that."

"Now, now," remonstrated Mariel.

But Aurelia was equally annoyed with her oldest sister. Fiona knew Aurelia didn't wish to have a society marriage arranged for her. It suddenly struck her as strange that enlightened women like Susan B. Anthony were attending the same gathering with others who possessed such old-fashioned attitudes.

"My marital status is not your concern, Fiona," Aurelia stated, hoping the topic would then be shelved.

Fiona drew herself to her full height. "Well, Aurelia, you are on the way to becoming as controversial as Aunt Phaedra."

Aurelia scowled and narrowed her eyes, but before she could come to her aunt's defense, Phaedra herself approached, two gentlemen in tow.

"Did I hear my name? Are you asking after me, darlings?"

Phaedra embraced and kissed each woman effusively. She gave Fiona a penetrating look that didn't bode well for her oldest niece who had the grace to appear discomfited. Then Phaedra indicated the quiet, unassuming fiftyish man with precisely clipped silver hair.

"You know Theo, don't you, Fiona? Mariel?"

They all murmured acknowledgments. Theo's gaze rested on Aurelia for a moment before moving back to Phaedra, who introduced her more flamboyant companion, a man with graying brown hair that brushed his shoulders.

"And this is Mr. William F. Cody."

His face weathered above his full mustache and gray-streaked goatee, the stranger grinned as he greeted the sisters. "You don't have to be so formal, ladies. Just call me Buffalo Bill."

"Buffalo Bill?" repeated Fiona, who stared at the man as if he had snakes in his pockets.

Aurelia had seen the famous man's image on posters. She would have recognized him anywhere, though he was now wearing a frock coat and a loose flowing tie rather than the buckskins he sported for his Wild West Exhibition. Set up on the parameters of the fair, the spectacle would be sure to draw crowds every day.

"I met Bill years ago in Kansas," Phaedra explained.

"Nearly thirty years," Cody added. "Phaedra was traveling with a theater troupe."

Aurelia smiled and Fiona winced. But then, her older sister preferred that actors stay safely backstage where they couldn't associate with any of her family.

"A theater troupe?" remarked Theo, who then looked uncomfortable, as if he were afraid he sounded disapproving.

Aurelia didn't know Theodore Mansfield well—he'd met her aunt through an art society and they'd become friends during the years Aurelia had been out of the country. But he seemed to be a shy man who would never dare speak ill of anyone.

"I painted backdrops and sewed costumes for the actors." Phaedra's tone was nostalgic. "My, those were the days. The country we traveled was rough but the life was fascinating."

Her nieces had already heard stories about Phaedra's experiences on the frontier. They also knew about the

Spanish husband Phaedra had left in California, although the situation was too much a disgrace for Fiona or Mariel to discuss. Going back to her maiden name, Phaedra had remained scandalous by eventually trotting off to study art in France and to learn about love in the arms of a nobleman.

"What kind of plays did you put on?" Theo asked Phaedra.

She laughed. "When I joined up with the group, they were doing Shakespeare. That proved unpopular, so we switched to melodrama, especially the kind where the actresses had to wear tights. Railroad men and soldiers and miners would turn out in droves."

Now everyone laughed, except Fiona.

"I remember those tights," put in Cody. "I seem to recall the name of the play I saw, too . . . *The Tragedy of Little Sadie.*"

"It is you who should be talking about your past, rather than me," Phaedra told Cody. "You had such exciting adventures scouting for the army."

Cody grinned. "Yep, I was working out of Fort Ellsworth in those days."

"And we were lucky you were still around when the troupe packed up the day after the play."

"You surely were," agreed Cody. "I stopped that Injun attack."

"Indians?" Mariel echoed.

Cody nodded and his voice vibrated with urgency as he added, "More than a dozen painted Comanches on the warpath."

"A dozen?" Phaedra raised her brows. "Warpath?"

"Well, maybe not a dozen," Cody admitted, clearing

his throat. Then he amended, "All right. A couple of rowdy braves." Unabashed, the frontiersman grinned at his small audience. "Why I guess Phaedra nearly caught me telling a tall yarn. Sometimes the pure and simple truth gets lost in the past."

Phaedra patted his arm. "Those Indians *were* dangerous. And you certainly haven't forgotten how to be charming, which is to your advantage as a showman."

"I hear that Indians take scalps as trophies of their victories," Theo muttered with a shudder. "Defiling the human form that way—so uncivilized."

Surprised the man was talking so much, Aurelia smiled in amusement as Fiona made a choked sound and Mariel changed the subject. She told Bill, "My son wants to see your Wild West Exhibition. I am hoping my husband will take me, as well."

"I can guarantee you a good time." Then Cody added expansively, "In fact, I'll be happy to give you all complimentary tickets."

"How wonderful!" enthused Mariel. "I have heard there's a real herd of buffalos, as well as roughriders and sharp-shooters and performing horses. Little Peter will be delighted!"

As Cody swung into a detailed description of one of the acts, Fiona leaned nearer Aurelia and whispered, "How *well* does Phaedra know this buffalo person?"

Aurelia raised her brows at her suspicious sister. "They were never more than friends as far as I know. Aunt Phaedra has always enjoyed platonic associations with gentlemen."

"Thank God!"

A little exclamation that made Aurelia wish she'd told Fiona that Phaedra had not only warmed Buffalo Bill's bed but also lived with the Indians for a while. Her sister had become too stuffy by far.

"Kansas, Colorado, Indian Territory," Phaedra was saying. "We were so young then, Bill, weren't we?"

"A lot of water has passed under the bridge since, I'll give you that," agreed Cody. "But you're still the alluring woman you always were."

Fiona gave the man a chilling look. "Please excuse me, but I must find my husband before he thinks I've been spirited away. Quite a rare experience to have met you, Mr. Cody." Backing away, she demanded, "Come along, Mariel."

Before her sister could protest, Fiona had grabbed Mariel by the arm and swept her off into the crowd, leaving the four people left behind staring.

And at that moment Liam O'Rourke popped out of the crowd in the company of his father, who looked to be as disgruntled with his son as Aurelia was. Though she would have liked to make a hasty retreat after her sisters, Aurelia stood firm as the two men approached.

The elder O'Rourke barely nodded politely in her direction before turning to her aunt. "Phaedra."

"Sean, how delightful."

Aurelia was immediately aware of the subtle change in her aunt, as if something had lit her from within. Phaedra positively glowed as she smiled at Sean O'Rourke, making Aurelia realize her aunt was as taken with Sean as the man was purportedly taken with her. Although he had iron-gray hair and a matching mustache, he resembled his handsome son and was a fine figure of a man.

Sean's spine straightened and his Irish lilt hardened when he said, "Liam, I'm sure 'tis pleased you'll be to make the acquaintance of Aurelia Kincaid, our new employee."

Though it was apparent Sean was telling his son to show some amount of enthusiasm, Liam barely hid the scowl that brushed his features before saying, "Miss Kincaid. I've been told you are a fine addition to the firm."

A fact he obviously found impossible to believe, Aurelia thought. "Mr. O'Rourke."

They stared at each other as if in challenge. Feeling heat creep up the back of her neck, Aurelia raised her chin as Phaedra introduced her two companions to the O'Rourkes.

"So this is your friend, Mr. Mansfield," Sean said. "And your illustrious acquaintance, Mr. Cody." He sized up both men as if he were determining whether or not they were competition. "I hope I'm not intruding."

"Of course not," Phaedra said. "Bill and I were just reminiscing about the good old days."

Sean's scowl matched his son's. "I'm not one to be looking back, but to be keeping an eye on the future. You won't object if I buy us all some champagne to toast the fair that is showing us what's to come, will you?"

"Champagne?" Phaedra smiled. "That would be wonderful."

Sean motioned for a waiter. Aurelia felt Liam's penetrating gaze still on her. Reluctantly, she faced him. His expression was carefully blank, but his green eyes glittered assessingly. He hadn't reiterated his objection to her working for the firm in front of his father and her aunt. Perhaps he thought she ought to force her resignation on him.

As the waiter poured their champagne, her anger renewed itself. She was a qualified architect and a talented one, not to mention a conscientious worker. And at least one of the O'Rourkes wanted her. She shoved aside her heretofore discomfort at her aunt's intervention in getting her the position.

All raised their glasses for a toast.

"To the future, then," Sean said.

"To the future," Aurelia echoed with the others.

In which she would keep her job if only to spite Liam O'Rourke and prove that a woman could successfully step down from her wretched pedestal and meet a man eye-to-eye.

3

Despite her reservations about Liam and her beginning draftsman position, Aurelia liked the offices of O'Rourke and O'Rourke. Located in the stepped-back tower of the Schiller Building, a new steel-framed "skyscraper" designed by Louis Sullivan, the suite was airy and bright, with huge windows opening out on all four sides. Aurelia sat in the central communal drawing area with several other draftsmen, but she had an excellent view of Randolph Street sixteen stories below, as well as the sky above.

Both the O'Rourkes had private offices at each end of the communal room, through which glass partitions in the doors allowed light and space to flow unimpeded.

Unfortunately, the glass also allowed Liam to spy upon his employees. Returning to the office the first workday following the Palmer reception, he hovered at his door to watch Aurelia. He'd already warned her that he needed the rendering she was working on and he hadn't bothered to hide his impatience.

By midmorning, he approached once again. "Haven't you finished that yet?"

Aurelia tightened her jaw, wishing she could rip the drawing into tiny pieces right before his handsome face. There was no indication that this was the interesting, exciting man she'd first met at the Palmer reception. And deep down, she regretted that man was lost to her forever. They had so much in common.

"Well?" he said, his eyes cool and hard as jade, his expression stormy. She tempered her righteous irritation. The other employees, all men, were sitting at their tables in the open room, an eager audience awaiting a scene.

Which she refused to give them. "If you would like this project less skillfully drawn, Mr. O'Rourke, I shall be most happy to hand it over to you in two minutes."

Liam frowned. "I want it executed exactly as it should be."

"Then the process will take at least another hour," she told him. "A quiet, uninterrupted hour."

His head jerked slightly when someone coughed, the sound echoing through the silent room like a coin dropped upon hollow metal. Liam glared about, then turned and stalked away.

Aurelia heard the door of his office close. Determined to be professional at all costs, she bit her lip and continued sketching. She didn't want to glance about her at all, but when she heard whispers nearby, she turned a furious gaze on two of her neighbors. The men flinched and looked startled.

Drat! She realized the two draftsmen had probably been talking about their own projects, not her.

Embarrassed, Aurelia stared at her pencil as she sketched in several more lines. She didn't need to make enemies. The devil take Liam O'Rourke and his prejudice toward her! For a moment, she actually entertained the idea of walking out of the offices and never looking back.

But that would be running from the enemy and Aurelia simply couldn't allow Liam the satisfaction of making her retreat.

With increased concentration, blotting out her surroundings, she lost herself in the rendering, thinking of nothing but how to show the house at its best, a suburban family residence combining Queen Anne with a little "seaside cottage," a mixed style that seemed popular nowadays.

She added just enough shadows to delineate the depth of the wide front door and used sweeping lines to emphasize the building's curving windowed turret. She wished she had a free hand to alter the structure's design somewhat—she thought the house could be more original—but she had to admit she truly did enjoy the process of drawing, if not the job of draftsman. There was something magical about summoning an image from an empty page.

She was almost finished when a purple iris suddenly appeared to float near the side of her drafting table. An iris? Then she noticed the hand holding the flower forth and she looked up into the attractive face of a young man with longish brown hair, unusual eyes, and an engaging smile.

"How do you do," he said. "If you would like this

flower, I shall be most happy to offer it to you for inspiration. I've always believed that the forms of nature are the architect's greatest teacher." He laid the iris on the sloping side of her table and peered at her drawing. "Not that you aren't doing an excellent job already. You are a very talented young woman."

His warmth and seeming sincerity touched her. "Why, thank you."

He reached for her hand and clasped it for a moment. "I'm Mr. Wright . . . Frank Lloyd Wright." He raised his brows. "You've heard of me?" His tone implied she should already be aware that he was well known and exceedingly well respected.

He seemed so positive and charming, she didn't mind a bit of egotism. "I've heard a great deal about the quality of your work." And also much gossip concerning it, the latest being a buzzing scandal that Wright had been let go from Adler and Sullivan for bootlegging houses away from his employers. She introduced herself, "I'm Aurelia Kincaid."

"Aurelia—a lovely name, flowerlike in itself. It fits you."

She smiled and found herself nearly blushing. To hide her slight discomfiture, she asked, "You had something to do with the design of this very building, didn't you, Mr. Wright?"

"I admit the detailing on the facade and window embrasures came directly from my pencil," he said pleasantly. His whole appearance was pleasing, from his smile to his well-cut brown suit worn with a wide trailing satin tie. And his continued eye contact bordered on the flirtatious. "We did some similar motifs on the gate to the exposition's Transportation Building."

"The Golden Gate is an imposing design," Aurelia said. One couldn't miss it: it was polychrome, and the rest of the building was terracotta, rather than white, like the other fair buildings.

"Sullivan was responsible for the entire structure," said Wright, who didn't sound in the least resentful of his former employer. "Most viewers find it impressive."

As was Wright himself. Aurelia was amazed at his self-possession, unusual in a man who seemed to be about the same age as she. If he approached the wives of prospective clients with such magnetic verve, he would sell many projects. And Wright's friendly warmth was a distinct relief to Liam's sharp coldness.

"I have recently set up my own offices in this tower."

"Really?" So a new business was his next move.

"That is, myself and my associate, Mr. Cecil Corwin, shall be working here in partnership." He added, "You must come by from time to time and brighten our days."

Aurelia was about to promise just that when Wright's gaze flicked behind her. She glanced over her shoulder. Liam stood in the doorway, his eyes assessing, one auburn brow raised.

Wright straightened. "Mr. O'Rourke."

Aurelia noticed Frank Lloyd Wright was several inches shorter than Liam as he stepped forward to offer his hand. Once again Wright explained he had set up new offices.

"It is fitting that architecture firms dominate a well-designed building like this," Liam commented.

A compliment? Aurelia noticed with surprise.

And Liam actually appeared openly interested and friendly.

"My partner and I are already busy with two important projects in Oak Park," said Wright. "I have heard that you are working at a site nearby."

Liam nodded. "We've broken ground and expect to be there throughout the summer."

"Which could be convenient. You see, my partner and I have found ourselves in a dilemma of sorts," Wright went on. "We are in need of some good mahogany, suitable for woodwork. I have ordered a quantity but cannot receive it for several weeks. I thought perhaps O'Rourke and O'Rourke might possess a stockpile from which I might borrow. For a short time, of course."

Liam considered for a moment. "Well, I don't see why not. I'll write an invoice that you may give to our foreman. He'll make sure you get what you need."

"Splendid." Wright grinned. "I shall appreciate the favor and, of course, pay you back as soon as possible."

Liam fetched some paperwork and gave it to Wright, who offered his firm thanks.

"You have a fine draftswoman here," Wright then told Liam. "I stopped to admire Miss Kincaid's work on my way to your office."

"Um, hmm." Liam glanced at the rendering, his tone noncommittal. "I see it is finished."

Wright waved a hand toward Aurelia. "Her skill has added volume that rises beyond the drawing's basic two-dimensionality. And the way she has portrayed the interlocking planes shows a true sense of design."

Liam didn't respond to the compliments heaped on his employee, but Aurelia smiled with pleasure. How gratifying to have the best draftsman in the city, the man who was called Sullivan's "pencil," praise her work. She hoped the situation was making Liam uncomfortable.

The two men talked about Oak Park for a few more minutes before Wright indicated he had to leave. At about the same time, Sean arrived. Wright also greeted the older O'Rourke and invited everyone to come by his new office, offering Aurelia a special smile that said visitation could be *any* time for her.

As soon as the young architect left, Sean asked, "And what was that all about?"

"He borrowed some mahogany from our site in Oak Park," Liam explained.

"Borrowed?" Sean looked annoyed. "I've told you more than once the man is notoriously in debt. Always has been. Why, that conniving little Welshman built his own house on Louis Sullivan's money. And he is always for living far beyond his means—look at his foppish clothes. He's a dandy, even wears high heels to make himself look taller—"

"He's never borrowed from us before," Liam interrupted smoothly.

Sean colored. "And he won't be doing so again if I can help it. He probably has no more credit with his suppliers. You wait and see, we'll never be repaid."

"Then I suppose my gesture will be a small loss," said Liam.

"Small? Who says the cost of mahogany is small?" growled Sean, running a hand through his iron-gray hair. "And just which partner has made a decision this time without consulting the other, I'd like to know."

As if suddenly aware of her presence, both men glanced at Aurelia. In turn, she focused on her drawing, staring hard as she penciled in her initials at the bottom. Again she wished she could leave the office and never come back.

The two O'Rourkes walked away, their conversation drifting back as they headed for Sean's office.

"I am sure we shall be repaid in other ways," Liam insisted. "Mr. Frank Lloyd Wright is a self-made man who knows what it's like to start at the bottom. I have a feeling he will go far in the world."

"Any man with common sense should be wanting to go far himself," Sean countered.

"Meaning I have no ambition? Let us settle this issue, please. You and I both know this disagreement concerns more than a few planks of mahogany," grumbled Liam before the door closed.

Wondering if the men were discussing her, Aurelia started working on another drawing. About a half hour passed before Liam came out into the drafting room again, his face so impassive, she couldn't guess what had transpired.

"May I have the finished rendering?" he asked politely, stopping by her table. "The client will be arriving shortly."

"Of course."

He seemed a little less cold in manner as he looked over the drawing. Despite herself, she admired the chiseled lines of his mouth and cheek and jaw. Unlike most men of the day, he wore no disguising muttonchop sideburns or beard or mustache.

"This is indeed nicely done."

"Thank you."

"And what are you working on next? The Ettlin house?"

"I have several projects." She didn't want to antagonize him, but she felt it only fair that she know if there was a hurry. "Is Mr. Ettlin coming by, too? If you would tell me beforehand that you have scheduled a meeting at a certain time, I would make sure that the necessary renderings are ready."

"All right." Face still impassive, he rolled up the drawing carefully. "I have no more client meetings today, but I could use the Ettlin renderings by tomorrow."

"Then I shall work on them first." Perhaps Liam had gotten the point, she thought with satisfaction. Maybe there was hope they could work together in harmony.

He started to go, then turned. "Mr. Wright seemed quite taken with your work."

She could almost hear his unspoken *and you*. "He's quite charming."

"He's quite married, as well, you know."

Startled, Aurelia flushed. "I did not mean charming in that sense."

His expression changed subtly. "I only wished to clarify things for you. Young women seem always to be measuring a man for husbandhood."

"I know how to separate my professional and private business, Mr. O'Rourke," she said testily. "And for your information, I am quite content being a spinster."

Liam's gaze raked over her appreciatively. "You are far from my idea of a spinster, Miss Kincaid."

Warmth spread outward from her middle as her

heart seemed to skip a beat. Nevertheless, Aurelia felt relieved when he turned and walked away. Like most men in the office, he'd removed his coat and his broad shoulders appeared strong and muscular beneath the thin white cotton of his shirt.

But Aurelia told herself she wasn't the least bit interested in Liam's manly figure as she went back to work. She wished she could have ignored his remark about Wright being married. If it hadn't been for Rosario, if she'd always been able to keep her private and professional life separate, the comment wouldn't have bothered her at all.

Though Aurelia was certain she hadn't meant to flirt with Frank Lloyd Wright, she still felt guilty. She only wished she could lay the past to rest. Perhaps a dab at romance in the present would help. With that in mind, she found herself accepting an invitation from Fiona for Sunday afternoon tea at which she would be introduced to the eminently eligible DeWitt Carlton.

Her husband out of town, Fiona greeted her guests enthusiastically and made certain DeWitt was safely seated by Aurelia before Mariel gave an impromptu concert.

At the end of the piano piece, DeWitt leaned closer to murmur, "All the Kincaid sisters seem to be artistic."

"In our own way," Aurelia agreed, having already confessed her professional involvement with architecture.

Phaedra, who'd needed the diversion enough to

come along and bring Theo, leaned forward in her plump, tasseled chair. "My nieces received their artistic influence from *my* side of the family," she said with a proud smile. "Though I wouldn't say Fiona had a particular leaning toward art."

"I beg your pardon," Fiona cut in, appearing at Phaedra's side. Though she professed to have different interests entirely, she preferred approval to disapproval from her aunt. "I am a connoisseur of art, if you please."

Fiona certainly was a connoisseur of fashion, Aurelia thought, admiring her sister's moiré Watteau-pleated tea dress, its soft pink and ivory lace the exact shades of the afternoon's tea cake frosting. As usual, her older sister looked beautiful.

Amused, Phaedra hastened to explain, "I wasn't criticizing you, Fiona. My apologies if you thought so."

"And my compliments on your connoisseur's taste," DeWitt made haste to tell Fiona.

In his late thirties, he had blond hair, a small mustache, regular features, and smooth manners. Not bad-looking, though not nearly as impressive as Liam, Aurelia thought.

"Isn't that a new painting I saw in the hallway?" he asked.

Aurelia had noticed the conservative, rather dark landscape in a heavy gold frame, which went with the equally heavy, elaborately carved furniture Fiona liked.

"Upton bought me the painting a week ago," Fiona said, appearing pleased, "after I complained of the bareness of the walls there. He is most thoughtful."

"A husband should spoil his wife," murmured DeWitt.

Fiona beamed, patting the pink silk roses nestled in her gilt hair. A second cousin of Upton Price's, DeWitt certainly knew how to impress his relative's wife.

"You are a connoisseur yourself, DeWitt," Fiona pointed out, looking to Aurelia. "The Carltons have many objets d'art."

DeWitt nodded. "Oriental vases, cut glass, and of course, some of the newer sort of paintings."

"Oh?" Aurelia was immediately interested. "Are you referring to the French school, the Impressionists? Such bright colors are exciting." As was simplicity in comparison to the usual Victorian clutter. "I've heard Bertha Palmer brought quite a collection back from France."

DeWitt raised his brows. "Impressionists? I've never heard of such a painting school. My mother and I prefer historical portraits or landscapes from the English academy."

Aurelia should have expected as much. But she knew she shouldn't pass judgment on the man simply because he was conservative . . . or chosen for her by her sisters.

As DeWitt and Fiona discussed DeWitt's mother, who'd had to miss the gathering because of a worrisome cough, Aurelia turned her attention to the servants pouring tea and offering platters of crustless sandwiches, scones, and more tea cakes. One of the maids was a tiny, young woman with dark hair swept back into a tight knot and shy, dark eyes. When a guest rose and jostled her, she mumbled something in Italian.

Familiar with the language, Aurelia tried to put the girl at ease. *"Grazie,"* she said, accepting a cake and going on in Italian about what a fine job the maid was doing.

The young woman smiled and Fiona drifted away to talk to the next cluster of guests. The maid served Phaedra, then Theo, who also spoke to the servant in Italian.

"You've been to Italy?" Aurelia asked him.

Theo seemed startled and, as usual, didn't meet Aurelia's eyes. "In my youth."

"Now who has mystery in his background?" remarked Phaedra. She patted his arm and he turned pink. "You're so unassuming, Theo. Were you traveling?"

The older man smiled wanly. "I was studying art. But I was not meant to be a creator, at least not the ordinary sort."

"You are a connoisseur like DeWitt and Fiona." Phaedra told Aurelia, "You should see his house, so many antiquities. It's like being in the Louvre."

"Hardly that," said Theo, gazing hard at the floor.

What a strange and quiet person he was, thought Aurelia. "I'm quite fascinated by antiquities myself."

Phaedra said, "Then you must accompany Theo and me on Thursday to a meeting of the Society for the Study of Ancient Mediterranean Cultures. They are considering my skills for a special project."

"I would enjoy that."

DeWitt had no opinion on antiquities, but agreed it was far too warm when Phaedra complained and rose to seek some fresh air in the garden with Theo and several other guests.

"Would you like to take a walk down the avenue?" DeWitt asked Aurelia.

She knew that he was hoping to find a way to be alone with her, but she agreed. And she chided herself for being so close-minded as to think he was boring.

In the hallway, Aurelia passed Mariel and another guest, Mrs. Norvill.

"I have indeed been asked to perform professionally, in an orchestra hall," Mariel said. "But I do not choose to do so."

"Why ever not?" asked Mrs. Norvill, expressing the surprise Aurelia herself felt at her sister's turning down such an offer.

From nearby, Wesley spoke up, "Because she has the more important responsibility of being my wife and the mother of my children."

"But surely you have enough servants—" Mrs. Norvill suddenly grew silent under the weight of Wesley's glower.

Aurelia turned away, careful to hide her own appalled expression of shock that Mariel would sacrifice her talent for her husband. How could any man demand that? Wesley surely appreciated his wife's genius; Aurelia had noticed how long and loud he'd applauded after today's concert. Upset and concerned, she quickly put on her hat and took a deep breath as soon as she stepped outside into the warm sunshine.

They strolled down Michigan Avenue, a wide thoroughfare separated by an island with trees and gas streetlights. Aurelia glanced back at Fiona's house, a fortresslike, Romanesque mansion of brown stone. The structure was only softened by shrubbery, bright flower beds, and a landscaped garden in back.

When they turned down a side street, the lake was visible in the distance. She put aside her worry over Mariel. "Lovely, don't you think? The water is as blue as the Mediterranean today."

DeWitt smiled, tiny wrinkles appearing at the corners of his mild blue eyes. "I shall have to take your word for that, I'm afraid. My mother's health has limited our travels."

When Aurelia stepped on a loose pebble, DeWitt hastened to offer his arm. He was very polite, she realized, remembering that *Godey's Lady's Book* said gentlemen could only do so if the footing were unsteady.

A little taller than she, DeWitt glanced at her frequently as they walked along. "You are very beautiful."

"And you are very flattering." Perhaps she *had* bloomed in Italy, changed in some inexplicable way. Perhaps the Blackbird had finally acquired a sheen to her feathers.

"You are so exotic-looking," DeWitt went on. "I caught sight of you with Phaedra last week at the fair. I knew I wanted to meet you whenever it could be arranged."

Not wanting to admit she hadn't noticed him, she changed the topic. "Please, let's talk about you, your department store. I would like to hear more about it."

DeWitt was delighted to expound on merchandising. Soon he'd launched into a speech on how to make one's fortune in the industry, something about obtaining enough money to expand the base inventory.

"But I must be boring you with all this talk of business," he finally said apologetically.

"I know something of business."

"Of course. You know much about many things. Yet, I am sure, you have the true heart of a woman." He went on, "Women are actually superior to men. They have far more depth of feeling. Thank God we have them to raise our children and make our houses homes—we males could never do that. We can only offer our protection in return."

Aurelia bristled at the way the conversation was going. He sounded like Wesley. Not that she was against motherhood or keeping house and not that she didn't realize many women of lesser means had no choice in the matter. But if a woman had a particular talent, it seemed criminal to hide it.

"How protected does a woman have to be?" she couldn't help asking. "Shouldn't women have interests outside of marriage?"

DeWitt chuckled, though he sounded uncomfortable. "I realize you love your architectural work and I believe you should continue with it as long as it suits you."

As long as it suited her. So he believed women's professions should be temporary, at best. But what else should she expect from an ordinary, conservative man?

They paused when they reached the long shore stretching down to Lake Michigan. In the distance, a steamboat full of sightseers puffed its way south toward the exposition. Aurelia couldn't help wishing she were on board as well. But, after enjoying the breeze for only a few minutes, she and her escort started their return.

"I would like to see you again," DeWitt told her, exchanging places, so that he was nearest the street. "Would you be available for an outing next Sunday? Your Aunt Phaedra, I'm sure, would also like to join us," he added. "Or one of your sisters."

Aurelia reminded herself she should at least appreciate DeWitt's good manners. After all, men and women of good repute did not usually venture out alone together. And he didn't storm about and blurt out outrageous opinions like Liam O'Rourke.

"Perhaps attending the fair would be nice," Aurelia suggested. "One day was hardly enough with all those miles and miles of exhibits. And Aunt Phaedra and I are particularly curious about the Midway Plaisance."

DeWitt frowned for the first time since Aurelia had met him. "There are rough people on the midway." He obviously referred to the lower classes. "Not a fit outing for ladies."

"We would be safe enough with an escort."

DeWitt shook his head. "Why, the midway is rife with pickpockets and, well, other sorts who are not reputable in the least. We shall do something more appropriate—take a carriage ride through the park." DeWitt planned on. "I shall come for you and Phaedra at two o'clock. I believe Mother would enjoy a carriage ride, too."

Aurelia quickly interrupted, "Actually, I didn't mean I could go anywhere at all next Sunday. Perhaps the week after."

DeWitt's frown returned, making him look petulant. "Perhaps? You aren't sure of the next week either?"

If truth be told, she knew she didn't want to see

him again at all. "I am only newly returned to Chicago and am coping with a very busy routine."

His thin lips tightened. "Then I suppose I shall have to talk to you again in a few weeks."

"That would be best."

They spoke little as they continued toward Fiona's house, DeWitt definitely sulking. How disagreeable. But then it was Aurelia's curse to be coping with disagreeable men of late. Of course, she knew that it was she herself who was to blame, that she no doubt brought out both Liam's and DeWitt's disagreeableness with her very independence.

At least Liam was more honest than DeWitt, if more prickly. Aurelia told herself she should remember to appreciate that fact when she went to the office the next morning.

4

Rather than deal with the infernal beautiful female who'd invaded his domain, Liam chose to work at the Oak Park site for three days, instead of the Schiller Building. Not one to shirk physical labor, he let open air and exercise temper his disposition. In addition, he had a meeting of the Society for the Study of Ancient Mediterranean Cultures to look forward to.

On Thursday evening, he stopped by his lodgings to bathe and dress before taking a carriage to Prentice Rossiter's monstrosity of a French Gothic mansion on South Drexel Boulevard. Late, he entered hurriedly when the elaborately carved door was opened by the butler.

Coming face-to-face with an unwelcome apparition in the huge vaulted entryway, Liam stopped short and nearly dropped his jaw. "Aurelia Kincaid!"

She nodded coldly, her soft lips forming a hard line. "Mr. O'Rourke."

"What are *you* doing here?"

She blinked but gazed at him steadily with those lustrous, slightly slanted dark eyes. "I am attending tonight's meeting with my aunt."

"You're both here?" Then he remembered hearing something about Phaedra having been approached to do the illustrations for a book the society intended to publish.

"It is a free country, Mr. O'Rourke," said Aurelia. "Even if women have not yet obtained suffrage."

"But you have no business with the society—"

"Not business, interest. I enjoy studying the past, something I have in common with the other members. I lived in Italy for two years, a country that has both an ancient history and a Mediterranean coastline." With a small toss of her head, she moved away. "Now, if you don't mind, I shall join my aunt."

He stared after her stiff back as she swept down the great stone passageway toward the library, where the meeting was being held.

Damn! He'd made an ass of himself again, he thought, entering the high-ceilinged room in her wake. Ten people already sat around the long mahogany table, everyone but Phaedra and Aurelia regular members. Decanters of sherry stood on the table's polished surface, ready to be served.

Although Liam took pains to greet his fellows, he remained overwhelmingly aware of the woman who'd flustered him. The deep gold of the dress she wore with only one piece of jewelry, a large but simple silver brooch set with faceted purple stone, made her appear glowing and jewellike against the dark leather of the surrounding shelves of books and the muted hues of the numerous ancient artifacts Rossiter liked to display.

It seemed that Aurelia Kincaid was going to haunt him wherever he went.

And, unfortunately, she was not only beautiful but self-composed, strong, and quite skilled at her profession. Liam had nearly had to eat crow after he'd made such a to-do over the rendering she'd completed on Monday. The only saving grace for that workday had been the truce he and his father had managed despite their opposing views.

He forced himself to turn his eyes from Aurelia as Dr. Rossiter brought the meeting to order. The society was very important to Liam. At the moment, his association with the group was the closest he could come to going on an archeological dig. He would never forget the joy and awe he'd felt visiting the ancient site of Mycenae in Greece two years ago or, a few months afterward, the thrill of sifting for shards of the past in the sands of Egypt.

Rossiter finished calling out the roll, his spectacles glittering and his bald pate shining in the light of the flickering gas sconces. Thin and a little stooped, the surgeon next introduced the speaker for the evening. "We are honored to have Jack Quigley back with us from northern Africa."

Liam's gaze slid to the big ruddy-faced man seated a few chairs down from Rossiter. Something of a bully and a braggart, Quigley was not popular, if quite educated, well traveled, and multilingual. As the only member who could afford to pursue archeology full-time, he was listened to with respect.

"Ahem, gentlemen." Quigley rose, his bulk and

booming voice immediately dominating the room. His thick beard and mane of hair also gave him a startling, semiwild appearance. "I am pleased to report that I have had great luck on a dig near Thebes in Egypt. I found a tomb, an intact and well-preserved mummy, and a complete set of canopic jars."

Many members' eyes widened. An undiscovered tomb and a mummy. Liam himself felt a thrill of envy. Of course, it was rumored that Quigley wouldn't be able to spend all his time in exotic countries if he hadn't managed to marry a wealthy lonely widow and ruthlessly appropriate her money.

"Was there any gold in the tomb?" piped up Ernest Williamson from the end of the table. Liam noted he earned Quigley's glare. A new member, Williamson obviously wasn't aware the archeologist preferred quiet during his lectures.

"I am in the process of sorting and labeling the many burial items," Quigley went on as if he hadn't heard.

"But you didn't find gold?" repeated Williamson.

Quigley's heavy brows drew into a ferocious scowl. "Gold? Any fool knows that most Egyptian tombs were already robbed by the damned peasants." He pounded one meaty fist into the opposite palm. "Why, I'd break every bone in their bodies myself if they tried the same thing in this century!"

The archeologist seemed to be hinting he'd be happy to break Williamson's bones as well. But then violence always seemed to lurk beneath Quigley's surface, Liam thought.

No fool, Williamson said nothing and sat back in his chair.

Quigley continued, describing the inscriptions on the tomb's walls. "The hieroglyphics indicate the mummy was buried during the New Kingdom." He picked up the glass of sherry before him and downed it in one swig. "The corpse itself is flexible and its bandages yellowish with a mat sheen."

"Hmm, also proof for dating the burial later in history," mused Rossiter. As the society's president and Quigley's friend, he *was* allowed to make remarks. "I only wish we knew the exact formula that Herodotus refers to, the specific substances and whether they changed through the decades."

"Those paltry details don't make any difference," said Quigley. He sat down, poured another glass of wine, and wolfed it. "They ripped open the corpse, took out its organs, and let the body dry out. That's all we need to know."

Rossiter cleared his throat politely. "I believe bodies were handled a bit more carefully than that." The surgeon was also allowed to disagree. "The Egyptians opened the corpse's abdomen with surgical precision. And they took much time and care on the preservation, usually at least seventy days."

Liam had heard it all before but wondered if the conversation would be too much for people with finer sensibilities. Like Aurelia. He glanced down the table. To her credit, she wasn't looking faint. Phaedra had her brows raised, and beside her, Theodore Mansfield listened with rapt attention.

"The method of removing the brain through the nose is especially fascinating," Rossiter went on. "Sometimes I wonder if the lack of that particular organ helped mummification proceed more quickly."

Quigley shook his head. "Egypt's dry climate made preservation natural. That was more important than balderdash like organ removal and chemical formulas."

"But the exact substances used in mummification could also have played a distinct part in the ritual," said Rossiter, a low level of excitement making his voice throb. "The order and the amount of natron, resin, bitumen, and balsamic oils. The Egyptians obviously refined the process by the New Kingdom, since older mummies tend to be black and desiccated."

Aware the macabre discussion could continue forever and preferring to go on, Liam asked, "Have you identified the mummy, Quigley?"

The big man glared at Liam. "Of course I've identified her—some noblewoman named Ptahnofret. Her name and portrait were on the coffin."

"Was she pretty?" joked Dr. Cunningham, another surgeon who was a member of the society. Short and dark, with an expressive face, he had a reputation for being droll.

"Who cares whether she was pretty or not?" Quigley growled. "She was silent—the best kind of damned woman there is."

Mansfield coughed heavily and stared at the table in front of him. Was he embarrassed? Mansfield had brought two ladies with him, after all, and was subjecting them to Quigley's rough language and attitude. But a man who usually faded into the wallpaper couldn't be expected to voice an objection, Liam supposed.

"Women were merely breeding stock in ancient

times anyway," Quigley stated, making things worse. He sounded as if he didn't think they were fit for anything else. Liam knew he kept his wife hidden away. Obviously, he had no more respect for her than the ancient women he deprecated.

The only other woman present besides the Kincaids, the only female member of the society, Mrs. Cunningham fidgeted beside her husband. "I believe there were several rather famous Egyptian queens, Mr. Quigley. At least nobly born women in antiquity seem to have been a bit more than breeding stock."

"Hah!" said the archeologist. "Queens only obtained their exalted positions by marriage. They were still broodmares, no matter their titles."

"Queen Hatshepsut a broodmare?" Now Phaedra entered the fray. Heads swiveled in her direction. "I believe she produced but one daughter. And she built the great temple at Deir el-Bahri."

"Hatshepsut was a widow who usurped her nephew's throne," countered Quigley.

"The accounts I've read say she willingly shared rulership with him," Phaedra came back.

"Then why did the Egyptians tear down her statues after her death, eh, and scratch out her name?" demanded Quigley. "They damned well knew the hag tried to rise beyond herself. She was better off a mummy with her meddling mouth wrapped in bandages."

Tension crackled through the room. Mrs. Cunningham was clasping her hands tightly, Phaedra was staring at Quigley with obvious venom, and Aurelia looked pale. And though Liam knew the Kincaid women were probably capable of holding their own, he also thought Quigley was out of order.

"I, for one, think many good things came out of Hatshepsut's reign," Liam stated before a shouting match started. "She encouraged decades of peace and funded wonders in the field of architecture. She was no doubt an exceptional woman." He pointed out, "However, I believe we're veering from the purposes of the society here, the promotion of open and nonprejudicial discussion of past cultures. Let's not preach sermons on our own personal views."

"If you're referring to *me*," Quigley argued, something cold and sinister behind his eyes belying his heated words, "I'm not preaching, I'm stating the facts."

"Then you must have found some papyri with irrefutable proof, documents that have evaded W.M.F. Petrie and everyone else who is working in Egypt."

Quigley beetled his heavy brows. His face was florid, though whether from anger or the sherry he was consuming, Liam didn't know.

"Anyone with a brain can ascertain the true order of nature," the archeologist growled. "Everyone knows what women are—"

"Enough!" snapped Liam. "You are being needlessly offensive to the ladies who are present."

Quigley half rose from his chair. "No one tells me to be quiet! Let's step outside and settle this matter."

"If that's what you want." Maintaining challenging eye contact, Liam was too angry to back down. But Rossiter immediately jumped up to intervene. "Gentlemen, gentlemen, please! This has gone too far." He patted Quigley's arm and said firmly, "We fully appreciate your report, Jack."

With a grumble, the big man sank back down.

Then Rossiter glanced at Liam questioningly. "And pray let us now proceed to other business."

Not having wanted a fight in the first place, Liam made no objection. As for Quigley, the archeologist was mostly wind. He usually forgot arguments as fast as he started them.

Rossiter opened discussion on several business matters facing the society. The treasurer made a report. Everyone seemed to settle down, especially Quigley, who mellowed his belligerence with even more wine.

Liam caught Aurelia staring at him, though she quickly moved her eyes away. He wondered what she thought of the evening, of his taking Quigley to task. Not that he'd done so for *her*, he told himself. It was the overall unfairness of the man's attitude.

As the meeting went on, Rossiter belatedly suggested that the guests be introduced, and Mansfield said a few words about Phaedra Kincaid. "She is an exquisite artist," he said in conclusion.

Smiling at the compliment, Phaedra, in turn, introduced her niece. "Aurelia is an architect and has spent nearly two years in Italy where she visited the site of the ancient Etruscan city of Veii."

"Another architect?" Cunningham remarked with interest. "Mr. O'Rourke will certainly have things to discuss with the young lady."

More than the good doctor could possibly know, Liam thought wryly. He hadn't told the other members about his business connection with Aurelia and he had no intention of doing so, though he wondered why Phaedra wasn't saying anything about it.

"Speaking of architecture," Rossiter addressed Liam. "Cunningham and I saw your completed project on the Midway Plaisance. We were pleased. Good work."

Liam nodded. "Thank you. Of course, I had to make many compromises, not the least of which were the lurid signs. But what can one expect from the midway?"

Rossiter smiled. "Cunningham and Mansfield and I are nearly finished with our contributions."

"I shall look forward to seeing them," said Liam. "Then the place can officially open."

Nothing else was said about the project and the conversation veered toward the subject of archeology in Anatolia and the late Heinrich Schliemann's discovery of Troy.

The last topic on the evening's agenda was the book the society was putting together, a tome of ancient history and translated poetry.

"I have recommended Phaedra Kincaid as an illustrator," Mansfield told the group, once more smiling upon his companion.

Phaedra explained the reason for her interest. "I have always loved ancient art and believe I am particularly adept at combining antique symbolism and motif in illustrations or paintings."

Then various members put forth their specific ideas for the society's book.

"Are you planning to pose your beautiful niece?" Dr. Cunningham asked Phaedra. "She would be perfect as an Egyptian or Greek lady."

Phaedra gazed closely at Aurelia. "She would, wouldn't she? I can imagine the effect of different hairstyles and jewelry. Would you be interested, Aurelia?"

Aurelia merely smiled, seemingly a bit embarrassed. "Perhaps."

Rossiter cleared his throat and Liam glanced at him, noticing that the surgeon's eyes gleamed strangely and his expression seemed disapproving. But then, Rossiter was a serious man who often wore a frown of concentration.

Several other members agreed that Aurelia would do wonderfully and asked her to consider. Which meant she would probably be attending more meetings, Liam realized. Fate seemed to be throwing her in his path whether he liked it or not.

The meeting lasted longer than Phaedra had promised, and afterward Aurelia went out onto the side porch to wait for the carriage to be brought around. Her aunt had gone back into the house, presumably to find Theo. Hoping to sight Phaedra, Aurelia peered impatiently at the windows where figures moved past like phantoms behind the lacy curtains. A tall, broad-shouldered silhouette came into view for a moment. She was certain she recognized Liam's strong chin and nose in profile.

Aurelia hadn't been pleased to meet Liam O'Rourke tonight, but she'd certainly been surprised when he sided with the women against Jack Quigley. Though she found the idea of physical violence repugnant, she had to admit she'd been impressed with Liam's courage and nerve. He'd simply refused to back down from the rough, opinionated man.

Not that Aurelia would allow herself to think Liam any more attractive. He possessed the sort of fiery, passionate nature that had already proved to be her detriment.

A crackle of leaves in the bushes suddenly drew her attention. Her skin prickled and she stared into the darkness, feeling uneasy. No breeze disturbed the quiet of the night. Then branches swayed and she had the distinct feeling that something, or someone was watching her. She could almost swear a dark form nestled in the leaves.

With a wave of panic, she caught her breath and stepped back in alarm. Her heart beat a staccato rhythm as she pressed herself against the wall of the house and inched toward the door.

But there was no other movement, save for the flickering shadows created by the single dim gaslight on the porch.

She had let her imagination play tricks on her.

Already chiding herself, Aurelia tightened her shawl around her shoulders and waited for her shaky breathing to slow. She wished she could forget about the night Rosario had been waiting for her to come back to her lodgings. Tree branches had danced to the rhythm of a capricious wind and there had been no one else around.

But now both Italy and Rosario were far away. Angry, Aurelia wondered how long she would allow herself to remain fixated on incidents that were over and done with.

Nevertheless, she couldn't help feeling greatly relieved when Phaedra finally appeared, obviously ready to leave. But her aunt was alone.

"Where's Theo?"

"He went out the servants' entrance to fetch the driver from the stables himself." Phaedra twitched her sharp little nose. "What an evening! That Quigley is truly an offensive beast."

"He is probably all hot air," said Aurelia, trying to be generous, though something about the man had made her deeply uneasy. More than his words, he gave off the aura of truly hating women. With all his blathering, he might as well have said that the only good woman was a dead one.

Phaedra shivered. "I wouldn't want to meet Quigley in a dark wayfare." Then she asked, "You did enjoy the meeting anyway, didn't you, darling? Despite him?"

"For the most part, I found it fascinating."

"That Dr. Rossiter was a bit macabre. He sounds obsessed with the details of mummification. I believe he'd love to try the art himself if he ever had the opportunity."

"I wasn't bothered. I am not faint of heart."

"Good, I would have hated for you to be unhappy over attending." Phaedra slung her small purse over her shoulder. "And are you really willing to pose for me?"

"If you like. We live in the same house, so it will be easy enough to arrange."

"I don't want you to do it only to please me. Modeling can be tiring."

Aurelia smiled. "I think it will be an enjoyable project . . . especially if you ask me about architectural details for the background."

Now Phaedra laughed. "That can be arranged. And you really are perfect as a model, you know. Have you finally realized that other people appreciate your unique beauty?"

"I am complimented." Which was as far as Aurelia could go. She'd lived for too many years as the blackbird of the family.

Phaedra moved closer to the carriage steps, which were several feet off the ground. She peered down the dark drive. "What can be taking Theo so long?"

"Who knows. He's a very odd man," Aurelia said, accidentally letting her secret opinion slip out.

"Eccentric," Phaedra corrected.

Aurelia knew it was none of her business but she asked, "How is it you remain such good friends with Theo anyway? I mean, considering his eccentricity?"

"You know how we met, darling, through that art society. And we have other similar interests. Theo's very urbane."

"I noticed you hadn't heard about his traveling in Italy."

"Theo is often shy, especially when in the company of more than one person. But he usually confides in me."

"And you are *only* friends?"

"Of course." Actually appearing a little uncomfortable, Phaedra smoothed her hair. "I believe you know my heart lies elsewhere."

"With Sean O'Rourke? You don't see him very often."

"Unfortunately, I do not know where that liaison is going." The older woman sighed. "Theo is a patient, undemanding escort, and a respectable lady does not go out alone. I am at least trying to be socially acceptable for your and your sisters' sakes."

Feeling a bit guilty, Aurelia wrapped her arm around Phaedra's slight shoulders. "You do not have to do that for me. You changed your life when you took me in. I do not wish for you to go against your real desires."

Phaedra chuckled, though she was obviously touched. She gave Aurelia a quick hug. "Save your worry. I am happy. I have sown quite enough wild oats in the past." Then she peered down the drive again. "Have Theo and the driver gotten lost? You must rise early for work tomorrow."

"I'm sure there is a good reason for the delay." As they continued waiting, Aurelia thought about her aunt's statement. "Theo is satisfied to remain a friend and no more. Why is he so undemanding, do you think?"

"You must have heard about such things in Italy. Europeans are more sophisticated."

"Do you mean he likes . . . other men?"

Phaedra didn't seem startled by the suggestion. "Hmm, no, I don't think that's the case. I believe Theo is the sort whose sexual nature is buried deeply. Perhaps he transcends the physical entirely, transfers his passion to other areas of life." Phaedra continued, "There are all kinds of people in the world. Theo is odd, but he is gentle and considerate."

"True." Now back to the other topic that aroused Aurelia's curiosity. "About you and Sean O'Rourke, Aunt Phaedra, how serious are your feelings for him?"

Again the older woman sighed and she looked distinctly relieved as the carriage finally appeared. "I will discuss that some other time, Aurelia . . . when we can also discuss your obvious problems with Sean's son." She explained, "I didn't mention the name of your employer because I sensed you were uncomfortable."

Aurelia was startled, not having told her aunt that anything was wrong. Because she feared Phaedra would approach Sean, she hadn't related the offensive remarks Liam had made at the Palmer House reception. She also hadn't spoken of the way he'd treated her at work. But she should have expected her aunt's usual perceptiveness. And had noticed that Phaedra had avoided mentioning O'Rourke and O'Rourke.

"You and Liam were staring at each other all evening," Phaedra pointed out.

"We were not! At least I wasn't—"

"I am not blind."

Now it was Aurelia who sighed, happy that the carriage was at the steps. "We can discuss it at another time."

Phaedra reproached Theo good-naturedly, "We were wondering if you had disappeared."

"I wouldn't leave you unescorted," he muttered. "There were problems with the harness."

He offered both ladies a hand into the carriage. His palm was soft and moist, and he didn't meet Aurelia's eyes. He certainly was a shy and nervous person.

On the way to Prairie Avenue, Phaedra launched into a discussion of Veii and the Etruscans. Aurelia was happy to join in, not wanting to think about work the next day. It might be in her power to avoid discussing Liam but she couldn't avoid seeing him.

She'd been lucky he'd spent the last three days working at a building site, rather than breathing down her neck. But she knew the situation wouldn't last forever.

South Michigan Avenue lay as quiet and empty as a graveyard in the middle of the night. The well-oiled wheels of his carriage made little noise as he drove along. Only the clops of his horse's hooves echoed through the darkness. The rows of great houses were silent, their windows blind eyes looking out onto the street.

But he was not blind. All his senses were heightened, alert, restless. Too restless to sleep, he had risen to prowl.

A little way from the mansion, he reined in and stopped beneath the whispering leaves of a maple tree. Three stories up, beneath the mansard roof, the servants lay abed. He thought of the dainty maid and what he'd learned about her—she was an orphan, all alone in the world. Behind cold stone, the poor little orphan was sleeping, her small face pressed tightly against her pillow.

He imagined that face still and quiet, only a little breath moving her lips and nostrils. Sometimes sleep closely resembled death.

Death . . . The image of cut flowers flitted through his mind. Flowers for wreathes or vases.

He loved cut flowers, the same way he loved still faces and cool flesh.

How lovely she would look with the life newly extinguished from her eyes. That exact moment was intensely fascinating to him. Sometimes the eyes opened even wider in a momentary look of surprise.

Of course, he always discreetly closed them for the rest of the ceremony.

The complete ceremony was intricate and long, as befitted a lovely lady. To his intense pleasure, he already had a ceremony in progress, nearly ready to be finished, a beauty waiting for him in the cellar of his home. So lovely, she was ripe and fragrant, wafting a perfume both sweet and strange.

He licked his lips.

Then he drove on with a shiver, wishing he could continue, could turn onto Prairie Avenue and pass a certain house, but knowing that doing so would only be disheartening. She, the most beautiful of all, she who would be the true gem of his collection, was not for his secret domain. Though he loved to imagine her there, as he had when he'd watched her earlier tonight.

Ah, the splendor. Her hair was like lapis, her arms more shining than gold. She was a sacred lotus in bloom.

He sighed deeply, never having been this frustrated before. But then he'd never before encountered a female like her.

So near and yet so far.

He forced himself to brood on the orphan instead, her dark eyes closed tightly, never to open again, and he quoted a few lines of his favorite poetry, "'My love has left me forever./ I am like a tomb.'"

5

"*I am sorry* to be late," Aurelia told Sean O'Rourke when she entered the office thirty minutes past the starting hour the next morning. She'd taken the State Street electric cable car rather than awaken old Fred, Phaedra's elderly driver. "It seems I did not judge my travel time properly. I hate to make excuses," she went on, embarrassed. "But there are so many people traveling to the exposition and then a dray overturned, forcing me to walk the rest of the way—"

"Ah, this fair has made a mess o'things," Sean interrupted with a wave, not looking concerned at all. "I noticed you have been prompt every other morning and in no hurry to leave at night."

She felt relieved. "I shall make up the time."

"O'course." He smiled warmly. "Don't be worrying yourself about it. Phaedra said you're a good and honest girl."

The relief turned a bit sour. Aurelia didn't want

Sean making an exception for her because of her aunt. But she smiled and turned to leave the private office, nearly colliding with Liam as he entered.

"Good morning, Miss Kincaid," he said, frost in his tone.

"Good morning, Mr. O'Rourke," she said just as coolly.

"I hope your responsibilities here haven't interrupted your busy personal interests," Liam added.

"Now, now." Sean intervened before Aurelia opened her mouth to say something horrid that would be sure to get her fired. "She has already explained why she was late."

Not bothering to hear Liam's reply, Aurelia tightened her lips and hurried away. Her face hot, she couldn't help being aware that all the other employees in the open room stared as she passed. Tossing her purse on the window sill near her drafting table, she took off her jacket and hat and pulled on a pair of sleeve protectors. Even so, she was too angry to get down to work and stared out the window at the busy street below.

Carriages, horse-drawn streetcars, and cable cars inched their way through a crowd of pedestrians. Free enterprise prospered in veritable walls of stone and brick buildings for as far as the eye could see. Chicago was growing every day. She knew she could find another job if necessary.

She didn't have to have a job at all when it came down to it. Though she certainly wasn't an heiress, Aurelia had enough of an inheritance to scrape by in moderate circumstances.

The only problem with the latter was that she

would be bored. No social butterfly, Aurelia passionately wanted to work in her profession. She loved architecture. From as long ago as she could remember, she'd been fascinated with the idea of building, creating shelter, changing the very face of the earth itself. As a little girl, her favorite toys had been blocks, not dolls.

And she didn't want to leave this position when she'd barely been there for two weeks. Not to mention that her defection might cause difficulties between the elder O'Rourke and Phaedra.

She sighed, then straightened up when she heard a couple of her neighbors discussing her directly this time. "Just watch, little Miss Bo Peep can do anything she chooses," muttered one draftsman. "She has the old man wrapped around her little finger."

"Well, we certainly can't compete with her pretty face."

The first man went on, "They shouldn't allow women to work outside the house anyway. It's inappropriate."

Furious, Aurelia turned around slowly, ready to affix the men with a Gorgon eye she hoped would turn them to stone.

But she was blocked by Liam, who was standing in the narrow aisle between the drafting tables and gazing down at her. "Are you enjoying your daydreaming?"

All the resentment and anger she'd felt toward him surged to the surface. Somehow, though, she managed to keep her voice low. "Are you enjoying your cruelty and sadism?"

His lip seemed to curl. "Sadism?"

She was beyond caring that she might be fired.

"What have you been doing the other days this week? Beating mules and workmen in the field?"

"I can't say that I've had that particular pleasure."

"You should try it. I'm sure it would agree with your basic nature."

He raised his brows. "My, we are in snit, aren't we?"

"*You've* been in a snit since the first moment we met. And though I have tried to ignore your jibes—"

To silence her, he leaned forward and gestured toward his office. "Miss Kincaid, please, let us continue this conversation in a more private place."

Where he was going to fire her for certain. Still uncaring, Aurelia rose and stalked down the aisle in front of Liam, her long skirts swishing against the drafting tables. As soon as they reached his office, he closed the door behind them.

She turned, suddenly aware of the dominating way his tall, strong presence filled the room. She felt cornered, her anger edged with a thrill of fear. But she straightened her shoulders and faced Liam proudly.

"You can continue your insults now, if you like," he informed her.

"I do not wish to continue anything. Fire me and be done with it."

"You will have to give me a better reason than that."

"I am speaking back to you and in a discourteous manner. Do you allow such from your employees?"

"In your case, I suppose I will have to." He remarked, "Speaking back, I'm sure, is merely an expression of your spirited personality."

She couldn't believe he was behaving so calmly. "What about my renderings? You seem to think I cannot complete them fast enough."

He shrugged. "I was a bit impatient the other day."

"I was late this morning."

"My father says you have a good excuse."

"Though you do not seem to accept it. I will not have your father and his connection with my aunt stand as the basis for my employment."

He nodded. "All right, then, you seem skilled at your work. That is another basis."

She was taken aback, wondering if she were hearing correctly. "You are arguing to retain me?"

"Are you arguing to be released from your obligations here?"

"No. Of course not."

His expression grew wryly thoughtful. "We seem compelled to take opposite stands with each other, do we not? I admit you bring out the contradictions in my thoughts and emotions." Then he actually laughed. "God, it does feel good to get that out in the open."

Her anger having slowly dissipated, she now felt confused. Aurelia shook her head slowly. "You are certainly a very complex man."

"Many have said so. You can add honesty and forthrightness to cruel and sadistic, I suppose." His smile was lopsided.

He appeared even more handsome when his features softened. She didn't return his smile, but she tried to apologize, "About that remark . . . well, I was exaggerating in the heat of the moment."

"Something I do frequently myself."

She respected him for admitting as much. She couldn't quite say she'd had this sort of experience with any other man. "I appreciate your courage, Mr. O'Rourke."

"I'll take that as worthwhile praise from one who has a surfeit of courage herself."

She couldn't help smiling. "Amazing, we seem to be complimenting each other."

"Which is probably better than hurling insults."

She continued smiling, though she felt awkward and still on guard. "Are we making peace then? I can go to my table and continue working without hostile surveillance?"

"You have had little reason to complain. I've been gone most of the week."

She noticed that he hadn't answered her directly. "I find it nearly impossible to work when someone is being—"

"Sadistic?"

"Difficult," she amended.

"And I find it nearly impossible to work with a beautiful woman around."

Beautiful? As usual when he mentioned her looks, warmth crept through her. She objected, "I have not in any way forced you to stop working."

"But you are a distraction."

"Then put a screen around me," she said with mild sarcasm. "Or wear horse blinkers."

"Blinkers are the better choice, I think." Again, he smiled charmingly. "But perhaps the situation will be different now that we have cleared the air."

"I sincerely hope so." That would be a relief. She glanced toward the glass-paneled door, noticing that Sean was observing them. "I'd better get back to work."

"I suppose."

An unusual tension hung between them, though it was nothing like the discomfiture she'd felt before. She started for the door, glancing at his desk as she passed. An architectural layout was spread out there—a simple ancient-looking building.

"Curious?"

Indeed. Aurelia paused.

"Last night you may have heard that I designed a project for the midway." He ran his fingertips affectionately over the layout. "O'Rourke and O'Rourke is not yet well enough known to have been invited to design a major exhibition building. But this structure wouldn't have been suitable anyway. It belongs on the midway. Today I will be inspecting the place one more time, taking measurements and having interior sketches drafted. Soon it will be ready for the public."

"How interesting."

"Hmm, sketches." He gazed at her assessingly. "I was planning to bring a draftsman. *You* could accompany me, of course . . . if the midway were an appropriate place for ladies to visit."

She immediately frowned. "Appropriate? I hate the word. I may be a lady, but I am not confined by old-fashioned opinions that limit my activities."

He crossed his arms. "So you are saying you heartily desire to accompany me?"

"Are you inviting me to do so?" she challenged in return. The game had changed, had taken a 180-degree turn and she was not displeased, though she thought she should be. "What about the distraction my presence might cause you?"

He laughed. "I shall simply have to force myself to concentrate." Then he pulled out his pocket watch and indicated the time. "If you're going, we shall need to leave shortly. Bring a sketch pad, pencils, and a tape measure."

Aurelia knew she was probably making a mistake, but refusing to worry, she exited the office to gather her supplies. Liam was waiting by the time she'd put on her hat and picked up her purse and jacket.

Sean came strolling down the aisle.

"I am taking Miss Kincaid to the field to do sketches," Liam told his father. "That is, if you can spare her today."

Not surprisingly, Sean seemed rather taken aback. "Well, yes, I can spare her."

"Excellent, although the midway project is small, it will be indicative of our firm's skill. I want everything done as well as possible."

All the other employees stared as Liam and Aurelia walked out the door together. What conjectures must be going through their minds! Aurelia herself could barely believe that she was voluntarily accompanying a man she professed to dislike.

Worse, she was actually looking forward to spending time in his company!

Phaedra straightened her studio, throwing away a used palette covered with paint and propping the canvas she'd been working on against a wall to dry. The entire third floor of the house, once a moderately sized ballroom, was now her private property. Several years ago, when Aurelia had chosen to become an architect rather than a debutante, Phaedra had taken over the room, furnishing it with painting supplies, theatrical props, a few pieces of furniture, and the crates that contained her artistic life's work.

Which was the bulk of her personal belongings. Having led a gypsy life for nearly twenty years, she owned very little. After moving into her brother's house, she'd refurnished a bedroom to her taste and left the rest of the house as she'd found it.

She glanced up when she heard the visitor bell chime three flights below. Sean was early! Smiling, she ripped off her smock and smoothed stray tendrils of hair as she hurried downstairs. The bell rang again and again.

"Such impatience!" she cried, opening the door wide.

Amorous-eyed, Sean slid his arms about her and kissed her deeply. "Too long! Too long!"

She pulled him inside, so the neighbors wouldn't gossip. As had been usual for several months of Friday afternoons, Fred and his wife, Mary, the housekeeper, had been given time off. Their living quarters above the coach house had also contributed to Phaedra's privacy.

Sean pressed her against him, murmuring endearments, then tried to pick her up. "I'll carry you upstairs."

She extricated herself and backed away, laughing. "My goodness, what impatience! Besides, you romantic fool, you will break your back."

His brows drew together. "You think that I'm getting too old, don't you? Well, passion doesn't die, just because a man ages a few years."

"I know exactly how passionate a man you are," she said in an attempt to soothe him, though she would seriously worry that he might strain something if he carried her so far. "Let's have some wine first."

"I'll not be needing wine." He clasped her waist and drew her forward again. "You're intoxicating enough, woman."

She placed her hands against his broad chest. "Just one glass."

He muttered to himself, probably Gaelic curses, but he let her go. She led him into the parlor and poured red wine from the decanter sitting on the sideboard.

He sighed heavily as she handed him a glass. "I long to see you more often."

She felt a twinge of guilt. "But you know it is important that I appear respectable."

"You can be as respectable as you want," he insisted, hinting he was quite willing to take care of that problem for all time.

If only her situation were that easy. Now it was she who sighed.

Sean glanced at his wine before taking a sip. "Can't we bring this up to the bedroom?"

"Soon," she said, enjoying the tension. Besides, she had another agenda. "Is everything all right at your office?" That had been on her mind for days.

"I'm not wanting to talk about the office." Instead, he began unfastening the top buttons of her yellow linen dress.

"Is my niece's work acceptable?"

He dropped his hand, abandoning the buttons for

the moment. "'Tis more than acceptable, 'tis very good. I believe even Liam accepts that now."

"*Even* Liam?" she probed. "Has there been a problem with him?" As if that weren't as clear as the nose on her face.

"My son didn't like my making the decision about Aurelia without him. But I believe we have come to terms with that."

"And Liam and Aurelia get on?"

"As of this day, they seem to."

That made her exceedingly curious. "This very day?"

"Why all these questions?" He scowled and reached for her. "Confound it, woman, I love you, I want to touch you and you are forcing me to do anything but. Life is too short."

She moved closer to kiss his nose lightly and tweak his mustache, but extricated herself when he tried to pin her against him. She circled a chair and reading lamp. "Come now, you are going to live for a few more years. Let us talk and get settled first. I have been worried."

He followed her and raised his brows to heaven. "Worried about what? And what is there to settle?"

"You said Liam and Aurelia have been getting on only as of this very day. Have they been at odds before?" She continued moving, keeping the chair between them.

Sean paused. "Ah, then, if you must know . . . I have heard raised voices between them at times. And o'course, the whole office is probably abuzz with it, your niece being the only woman present except for the cleaning char."

"I knew there were problems, though she wouldn't tell me. I was certain of it. Poor girl."

He tried to catch Phaedra by circling the obstacle in the other direction, but she was too quick. "Don't be worrying. Aurelia is bearing up quite well. She holds herself proudly and does her work. She is quite the professional lady."

"But there has been some change today, you indicated . . . have Aurelia and Liam made peace?"

"I would assume so." He caught hold of the flying edge of Phaedra's skirt, his eyes alight at the sight of her lacy petticoat. "They left the office together to work on a project."

"Really? Hmm, that brings up another question." She let Sean pull her toward him as she searched for the right words. "Er, do you think there's any possibility of romantic feelings between them? Sometimes being at odds disguises that."

Phaedra suspected Aurelia had had some disturbing experience in Italy. The edginess her niece displayed at times was surely due to more than increasing maturity.

"Romantic feelings?" At the mention of that, Sean immediately let go, appearing stunned. "Between Liam and Aurelia? Lord help me, I hope not. That would complicate matters, wouldn't it?"

"Probably."

"I am having enough difficulty with getting down to romance meself."

"Not such difficulty," she said silkily, finally approaching to press herself against him. He tried to kiss her, to cup her breasts, but she slid sideways and led him toward the stairs. "Come, my lovely man." She'd finally gotten the information she wanted.

Afire for what was to come, he murmured huskily, "I can't wait to touch your soft, soft skin!"

He embraced her from behind, grasping her hips as they started to ascend. She moaned softly and arched her spine, showing him that he excited her. She knew he would adore the new silk French undergarments she'd donned for him today.

Not that Phaedra's feelings for Sean were studied. She might be more patient, but she looked forward to their trysts as much as he. She'd fallen in love with Sean O'Rourke very soon after they'd first met, though they hadn't gone to bed for many months. He was a passionate lover and an intelligent, open-minded companion. When she'd told him she'd been an "actress," had hinted she'd had other lovers, he hadn't cared. She knew he would like to offer marriage.

Marriage.

Phaedra wasn't sure what she would say after the most fevered moments had passed and they lay in each other's arms. Though it hurt her, she had been intentionally limiting the time they spent together because Sean had become more and more serious.

Remembering the mistake of her life, the man she'd abandoned in California, Phaedra only wished she were free to make a serious commitment.

6

Liam found he could no longer be irritable with Aurelia after their open discussion. Strangely enough, he didn't mind being distracted by her presence. He was fully aware of her loveliness as he paid forty cents for two tickets and they took the Illinois Central Railway to the nearest gate of the Midway Plaisance in Jackson Park.

"Are we going to discuss the project?" Aurelia asked him at one point on the short journey. "What it is you want me to sketch?"

"I would rather wait, let you see the building first."

"A surprise, hmm?"

Which was about the extent of the conversational possibilities as they were buffeted and interrupted by the railway's many other travelers, most of whom were tourists. Liam tried to ignore the soft curves of her body whenever she was pushed against him.

When they got off at their destination, they headed for the fair gates, where Liam showed the special business pass that saved him from paying the rather high entrance fee of fifty cents apiece.

Having wondered about her background from the first, he asked Aurelia about her training in Italy. "How is it you were able to study in a country where women are, ah . . . not always in the forefront of the industry?"

"Women are not in the forefront anywhere," she pointed out. "But Solini is a man with three daughters and no sons. He is training his youngest in the art."

"An older mentor."

"And someone my aunt knew years and years ago."

"Your aunt is very helpful," Liam remarked, then noticed the sidelong look she gave him. "As is my father. He was a builder in New York, though he never had a formal education."

"Which is not unusual for today's architects."

"Father sent *me* to school to learn the finer points."

"And you wanted to do so. You love the subject, I assume."

"I love it," he admitted, thinking of archeology, which he loved as well but could not pursue.

She might have heard the hesitation in his voice, as she gazed at him curiously.

"I'm not only my father's only son, I'm his one surviving offspring." Which was why he didn't want to disappoint the older man. "I had a sister and a brother who died as children."

"I'm sorry."

"Then I lost my mother before I was eighteen. My father and I have been on our own for quite some time."

"I have dealt with loss myself," she said, her face serious. "By age sixteen, both my parents had passed on. Aunt Phaedra took me in. She has been a loving and generous guardian."

As they strolled along, he thought about how easy their conversation seemed to flow, once they'd made a truce. Liam really liked the "feel" of Aurelia. She was an intelligent and refined companion, not a puppy-eyed female who hung on his arm and his every word.

Though over twenty-one and independent, Aurelia wouldn't appreciate the attentions of some of the rough-looking men who were lined up at the midway's entry gate. Liam gave them warning looks that told them to keep their distance.

Inside, music tinkled and the smell of exotic foods wafted through the air. Noisy families, as well as clusters of women and men, crowded the walkways. Hucksters tried to sell trinkets wherever one turned.

"Everyone looks excited," said Aurelia. "Already the Midway Plaisance seems more vital somehow."

"That's because these people are seeking entertainment, not architectural examples or educational exhibits to awe them." He chuckled as they passed a Swiss-style chalet with a huge garish cuckoo clock hanging above the front door. "These temporary shacks probably came from other fairs in Europe, but no one cares. The midway is going to be far more popular than the rest of the exposition and will bring in more money, too."

Aurelia stared at the "Blarney Castle" as they passed it, then pointed out a sign advertising Hagenbeck's animal show that would be taking place in a great steel arena.

"That German has lions riding horses, I hear."

"There is something for everyone." She indicated another sign. "I see they have an ice railway, a skating rink, and a toboggan slide. Personally, I would like to try the Ferris wheel."

No one could miss the great engineering marvel towering over all. The 265-foot girdered wheel had been designed by the same bridge builder who created the Eiffel Tower.

"Perhaps when we're finished, we shall see if there is room for us," said Liam. Not that the glass-and-veneer cars weren't roomy; each carried sixty people. But the queues waiting to get on were rumored to be long. "I hear it only lasts for twenty minutes, but there's quite a view."

They turned past the reconstruction of the Viennese street Der Graben as it appeared in 1750. Notes from a harpsichord blended with the drumbeat coming from the African exhibit nearby, a village of Dahomey.

The most popular area of all was their final destination, a street in Cairo.

Aurelia openly admired the exotic bazaars. "My goodness, there are real camels and donkeys."

"Authentic touches. The climate is much nicer here than in Egypt, though."

"You've been there?"

"Once."

"It must have been fascinating." She actually sounded thrilled.

"Do you think so? Would you be adventurous enough to visit such a country?"

"If I had the chance, I certainly would."

He thought she was being truthful and had to admit he was intrigued.

Aurelia started, bumping into Liam as one of the camels rose to its knees and made a loud, groaning noise. "Good heavens."

"The animal isn't unhappy," Liam assured her, once more trying to ignore her soft curves. "Noises like that are normal. And he's sticking his throat out there, not his tongue."

She made a face. "You're an expert on camels, hmm?"

"We used them as pack animals in Egypt."

"Were you crossing the Sahara?"

"Something I deem even more exciting. We were looking for the past." He went on to explain, "The English archeologist Petrie took me on as an assistant for several months. I accompanied him to the Valley of the Kings, sifting sand for ancient artifacts."

"My, you have had real archeological experience."

"Though I'd like to have even more. Archeology is the other love of my life."

"No wonder you are a member of the Society for the Study of Ancient Mediterranean Cultures."

"Speaking of the society . . ." He made an expansive gesture toward the building they were approaching. "Here is O'Rourke and O'Rourke's project."

"Oh!" She caught her breath, her eyes bright. She stepped back and sideways to get the best view. "An Egyptian temple."

"Of sorts. It's no Karnak."

"I was certain the layout on your desk was some sort of ancient building."

"Do you like it?"

"I love it!"

Liam knew she wasn't the type of woman who would effuse in order to impress him. "I had the exterior painted an authentic reddish sand color." Liam indicated the two towers in front. "As you may have noticed, the pylons are small. And there is no inner courtyard or sanctum."

"But it looks quite authentic to most eyes, I'm sure," she hastened to add. Then she read aloud the bright lettering on the side of the temple, "See the sacred ancient mummies! Four-thousand-year-old kings buried with their gold!"

"Real temples, of course, didn't have garish signs," he said with a laugh. "Unless they were in hieroglyphics."

"Are there really mummies on display?"

"Not yet, that's why we're here. The building was barely up by the time the fair opened. Rossiter and some of his associates are still sculpting and decorating several coffins in heavy papier-mâché. You and I are going to design the niches for them."

"I'm honored."

Pleased himself, he unlocked the door of the little temple and started to take her inside.

A man meandering by called out, "Can we see those dead mummies?"

Liam exchanged glances with Aurelia. "Come

back in a few days!" he shouted, then muttered under his breath, "God help us if mummies were alive."

Aurelia joined his laughter. "Are you actually going to present your exhibit as ancient Egyptian?"

"Let's just say we are not claiming anything is fake. The coffins are fairly realistic, considering the material for those of the New Kingdom were similar—cartonnage."

"But there won't be any bodies inside, alive or not."

"Of course there will. Rossiter is also wrapping up some sample mummies. As you may have noticed the other night, he's quite the stickler for detail and insisted on ripping up yards of real linen for the bandages."

"I noticed." She gazed about the dark interior of the building. "This exhibit will certainly appeal to the macabre imagination."

"That's why I want to plaster in niches that will place the coffins in deep shadow." Liam turned on the building's two small gaslights, revealing plain walls. "We need five display areas, two on one side and three on the other. The coffins will be propped inside them. Each coffin is approximately six by two feet."

She was already pulling out her sketch pad and pencil.

"A basic draft will be fine for the moment. You can complete the rendering in the office."

A tendril of dark hair escaped her Psyche knot as she sketched. Fascinated with the way it curled against her slim neck, he had to tear himself away. Determined to take measurements, he took out some paper from his case. When he had finished, he approached Aurelia again and gazed over her shoulder, catching a whiff of her light scent.

"I see you're adding some imaginative touches." Elegant rows of lotuses and scarabs were evident around the niches' borders.

"Don't you think this would be more decorative?"

He considered. "The borders would be eye-catching enough, but time-consuming to sculpt in plaster."

"I wasn't thinking they should be in bas-relief." She waved her pencil. "What about a two-dimensional stencil? I believe the Egyptians were partial to wall paintings."

"True." He had to agree. "I like that. We shall try it." As she continued, he added, "You draw Egyptian decoration as well as the more common Baroque and Renaissance."

"I may not have visited Egypt, but I've studied her art. If you like, I could create lotus and scarab stencils myself. Then anyone can paint the borders in."

"That would be wonderful." But he pointed out, "You'd be doing more than your job requires."

"I don't mind."

Was the truce to become a long and lasting peace? From the look on her face, he believed they may have overcome any previous tensions.

While she finished up the sketches, he inspected the rest of the interior and revealed some of his philosophy. "Ancient architecture appeals to me. I like the simple lines. I believe the ancients worked much closer to nature. Egyptian buildings were either constructed of dried mudbricks from the Nile or sandstone from the country's mountains."

"Their architecture seems to be an intrinsic part of the environment," she agreed.

"Even Egyptian wall paintings reflected the colors of the surrounding land—jade green and brown for the Nile, turquoise and lapis blue for the sky, carnelian red for the desert." Colors which would also look good on Aurelia, Liam mused.

"Do you think the Greeks and Romans worked close to nature as well?"

He forced his mind back to the subject at hand. "Interesting question." He rubbed his chin. "Well, the Greeks anyway. Though their marble temples reflected their philosophy of grace and balance as much as their elemental land."

"They were an intellectual yet passionate culture."

Just as she was an intriguing mixture of intellect and spirit. But Liam stuck to the topic. "As for the Romans, in my opinion, they got carried away, added too much decoration. They tried too hard to impress the world."

She smiled wryly. "Then you probably don't like the Beaux Arts style of the main exposition area."

He had to be truthful. "Where every possible style is mixed with every other style, then merely applied to a basic structure underneath? No, I can't say I approve."

"But the white buildings are rather magical-looking, don't you think? They seem to float on the horizon."

"They will do for exhibits that are meant to fade

away," he agreed grudgingly in respect for her positive outlook. "Hopefully they will not influence future architects' ideas of modern design."

She laughed softly and finally closed her sketchbook. "You are a follower of Sullivan's 'form follows function.'"

"In both ancient and modern architecture. Not you, though?"

"I do not dislike Beaux Arts but neither do I wish to use the style as a prototype for the future."

A thoughtful answer, but he had strong opinions on the matter. "I believe it's imperative to consider the needs of the modern world."

"And you think you know what those needs are?"

"I can make a good guess." He smiled. Then he told her, "You have nerve, implying your employer might not be correct."

But she only laughed more in reaction.

"You stand up for your views, don't you?" A trait that garnered his respect.

"Usually, though I try to avoid being strident with clients." She pointed out, "I don't think we have opposing opinions anyway. I prefer simplicity whenever possible, a view Sullivan would agree with."

Aurelia was a woman whom Liam found very agreeable indeed. He was certain he could converse with her for hours and never be bored.

As they got ready to leave the temple, she brought up another related subject. "What architectural philosophy does your father hold?"

"My father? He is practical enough to like functional form and broad-minded enough to let me guide the design direction of the firm."

Which would tell her whom to look toward when she wanted to advance in her position.

Liam thought he'd indeed be considering her for a higher level in the future. Aurelia Kincaid was not only a woman of beauty and grace, but ideas and talent.

"Are you still willing to wait for a ride on the Ferris wheel?" Liam asked after they'd left his Egyptian temple.

"Are you?" Aurelia came back, feeling amazingly at ease with him. She was tempted to pinch herself to make sure she wasn't dreaming.

In answer he shouldered forward to purchase tickets and they got in line. As did two well-dressed ladies and three gentlemen. Aurelia glanced politely at the small group. Obviously the upper classes sometimes enjoyed the midway, too.

"Anyone you know?"

She shook her head.

"I'm surprised."

"Why? I am not at the forefront of Chicago society and never have been. There are many people I do not know."

"You don't attend a round of dinners every week or hostess teas on Sundays?"

"I don't have the time or energy. I prefer pursuing my profession."

"That's an unusual decision for an heiress."

"Heiress? Where did you get that idea? I have a moderate independent income, that is all."

Which ended that line of inquiry. Aurelia supposed

Liam was like anyone else in wondering about her financial circumstances. The difference was he actually asked questions.

They surged forward a few moments later and entered one of the enclosed cars of the Ferris wheel. Liam made sure they would have a good view by obtaining plush seats next to the expanse of glass. When the car began to ascend, the crowd pressed him against her.

Whether she liked it or not, she was all too aware of the warmth of his body, but then that was probably because she wasn't as innocent as most women in her position. And when the westering sun blazed through the glass, she noticed the gold flecks in Liam's green eyes and admired the red glints in his auburn hair.

The whole carload of sixty oohed and ahhed when the car stopped for several minutes at the very top to give them a panoramic view. On one side, the silver-blue lake stretched out toward the hazy horizon; on the others, the gray of the city mixed with the fairy-white of the exposition buildings. The sun was a brilliant orange ball.

Liam leaned closer, his breath feathering her cheek. "The future will be as bright as this day."

"Are you making a prediction?"

"I'm expressing a hope . . . just like the Egyptians. They painted a joyful view of the afterworld in their tombs, you know. They weren't as concerned with death as everyone thinks. They were only passionately hopeful that life would continue."

Liam was just as vital and passionate, Aurelia thought, as the car slowly descended. When they got off, he offered her a helping hand, then his arm, obviously not caring what *Godey's Lady's Book* had to say about anything.

Aurelia admired his physical strength, apparent in the muscles that flexed beneath her fingers and the calluses she'd felt when she'd taken his hand.

They strolled back toward the railway, passing a pair of pretty, young lovers kissing in a shady area in the bushes. Aurelia's breasts tightened and she stared hungrily before becoming decidedly concerned about herself. Was she so wanton? Before he had betrayed and frightened her, Rosario had introduced her to the intense pleasures of love.

Recalling languorous hours spent in a man's arms, she sighed, then flushed when Liam gazed at her.

"Is something wrong?"

"Everything is quite fine," she told him. Terrible! Untruthful! She imagined *his* arms around her.

"Good, because I've had a wonderful time with you this afternoon. You are a very exciting woman. I like your directness, your intelligence," he went on.

"And I, yours . . . Mr. O'Rourke."

"Please call me Liam," he told her. Then he laughed. "So you like my directness . . . even when you've thought it sadistic."

"Perhaps I haven't always seen you at your best."

"That is certainly true."

A passing group of men crowded Liam, forcing him against her. He slid an arm about her shoulders to steady her and she vividly imagined what spending hours in his arms might be like. She grew breathless as the crowd grew thicker nearing the entrance gate.

"We seem to be trying to swim upstream, don't we?" she noted.

"Perhaps we should wait for a break in the rush."

Still holding her lightly with one arm, Liam moved her off the path. All the benches were taken, so they couldn't sit down. Instead, they took refuge beneath a flowering tree. The low-hanging petals smelled sweet.

"This is lovely," she said.

"Very."

Liam picked one of the small flowers and gently rubbed it against her cheek. The simple, sensual gesture disarmed her. Semisecluded from the passing world, they gazed at each other for a moment before he lifted her chin and kissed her lightly on the lips. She took a shaky breath, but couldn't bring herself to pull away.

His eyes darkened as his expression changed. He drew her toward him and angled his head to take her mouth. Their breaths melded as Aurelia was pressed against his broad chest. She touched him, felt the warmth of his flesh beneath his shirt. He was all too achingly real. Opening her lips to allow him deeper access, she wound her arms about his neck. Her hat tumbled off but she didn't care.

It had been so long and he was so very attractive. She shivered as he ran his fingers along her spine— she could feel the delightful pressure even through her camisole and corset. Liam pressed one hand firmly against her waist, causing her back to arch. He was masterful and sure of himself, sure of her body's reactions.

Lost to sensation, unconsciously she moved her

hips. She didn't realize he had cupped her breast until she was achingly, wantonly aroused . . .

But her mind still functioned. And through the blur, she knew she should be very upset by the over-familiarity.

She placed her hands firmly against his chest and pushed away, breathing raggedly. "We have gone too far, Mr. O'Rourke."

His breath was also uneven. After a minute, he said, "I thought we had established you were to call me Liam."

She ignored the reminder but couldn't fail to notice the prying eyes of passersby. She quickly smoothed her hair and dress. "We are in a public place."

He glanced about. "Is that what has upset you?" He reached for her. "Then I can easily provide more privacy . . ."

But Aurelia drew away. "We have established much too much too soon."

He frowned. "I was only going to place my arm about your shoulders . . . in a soothing gesture."

"I am not sure I could trust you to keep to that." She certainly couldn't trust herself. "Considering the kind of man you are." Passionate and daring.

"Kind of man?" His frown deepened. "And what do you mean by that remark? I wasn't born and raised a gentleman—does that make me ineligible to be your suitor?"

His obvious anger caused her to step back. "I do not grant liberties to any man, gentleman or not."

"Well, you granted a few to me a moment ago. You must have forgotten yourself."

Her face grew hot. Had some gossip managed to travel to this country? "I forgot myself, yes, but so did you. Now I think we should both forget about this situation entirely."

Especially since they worked together.

"I will never forget," Liam promised.

How embarrassing and unpleasant!

Blaming herself more than Liam, whose intense personality could nevertheless change with the direction of the wind, Aurelia maintained a cool silence as they took the train back to Randolph Street. She was glad of the surrounding crowd that kept them from so much as making eye contact.

She was also happy that Fred had brought the carriage to the Schiller Building to fetch her. It being late in the afternoon, she didn't have to reenter the office.

She and Liam didn't say good-bye.

He'd claimed he would never forget their kisses. And, unfortunately, neither would she, no matter how much she wanted to.

Liam was a man she couldn't ignore, fascinating if difficult. She knew it would be very easy to get involved with him, and she feared it would be absolutely the wrong thing to do.

7

Aurelia finished the renderings of the Egyptian temple's interior on Monday. Far too aware of Liam for her own comfort, she was somewhat relieved when he seemed distant and cool.

"Thank you," he said simply when she handed him the drawings.

She knew he was watching her closely as she reached inside the folder she'd brought from home. "And I have the stencils completed."

His gaze moved from her to the scarab-and-lotus design cut out of medium-weight paper that had been coated with linseed oil. "You made these on your own time?"

"I told you I would do so." She hadn't considered going back on her promise merely because they'd had a heated exchange.

"Very nice . . . though it wasn't necessary."

"I believe the display will be enhanced by decoration."

"I'm sure it shall," he agreed. After one more long glance, he turned on his heel and returned to his office.

While Aurelia started on another project. And berated herself—how could she have allowed Liam such liberties? She had certainly given him the wrong impression. He no doubt believed she was a wanton woman. What if he gossiped about her to other men? She didn't want to be more uncomfortable at work than she already was.

Mixed with her professional worry, however, was personal disappointment. They had so much in common and had been getting along so well that day they visited the fair. Liam O'Rourke was not only highly attractive, but mentally stimulating. He had a unique, unconventional view of life. She'd been hurt when he said he was unwilling to forget their indiscretion. And she'd been surprised when he'd accused her of ruling against him because of his working-class past.

Ruling against him as what? A lover?

She glanced back at Liam's office, where he was sorting papers and jotting down figures. Did his untraditional attitude mean he was broad-minded about love? Perhaps he didn't think it wrong for two independent, unmarried people to have a discreet affair.

Not that she desired to do so, she told herself, not for some time in the future and not unless she truly cared for a man. And if that were the case, she thought, surely marriage would be included in the plan.

She'd had enough of illicit liaisons, forbidden

pleasures, honey-sweet kisses that no one was supposed to hear or see.

If only she could convince her sleeping mind of that logic.

This morning she'd awakened from a dream about Liam, half remembering the warmth of his skin, the thrill of his caress, the excitement of his tongue lightly touching hers. They'd been only partially clothed as they lay beneath the flowering tree .

Aurelia flushed at the memory.

She'd been upset about the dream and absolutely refused to allow it to interfere with her work now.

To force her thoughts into some semblance of order, Aurelia carefully arranged all her pencils and papers next to her drawing board. Then she sorted through her assignments. One was rather important, a large and expensive house to be placed on a woodsy Oak Park property. Documents hadn't been signed yet, so it was hoped detailed sketches of several elevations would sway Jerome Gray, the wealthy client.

Inspired by the simple-looking but complex design that again reminded her of ancient buildings, Aurelia wished she had the liberty of visiting the site herself. The actual lay of the land was vital for good renderings. And she'd always preferred experience to figures and measurements anyway.

Putting the Gray assignment aside temporarily, Aurelia toiled through the rest of the morning, only taking a light lunch before getting back to work that afternoon. Liam left her alone and the other draftsmen paid her no mind, possibly because they were now used to her presence or had nothing interesting to gossip about.

When Aurelia dropped her pencil, though, a bashful-looking, bespectacled young draftsman named George picked it up. His smile when he handed the pencil to her seemed sincere.

"I know what it is like to be new. If you need any help, please let me know."

"Why, thank you," Aurelia said, appreciating the first kindly gesture she'd received from another employee.

George went back to work and Aurelia smiled, her faith in humanity renewed. One person, at least, did not resent her. She was still feeling sunny when the firm's front door swung open to admit Frank Lloyd Wright.

The architect passed by her table and exchanged a quick but friendly greeting. "I am disappointed you haven't stopped by yet."

"Then I shall try to do so very soon."

"I have several projects you will enjoy looking over."

"Really? You're willing to show work in progress?" said Aurelia enthusiastically.

Wright lowered his voice conspiratorially. "To *you,* of course. Try to come by tomorrow afternoon."

Aurelia promised she would, then Liam caught sight of Wright, showed him into his office, and shut the door.

She wondered if they were making arrangements to pay off what Wright owed for the mahogany. Considering the young architect's reputation, he was probably borrowing some additional materials. Indeed, he was so charming and complimentary, Aurelia figured it unlikely that anyone could turn him down unless he took advantage one too many times.

And if she said as much to Liam, he would undoubtedly once more accuse her of being interested in a married man!

Trying to put both men out of her mind, Aurelia got down to her work. She was so engrossed in her rendering that she was startled when Wright stopped by her table again. As before, he leaned closer to examine her work.

"About those projects I mentioned . . . could you use some extra income?"

She raised her brows.

Wright went on without waiting for an answer. "My partner and I are so busy, we hardly have time to complete our own renderings. I should very much like to hire you for a job or two . . . on your own time, of course."

So that was what he'd been getting at. "I am flattered."

"But are you willing?"

"I'm not sure." Though she thought it would be exciting to work with Frank Lloyd Wright, she did owe her loyalties to the O'Rourkes. "I am very busy."

"Well, please think about it." He waved an expansive hand. "And let me know. Your fee would be based on speculation—paid only after the client pays. But there is no need to worry. My business is growing every day."

She thanked Wright for considering her and he left rather quickly, perhaps because he'd realized Liam was observing them. Aurelia's heart sank when Liam approached to sit down on the windowsill beside her.

He crossed his arms and didn't bother to tiptoe around the subject on his mind. "You would do well to limit yourself to projects for your own company. Mr. Wright was fired by Louis Sullivan for 'bootlegging' houses. Are you planning to follow in his footsteps?"

Her face grew warm.

"Were you eavesdropping?" she demanded. "If so, you didn't hear correctly. I have no intention of designing houses for Mr. Frank Lloyd Wright."

"You're merely doing a few renderings for him."

"I did not agree to that either."

"Not yet."

Probably not ever. But she refused to admit that to Liam. "O'Rourke and O'Rourke is in no danger of losing business from my activities. Unless my work is in direct competition, I believe I can do what I like."

"That's what Wright told Sullivan—his designs were for domestic dwellings, not the business structures in which the company specializes."

"Then Sullivan was in the wrong," she concluded.

She raised her chin and glanced at her opponent out of the corner of her eye, noting Liam's burning expression. For half an instant, she could imagine he was jealous. But that, of course, was ridiculous.

"So you won't agree to limit your work to this company?" Liam asked.

While she had already made that decision, she did not appreciate his insisting. "Not unless you pay me for every hour of the week."

"Hmmph." He rose with a scowl. "If you ever lose this job, you will have to be ready to live on that moderate income you say you have. For if you think you will ever get money from Wright, you're dreaming."

Dreams.

Aurelia stabbed her pencil at the paper, wishing she'd dreamed of choking Liam the night before, rather than enjoying his embrace.

"You will not have to stay late and the social experience will be diverting," Fiona assured Aurelia on the way to dinner at Mariel's that evening. "You are far too serious about your work."

Aurelia yawned, not bothering to take offense. "Your driver will have to be willing to take me home when I wish. Otherwise, you are carrying out a kidnapping."

Fiona merely rolled her beautiful blue eyes and toyed with the lavender fan that matched her beaded dinner dress.

Aurelia hadn't expected to find her elder sister waiting in the hallway when she came home. Nor had she expected Fiona to be able to convince her to go out for the evening. But she'd felt guilty when Fiona had reminded her that it was Mariel's anniversary. Aurelia might not care to celebrate the occasion, but she knew Mariel would be hurt if she didn't.

"I can't believe you didn't read the invitation that was delivered to you last week," Fiona went on.

"I sorted through the envelopes and only opened the bills."

Fiona sniffed. "Really, you and Phaedra lead such strange lives, if you *do* manage to avoid notoriety."

"We are difficult to understand, I am sure."

Phaedra herself would be missing this event, having already left the house before Aurelia had gotten home. Her aunt would receive an admonishment from Fiona at another time, Aurelia was certain.

"Is that truly one of the nicest dresses you have?" Fiona looked over the simple deep gold silk that Aurelia had worn to the Society for the Study of Mediterranean Cultures. "It isn't even in style."

"But it suits me." Having socialized with the Solinis in Italy, who were a rather avant-garde family, Aurelia had honed her own style.

"Hopefully, DeWitt will think you pretty anyway."

"DeWitt?" said Aurelia. "He is a guest at this dinner? I thought he was your friend, not Mariel's."

"He is a friend of us both."

And Aurelia had not one doubt that she'd be seated next to the man.

But by the time they reached Mariel's house, she had convinced herself to give DeWitt another chance, especially after the words she'd had with Liam. By comparison, DeWitt would make a polite and considerate dinner companion.

Both Wesley and Mariel greeted the sisters so warmly, Aurelia was glad she'd come. She complimented Mariel on her new diamond earrings, Wesley's anniversary present.

A little while later, Aurelia even offered a sincere

smile to DeWitt when he pulled out her chair at the table. Then he made small talk, raving about the first course, cream of asparagus soup, as well as the second, broiled quail on toast. Aurelia merely picked at the food on her plate. Too many disturbing thoughts about Liam and her seesaw situation at work crowded her mind.

"Are you feeling well?" DeWitt asked when he noticed her lack of appetite. He smoothed his napkin over his mustache carefully to remove any stray crumbs.

"I'm fine, merely tired."

"You have been busy with your architecture?"

Aurelia stifled a yawn. "I completed several renderings today and another project over the weekend."

"You should be careful. Ladies need their rest. They are like pretty flowers and as easily crushed."

Wondering where DeWitt had obtained his philosophy regarding women, Aurelia stared down the table at Mrs. Carlton. Her white elbow-length gloves rolled back to free her age-marked hands, the elderly Southern belle ate dainty bites and simpered at the gentlemen seated on either side.

DeWitt exchanged pleasantries about the weather until the main course arrived. Then he asked Aurelia about her renderings.

"The two I enjoyed most portrayed the interior of a small Egyptian temple."

"A temple?" He paused between bites. "Do O'Rourke and O'Rourke build in the Orient? I had no idea."

"Actually, the temple is on the midway." She thought of Liam and their outing with a sharp twinge of nostalgia. "The building is located on the Cairo street and when finished will display coffins and mummies."

Then she remembered that DeWitt disapproved of the midway and expected him to offer censure.

Instead, though, he seemed interested. "How extraordinary. I suppose such a place is meant to spook the observers, but I must say I've always admired the Egyptians. They treated their lost ones with respect."

"Lost ones? Oh, you mean the dead."

"The Egyptians' tombs were so well constructed and nearly as elaborate as the mausoleums of New Orleans . . . my mother is from Louisiana."

"I've heard the cemeteries are quite interesting there, everyone having to be buried aboveground and all."

The bewhiskered man on Aurelia's other side glanced at her and then at DeWitt with a frown. But the unusual conversation didn't seem to bother DeWitt.

"The Egyptians took such time and trouble with those who passed on," he went on. "I've read much about it. Today's undertakers could learn something from them." Then he admitted quietly, "There have been several of that profession on my grandmother's side of the family."

Perhaps that's where DeWitt's uncharacteristic interest came from, Aurelia decided. Wherever, the subject had prompted the most scintillating conversation she'd ever had with the man. How different he was from Liam, who could barely exchange two words with her that didn't cause sparks to fly through the air.

Aurelia skipped dessert but DeWitt dug into the lemon custard pie. Unable to stop a yawn this time, she hid it behind her hand.

"You *are* tired," said DeWitt.

"I'm sorry."

"You must make time for other activities besides work." She knew he could tell she didn't like his tone. He softened the remark by explaining, "I myself try to limit my hours at the department store. Otherwise, I would be there day and night."

She nodded. Which must have given him enough encouragement to launch into another lecture on the current state of merchandising. As he finished his pie, he discussed Chicago's merchant prince, Marshall Field, and his success, then his own goals for expansion in the future.

"I see no need for ladies to travel to Paris or even New York for the newest in fashions. They should be able to buy them right here. Of course, one would need quite a large sum of money to lay out for such an inventory."

"Umm, hmm."

Aurelia stared at the flickering candelabra in front of her to keep her eyes from closing. She couldn't wait until dinner was officially over and she could ask Fiona's driver to take her home. She had a long day planned for tomorrow.

"Aurelia?"

She suddenly realized that DeWitt was waiting for some response from her. "Pardon me. Now what was it?"

Looking annoyed, DeWitt repeated his question. "Where do you buy your dresses?"

"I had this one made by a seamstress in Italy."

"From a French pattern?"

"I believe she drew up the pattern herself, after I described what I wanted."

"That's unusual."

"I do not believe every passing fashion would become me," she explained. Though she dressed in the usual conservative workaday skirt and shirtwaist during the day. "I prefer an individualistic style."

"Then you are a difficult woman for a merchandiser to approach."

Noting his tightened lips, she realized he disapproved. "I am not the best customer for department stores."

Actually, she wasn't the best woman for DeWitt Carlton. So why was he pursuing her?

After dinner, as should have been expected, the other guests implored Mariel to play a piano piece. Aurelia determined that she would stay a little longer to please her sister. Once more she lost herself in Mariel's playing. Such talent. Aurelia only hoped that she had the potential to be as talented an architect.

When the piece ended, Wesley stood and led the applause. Then he made a toast, "To the sweetest, loveliest . . . and most talented lady. I am honored to share my life with you, Mariel. I cherish every day."

Tears glistened in her sister's eyes and Aurelia felt touched by the sincere emotion husband and wife shared. But she was also a little surprised to hear Wesley announce so strongly that he valued Mariel's talent. Perhaps he wasn't such a bad life partner, after all. And Mariel obviously loved him. In addition, Aurelia had to admit the idea of being cherished was rather appealing.

A few minutes later, she finally made ready to leave, only to be caught by DeWitt near the door.

"Mother and I will be pleased to take you home," he insisted to her dismay.

On the other hand, DeWitt's mother didn't seem impressed with her son's choice of ladies at all. After being seated in the carriage and tucked in with a lap robe, she stared closely at Aurelia. "Do you have any relatives from, ah . . . southern Europe?"

Though Mrs. Carlton worded the question carefully, Aurelia could feel the impending censure. "I had one grandmother who was Greek." A detail that Fiona regarded as a family skeleton that needed to be locked in a closet.

"Greek?" said Mrs. Carlton faintly. "Oh."

The elderly woman certainly didn't sound pleased. Perhaps she would tell her son to cease his attempts at courtship. Not that Aurelia would mind.

"How long has your family been in this country?" DeWitt's mother went on.

"Most of them have been here for two generations. They settled in Massachusetts and Ohio before coming to Chicago."

"Hmm, always in the North." Mrs. Carlton sounded even more disapproving. "Did any of your relatives happen to take part in the, ah . . . recent unpleasantness?"

Unpleasantness? Then Aurelia understood. "You're referring to the Civil War? I had an uncle who served in the army."

"Union, of course."

"He was an officer under General Sherman."

That nearly took Mrs. Carlton's breath away, Aurelia could tell, certain the woman was imagining the burning of Georgia in vivid detail. For a few minutes, the atmosphere was charged but silent.

Then DeWitt finally spoke up in her defense. "Actually, Father was a Northerner, too."

Mrs. Carlton broke in quickly, "My late husband was a good man, no matter his relations. He was generous with his wealth and his social connections."

What she really meant, Aurelia realized, was that her husband's money made up for his background.

"Social connections are the most *important* part of people's lives," Mrs. Carlton stated, as if reciting a commandment. "We must honor and nourish them like a beautiful garden. The flowers and vegetables and fruit will reward you someday. DeWitt's late wife understood that."

Fiona had told Aurelia that the younger Mrs. Carlton had died of a fever. At the moment, Aurelia wondered if DeWitt's poor wife had died to escape his mother, who'd always lived with them. An uncharitable thought, perhaps, but appropriate.

Again, she wondered why DeWitt was attempting to court her. She wasn't a good marital prospect and he surely had enough sense to know that. Unless there was some social connection DeWitt could gain through her, a connection more important than his mother's objections.

DeWitt was already distantly related to the very wealthy Upton Price. Might a merger with Fiona's sister cement a closer relationship . . . and make possible a hefty business loan? DeWitt had twice mentioned he would need a great deal of money to pursue his highest goals.

When they reached the house, DeWitt insisted on seeing Aurelia to the door. They stood on the broad, roofed porch for a few moments. "Fiona is having an at-home tomorrow evening. Of course, I'll see you there."

"No, I am planning on taking a field trip after work hours," she explained.

"A field trip? Must you soil your hands, too?" He didn't try to hide his disapproval.

"It isn't required by my employer. But it is important to me, as I have some very important renderings to do on a project in Oak Park."

"Oak Park? You would travel so far to sketch? You seem literally consumed by ambition."

"I love my work," she told him. Even at the draftsman level, she'd decided, and even if she had to deal with Liam O'Rourke.

"But work will be a very cold companion as you grow older. You are not a young girl anymore."

Now Aurelia was growing annoyed. "If you do not like my attitudes and interests, why do you pursue me?" she asked bluntly.

"Because I believe you have much sensibility underneath," DeWitt stated. Before she could reply, he continued, the determination he usually hid coming to the fore, "You should be happy I pursue you. I can offer you much, take you away from the dreary life you lead." He grasped her arm with a strong grip, surprising her. "And I *will* pursue you. I will change your mind and reach that soft, sweet heart." Then and only then did he release her to step away. "Good night."

Chilled, having heard similar statements from Rosario, Aurelia stood in the darkness and watched the carriage depart. Her concentration was so complete, she almost jumped out of her skin when Phaedra suddenly appeared out of nowhere.

"Sorry, darling, we arrived at nearly the same time as you," Phaedra apologized. Theo followed directly behind her. "We didn't want to interrupt your little tête-à-tête, so we sat in the driveway."

"I would have been happier if you had interrupted."

Phaedra laughed at the sarcasm and touched Aurelia's cheek affectionately. "Let us go inside and have a little nightcap of brandy." An unladylike habit Phaedra had acquired in Europe. "Would you like some, Theo?"

"No, thank you. I fear I must leave."

"Then good night," said Phaedra. "As usual, I am grateful for your kind and thoughtful companionship."

"Good night, Phaedra. Aurelia."

Inside the softly lit house, homey and familiar, Aurelia relaxed and put DeWitt's remarks into context. He was obviously an arrogant man who thought he could influence a woman with strong words. Well, if he ever spoke to her that way again, Aurelia would show him how a strong woman reacted and tell him off in no uncertain terms.

Phaedra went to the parlor to fetch the brandy.

"I can only stay awake a short time," Aurelia cautioned, following her. "I dare not be late again. And I prefer mixing a little water with my brandy."

"As you like. The liquor will help you sleep better and more deeply."

Hopefully, so deeply she wouldn't dream, Aurelia thought. She didn't want to spend another night having nightmares about Italy . . . or erotic encounters with Liam. At the moment, she wasn't certain which was worse.

8

On Tuesday, Liam dropped by the turreted mansion on South Drexel Boulevard to check on Rossiter's mummies and coffins. No one answered the bell, but the great front door was unlocked, so he went in.

The house seemed deserted, not even one servant in sight. Feeling a bit uncomfortable, Liam walked past the front parlor, glancing at the plush maroon upholstered couch and its facing brown leather chairs, then stopped to peer into the library before continuing down the long central stone passageway. The going was dark and Liam hoped he wouldn't stumble over any furniture. Very little sunlight seeped in from the rooms on either side, blocked as it was by leaded windows, heavy drapes, and thick lace curtains.

At the back of the house, in a narrow room off the kitchen, he stopped dead at a startling sight.

His massive back to Liam, Jack Quigley bent over a still, unmoving, tightly bandaged form stretched out on a table with carved clawed legs. His hands were around the body's throat.

The scene looked so real, Liam let his breath out in a huff, which attracted Quigley's attention.

Scowling, the big man released the mummy and turned. "O'Rourke."

"I hope you mean that as a greeting."

"What else would I mean?" Quigley growled. He grabbed the mummy's throat again, lifting it partially off the table. "Damned realistic-looking, don't you think?"

"Indeed."

"There's a human skeleton inside, that's why. The one that was hanging in Rossiter's office."

"I see." Liam let his pulse slow, embarrassed he'd misunderstood the situation. But there was always that undercurrent of doubt lurking in the back of his mind about Quigley. "Rossiter has you working on this project with him."

"As long as I'm in the city, why not? I've seen more real mummies than anyone else."

Liam stepped closer to inspect Quigley's handiwork. The archeologist stood aside proudly, obviously not holding a grudge after the argument he'd had with Liam the other night.

"It looks very authentic," said Liam, noting the arms were crossed over the chest, as should be, and the feet bound tightly together. "Excellent work."

"We could have done even better with a real corpse. Rossiter wanted to use his connections to claim one from the morgue."

"And mummify it?" Liam raised his brows, thinking of the unpleasant repercussions such a shocking act might cause. "Too questionable."

"Questionable, as well as impractical. We didn't have seventy days. Lack of time made many details impossible." Quigley pointed out gruffly, "There aren't half as many layers of bandages as there should be. To make up for it, we used a coarser grade of linen."

"No one but you or another expert would notice that."

Quigley punched the mummy in the chest. "And this one should at least have the vestiges of breasts. It's supposed to be a woman."

Naturally. Who else would Quigley want to mummify? But Liam didn't say so.

"The Egyptians used to slit the sides of a dead woman's breasts and stuff in linen pads to give her a more voluptuous appearance." Quigley guffawed. "Lust and lechery have always existed, eh? Who knows, maybe the embalmers had a good time with them before they wrapped them up."

Repulsed by such images, Liam nodded, then glanced about for a quick exit. "Where is Rossiter, anyway?"

"Out in the garden finishing the coffins. The other mummies didn't turn out as well as this one—but then, they contain only boards and wads of fabric."

"We'll have to put yours in the center of the display," said Liam, who then took polite leave of the archeologist and went out the back door.

The scene in the garden was also macabre, if a bit more amusing in its incongruities. Four other mummylike forms lay propped against the lawn furniture, and three men in their shirtsleeves sat on the grass busily painting human-shaped Egyptian coffins while a butler wandered among them serving coffee and tea. In the background, across the alley, another French Gothic house raised its pointed towers and steep roofline to the sky, adding to the unreality of the situation. If he didn't know better, Liam could imagine he was having a bizarre dream.

Rossiter, nearly finished with one of the projects, was the first to notice their visitor. "O'Rourke? Come to help us?"

"You don't appear to need any help."

Theodore Mansfield and Dr. Cunningham glanced up from their task of painting a sculpted face on a coffin lid.

Liam greeted them, gazing admiringly at the men's work. "This is even more than I expected—such beautiful designs and colors."

Including sections of what appeared to be real gold. Isis spread her wings across the chest of each coffin, surmounted by sacred *udjat*-eyes and hieroglyphics.

Rossiter used a small brush to add gold beads to the decorative collar of the lid on which he was working. "This paint has gold leaf in it. Cost me a pretty penny," he admitted.

"I shall have to find a way to give every one of you artistic credit," insisted Liam.

"How can you do that? They're supposed to be real mummies, aren't they?" said Cunningham.

"The temple will impress more visitors that way.

But I see no reason your names cannot be listed as contributors to the interior design of the building."

Mansfield smiled. "Thoughtful of you, but not necessary."

"No, really, I insist." Then Liam went on, addressing Rossiter, "As to transporting everything to the site, I have notified the chief night guard, given him your name. You won't have any problem with the delivery."

Cunningham wiggled his brows in an intentionally silly manner. "So we're to move the bodies in by night, hmm?"

Liam laughed and pulled an iron key from his pocket to hand to Rossiter. "And this will get you into the temple."

"No secret password, then?" Cunningham asked, always ready for a joke.

Mansfield smiled at his companion's humor, but Rossiter seemed very serious.

"In a way, gentlemen, I feel this is a sacred task," the surgeon pronounced.

"Sacred mumbo jumbo is more like it." Cunningham laughed uproariously, then as quickly sobered when Rossiter gave him a cold look.

Liam repressed his own smile.

Cunningham cleared his throat. "Actually, working together has been very interesting. More enjoyable than spending one's time alone translating poetry or essays for the Society's illustrated book."

"Perhaps you could become involved in some task that would involve others," Liam suggested.

Mansfield offered, "You could organize and serve on an approval committee for the illustrations, if you like, Dr. Cunningham."

"You mean look over the paintings and how they'll be laid out?" Cunningham smoothed his mustache. "Hmm, could be intriguing, especially viewing Miss Kincaid's niece. I presume the clothing she'll be wearing for the artwork will be of insubstantial weight."

Liam frowned. He'd forgotten about Aurelia's involvement with the poetry book and hadn't even thought about her costumes. Although he was liberal-minded, he couldn't say he'd be pleased to have other men drooling over her half-clad body.

He put in quickly, "The illustrations needn't be exceptionally revealing. I'm sure Phaedra Kincaid will proceed in good taste."

"Are you certain?" said Cunningham, laughing again. "Her niece doesn't seem to have a husband who would object." He looked at Mansfield questioningly. "Or a fiancé?"

The soft-spoken man examined his paintbrush. "Only a suitor."

With a twinge, Liam swiveled his gaze on Mansfield. "A suitor? Who?" He'd heard nothing about it.

"The younger Miss Kincaid has been escorted by Mr. DeWitt Carlton on occasion," explained Mansfield. "The man is a wealthy widower who owns several department stores."

When had this come about? Liam wondered. But then, he supposed, he wasn't privy to Aurelia's secrets and he didn't keep company with Chicago's social elite. The kiss beneath the flowering tree came back in full detail, along with Aurelia's rejection.

Cunningham gave a mock sigh. "A wealthy suitor?

Then I suppose the illustrations will *have* to be conservative. How disappointing."

Rossiter, who'd been working quietly and showing little interest in the conversation, finally admonished the other men, "Are we going to finish these coffins today or not? It takes several hours for the paint to dry."

The crew got back to work and Liam started to leave, his mood a few shades darker than when he'd arrived. As he stepped away, however, he took a closer look at the face on which Cunningham and Mansfield were toiling. It was lovely, with a straight chiseled nose and wide-spaced dark eyes . . . and reminded Liam of someone. He narrowed his gaze, imagining the Egyptian face surmounted by a different hairstyle . . . my God, Aurelia!

"Is something the matter?" asked Rossiter, who'd risen from the grass to clean his hands on some rags.

Liam quickly masked his expression. "No, nothing." It was only his imagination getting away with him.

Later, he walked down sunny, magnificent Drexel Boulevard still thinking about the woman who obsessed him night and day. He had established better terms with her last week, only to have their tenuous friendship crash about his head.

But he and Aurelia Kincaid could never be friends.

There was too much ripe attraction between them, he'd realized after tasting her lush lips, holding her soft body against his. They could be lovers perhaps. He'd sensed she'd wanted him almost as much as he'd wanted her.

Yes, they could be lovers, if he were deemed good enough for a lady with society connections.

Aware he could have overreacted due to his past experiences, Liam had almost given her the benefit of the doubt, had thought perhaps fear of her own desires had caused her to claim insult after kissing him so passionately. But that was before he found out about the estimable DeWitt Carlton.

Not stopping to admire the two-hundred-foot-wide grand drive on which he strode, Liam gazed into the distance, looking for a streetcar. Borders and beds of spring flowers flaunted their new blossoms about him to no avail. In the wide center of the boulevard, two side-saddle riding ladies waved at him from the shady, winding bridle path, but he merely turned his eyes away.

Only one woman occupied his mind. And though he wouldn't be seeing Aurelia today at all, since he wasn't going into the office, he knew he wouldn't be able to stop himself from brooding about her.

As she'd planned, Aurelia took the electric streetcar to Oak Park right after work. Although the western suburb was some distance from the business area of Chicago, the speed of modern transportation made it possible to travel there in a moderate amount of time.

This convenience also attracted permanent dwellers, both ordinary families who wanted to live closer to nature and wealthy ones who preferred more space surrounding their great houses.

Aurelia's most important set of renderings would display the latter category, an excellent sales possibility for O'Rourke and O'Rourke and a challenging project for her. If she did an impressive job, she daydreamed, she might even be earmarked for a promotion by Sean or at least prove she was worthy of a better position.

Her streetcar stop was nearly at the end of the line, where the rails intersected a gravel road, and Aurelia was surprised to find the surrounding area so countrylike. On at least three sides, the land rolled toward an open horizon, a meadow dotted with clusters of trees and clumps of brush.

It was also quite a walk to the acres on which the house would be built. Glancing at the small map she'd drawn for herself, Aurelia followed the road. The sun sank toward the west, but there was still plenty of light. And she was soon enjoying herself in the fresh air. She loosened the collar of her plaid blouse and hitched up her black skirt.

A red-wing blackbird flew up from the long grass in the ditch beside the road and a meadowlark trilled a few yards farther on. How lovely! She should get out to the country more often, Aurelia told herself, inspired by the walk and the endless sky as much as the project.

When she finally reached her destination, she carefully inspected the plot and took out her sketchbook to draw. Thankfully—for she hated seeing grand new houses built on barren lots—Sean and Liam had agreed to leave the lovely oaks growing on the southern and northern sections. She would include those in her drawing.

Working away enthusiastically, she decided she'd

definitely made the right decision to come here in person. To give herself as many options as possible, she would sketch the basic landmarks from several directions.

Aurelia became so involved, she forgot about the time until she noticed the shadows lengthening. The birdcalls had been replaced by the insect noises of evening. Closing her sketchbook, she made ready to leave, only to hear a distinct crunching sound, as if someone were walking down the gravel road some yards behind her.

Startled, she whipped around to catch quick, furtive movement from the corner of her eye . . . though the road now stretched out empty.

"Is there anyone there?" she called.

No answer.

Perhaps it had only been an animal . . . or her imagination.

But she couldn't help feeling spooked. Gazing about, she realized how alone she was in the great stretch of woodsy meadowland. There was no one to hear a shout for help. Even the electric streetcar rails were quite some distance away. For some reason, her very skin crawled.

Intent on leaving immediately, Aurelia headed for the road. But as she did so, she saw a shadowy figure slowly rising from the ditch to glide behind some bushes.

She stopped short. Someone *was* there! And he was watching her!

Her heart beat so hard she feared it would burst her chest, yet she tried to calm herself. Perhaps the skulker was only a farmer or a traveler and meant her no harm.

But then, why should he hide from her?

Perhaps the man was a hobo, Aurelia reasoned next, though the thought wasn't very comforting; hobos were sometimes escaped criminals.

Attempting to avoid the brush where the skulker was hiding, Aurelia cut diagonally across the lot. She lengthened her purse strap and fastened it over her shoulder, placed the sketchbook under her arm, and hitched up her skirt even farther, in case she had to run. Not caring where she stepped, she felt burrs and thistles attach themselves to her stockings above her sturdy walking boots.

The minutes seemed to drag by until she came out onto the gravel. Glancing over her shoulder, she was just in time to see the skulker following her. When he realized she was looking at him, however, he bolted and slipped into a copse of young trees where he disappeared.

Oh, God!

The man was definitely in pursuit.

Tempted to panic, Aurelia forced herself to concentrate on walking faster. The light was dimming so quickly, she soon wouldn't be able to see her pursuer at all, neither how close he had gotten, nor if and where he was hiding. Night was coming on and she had no way to protect herself.

Sighting a thick branch lying in the ditch, she stooped to grab it with an iron grip. If the man attacked, she thought desperately, she'd fight him to the death!

She had to follow the gravel road. There was no other choice. But she couldn't run. Not yet. She would wear herself out too soon. So Aurelia strode swiftly, swinging the branch beside her threateningly. Perhaps her pursuer would see it and be frightened.

Not likely.

For what kind of a man would be frightened of a woman with a tree branch?

Unable to curb her morbid curiosity, Aurelia glanced over her shoulder again, once again sighting the figure before he disappeared into some brush.

But she was certain he had gained on her.

And there was something familiar about him. Aurelia turned her face forward, picked up her skirt, and walked even faster. The plaid-banded straw hat that matched her outfit flew off, but she didn't bother to retrieve it.

How far to the streetcar stop? she wondered. She was so harried, she was unable to calculate the distance. And even when she reached that goal, there might be no one else around.

It became more and more difficult to remain calm. In her semihysteria, she imagined Rosario—no, perhaps it was DeWitt Carlton in the dusk behind her. That was why the figure seemed familiar.

DeWitt had told her he would pursue her the night before.

Though she hadn't thought DeWitt meant real harm.

And she somehow sensed the man pursuing her *was* dangerous.

Her foot hit a loose piece of gravel and she stumbled, nearly taking a fall. Again, she wondered how far she was from the streetcar stop.

When she finally sighted the intersection up

ahead and a gas streetlight, she broke into a full run. No streetcar was in sight but the light gleamed like a beacon.

Aurelia gasped for air, feeling as if her lungs would burst . . . yet she still was able to cry out when someone stepped directly in her path. Unable to stop her momentum, she crashed into a solid male body!

"No!" She struggled and struck him with the branch until he knocked it out of her hand. She dropped the sketchbook as well. "Leave me alone!"

"Aurelia?"

Liam?

"Aurelia, what's the matter with you?" He pinned her flailing arms behind her back. "What the hell are you doing out here?"

She instantly relaxed as she realized Liam wasn't the pursuer—that man was still in the twilight gloom behind her. Near hysteria, she laughed to think that, even for an instant, she could believe Liam subtle enough to sneak about in the dark. But when her laugh turned into a sob, she hushed and clung to him.

"My God. What's wrong?" He cradled her against him.

She was shaking, but willed herself not to cry. Swallowing another sob, she struggled to catch her breath. They stood there together, she nestled in his arms and listening to the strong solid beat of his heart. Her breathing slowed, but she didn't let go. She feared her knees would give out. Keeping his grip on her solid, he made murmuring, soothing sounds. She felt safe and protected, warmed.

She wanted to wrap her arms around him and stay there forever.

But as she recovered, Aurelia felt her attraction for Liam come to the fore. She was aware of her breasts flattened against his chest and imagined he did, too. She caught her breath and immediately pulled away.

"A man was pursuing me," she finally managed to say.

"Who?" He glared down the road. "Where?"

She, too, glanced back at the road, not surprised it was now empty. "I don't know who he was or where he went, but I am certain he meant me harm."

"Well, he seems to be gone now. He's probably run away. Did you see what he looked like?"

"He was too far away and it was already too dark." She bobbled slightly, her knees still shaky.

Liam reached out to support her.

She stepped out of range. "That's not necessary."

He dropped his arm. "As you wish." Then he said decisively, "The man was a pickpocket, no doubt. He probably wanted your purse." He watched her loosen the folds of skirt she'd stuck in her belt and try to straighten herself. "What are you doing in Oak Park anyway?"

"Sketching the property for the Gray house."

"The firm didn't ask you to do that. Or did my father—"

"I wanted to see the land for myself," she cut in, defending her actions. "I like the design and I wanted to do a good job. I am used to being ambitious."

"And you're out here all by yourself?"

"Well, one usually thinks of the suburbs and the countryside as being safe."

"Not for a woman alone," said Liam. "And there are all kinds of strangers in the area because of the exposition."

"If this *was* a stranger." The words came out before she thought.

And immediately captured Liam's interest. "You're saying it was someone you know?"

"I am not sure. As I've already said, I couldn't see well. It was only that something about him seemed familiar."

"Familiar how?"

"The way he carried himself." And something else she couldn't quite put her finger on.

"But you can't put a name to the familiarity?"

"Unfortunately, no." She didn't want to accuse DeWitt without foundation. After all, if she were wrong, she could ruin his reputation.

She touched her hair, which had fallen nearly down to her shoulders, pins and all. She attempted, without success, to put the heavy mass back up until Liam helped her. His hands grazed her neck, causing her skin to tingle, but she was too exhausted to make another objection.

"I must look a mess."

"You are quite the wild woman," he agreed lightly.

"I thought I was running for my life." And she wanted to give Liam his due. "I am so thankful you appeared. What are *you* doing out here anyway?" She'd been so caught up in her own fears, she hadn't thought about it.

"O'Rourke and O'Rourke also have a site about a half mile that way." He gestured to the south.

"I was aware of that, I guess." She simply hadn't expected to encounter Liam.

The light from the streetcar suddenly appeared far down the rails.

"Look! Here is our transportation."

Aurelia breathed a great sigh of relief. She couldn't wait to be homeward bound.

But Liam's gaze was fastened on the dark gravel road. "I thought I saw something moving over there."

Her blood chilling, Aurelia immediately turned and stared into the night. Thankfully, nothing and no one was visible. She shuddered.

"I don't see anything. Hopefully, as you said, the man's run away. Perhaps he was only a hobo, after all."

"Except you said something about him seemed familiar." As the streetcar continued to approach, he probed, "Who did you imagine might be following you?"

"No one you know," she said vaguely.

But Liam was insistent. "What is his name?"

"It is none of your business."

"Is he some poor stableman or servant you have managed to charm?"

Her face grew warm. "I am not a temptress. And the poor are not the only ones who skulk after women."

Liam's expression changed. "Not poor, hmm? But why would anyone else want to sneak about in pursuit of you?"

Aurelia knew she didn't owe him an explanation but she felt compelled to say, "Men can sometimes be strange about their feelings for women."

Liam's eyes glittered. "Really? Are you hinting this man has feelings for you? Could he be a suitor?" His tone was tinged with bitterness. "Is that the *kind* of man you prefer, perhaps? Wealthy and strange?"

At first she didn't understand, but as his words sunk in, she realized he was accusing her of some sort of perversion! "This conversation has gone far enough, Mr. O'Rourke!"

"Liam."

She paid no attention to his request, stating in no uncertain manner, "I like men who treat women with respect."

And at the moment Liam was being disrespectful. She didn't understand his anger, which had also flared after the kiss at the fair. It seemed to be connected with his humble social background.

With a clack of wheel and rail, the streetcar loomed only yards away.

"Thank goodness," murmured Aurelia, wanting to escape the uncomfortable situation.

"Strange and wealthy," mused Liam, not letting the subject rest. "Unusual requirements for husband material."

All her emotions close to the surface, she couldn't hold back her anger. "I have not once spoken of husbands. You are completely out of order, Mr. O'Rourke!"

"Liam."

"Mr. O'Rourke." Then she added, "If you truly believe I like men who are strange and wealthy, I can assure you that you yourself have enough money to attract me." No matter his background. "And are certainly very *strange.*"

"So you're saying I'm husband material?"

She wouldn't answer directly. "Perhaps you had better keep your distance."

He was silent after that, though he offered to help her get on the streetcar. But she avoided touching him and took a seat near the front of the nearly empty vehicle. Liam sat nearby and they traveled silently back to the city.

Was he actually trying to keep his distance? she wondered, perversely hoping she'd frightened him with the remark about husband material. Liam O'Rourke had a foul mind and deserved to be made uncomfortable.

He lit oil lamps for the last and most important part of the ceremony, placing them throughout the dark room. Their warm glowing smell would blend with the other sweet, heavy odors. The flames flickered, tiny red tongues of fire in the inky blackness. From his niche, the god Anubis gazed down benignly.

Then he approached his lovely one, falling to his knees. Tears fell from his eyes and rolled down his cheeks as he touched the still, cold form. His hand shook.

"Open your eternal gates, ye gods," he prayed. "And take my beloved. May her beauty shine and be reborn like the sun."

For that had been his purpose from the very beginning—a beautiful lady must stay so forever!

When his mourning had been somewhat assuaged, he rose to anoint the still form, to sprinkle her with drops of precious frankincense and myrrh. The scents would help mask the spicy resins underneath.

She was a perfect work of art. The best of all he'd done thus far. Simply gazing upon her gave him intense, erotic pleasure. His heart palpitated, his blood raced.

He touched her face, traced the lines of her cheekbones, leaned over to kiss her lips through the thick fabric. The taste was salty and satisfying. His entire body shook. Overcome, he stretched himself along her length, feeling his shuddering release beginning.

Oh, ecstasy!

He lay still for quite a time, reveling in the far too infrequent triumph, then finally rose.

The experience had been ecstasy, true, but not as pure or sweet as it had been before.

Because of *her*.

Why had *she* come into his life? She whom he could never touch, never exalt, never truly worship like the queen she was?

Wet with perspiration and other bodily secretions, he trudged up from the cellar to bathe and dress for bed. Despite the pain he knew it would cause him, he paused to open a drawer and pull out the treasured memento he'd managed to obtain. He rubbed his face lightly against the black straw hat, inhaling her odor. He fingered the plaid band.

If he couldn't have her, she would at least have him . . . his dedication, his hovering presence. He knew she had seen him when he'd tracked her out beyond the city limits. He'd enjoyed observing such exquisite loveliness, beauty that soared with the songs of the birds.

And he had wanted her to see him, if not to recognize

him. He'd wanted to impress himself upon her somehow.

But he longed for more.

He wanted to show her that he was powerful, worthy.

He wanted to prove that he and he alone could capture her essence and preserve it beyond time's thrall.

"'Come, pretty birds,'" he mused, then quoted the entire poem, "'Come, pretty birds of passage./ Wing your way from beyond the lands of the Great Green./ Come to my nets, lovely ones./ Lie as offerings on my altar of gold.'"

And she was the prettiest bird of them all.

9

"*Ladies and gentlemen,* permit me to introduce to you a Congress of Rough Riders of the World," boomed Buffalo Bill Cody in the center of the huge arena that had been fenced off for his Wild West Exhibition.

The trained white horse Cody rode rose on its hind legs and the buckskinned rider swept off his broad-brimmed hat. In the background, the Cowboy Band struck a high note.

Seated on bleachers beneath a canvas tarp roof, Aurelia applauded along with the rest of her party and the surrounding crowd. A host of mounted riders carrying flags circled the arena—cowboys, or "roughriders," and soldiers from the United States, England, France, Germany, and Russia.

"Quite a colorful display, don't you think?" Phaedra whispered. Aurelia smiled. "And I hear this is only the beginning." She was glad she'd decided to come after all.

Not that she'd balked at spending Saturday afternoon with her sisters and their families, but she wasn't thrilled that Phaedra had insisted that two of Cody's complimentary matinee tickets be given to the O'Rourkes, people she saw quite enough of every week.

Phaedra had maintained it would only be polite to bring everyone she'd introduced to Cody at the Palmer's reception, in addition to the children. Only Theo Mansfield had declined, saying he had other plans.

Two seats away, Liam O'Rourke was sitting next to his father. Wondering what he thought of the spectacle, Aurelia leaned forward slightly for a peek. Liam turned to meet her gaze and she quickly ducked back to face forward again. She didn't want him thinking she was in the least bit interested in what he was doing.

The riders finished their grand review and the second act began, with sharpshooting by Annie Oakley. Wearing a knee-length fringed skirt over leggings, Oakley appeared to be a frail young girl with long curls brushing her shoulders. She smiled and waved at the crowd.

"She looks like a child," commented Fiona from behind Aurelia.

"She's actually thirty-two," Phaedra stated, privy to such details because of her old friendship with Cody.

"Will you both be quiet, please?" said Upton, who'd returned to Chicago the night before. "I want to hear the ringmaster."

"Ringmaster? This isn't a circus," Fiona grumbled, as usual, never willing to be quiet. But she smiled affectionately at her husband.

Phaedra leaned back. "That man out there is Annie's husband and partner, Frank Butler. Bill calls him the human target."

"Shhh!" hissed several people sitting nearby.

Upton laughed and lifted his youngest, the little blond five-year-old, onto his lap so she could see better.

"First Miss Oakley will shoot a cigar out of my mouth," Butler was announcing in the arena. "And then she will put bullets through several card targets."

Aurelia watched, amazed, as the petite Oakley did just that. The two-by-five cards with holes neatly drilled through their heart-shaped bull's-eyes were then thrown into the audience as souvenirs.

Aurelia whispered to Phaedra, "Are they using real bullets in this arena? A bit dangerous."

"The shot is lightweight so it doesn't travel far," Phaedra whispered. "More women should learn sharpshooting skills, don't you think?" She lowered her voice another notch and spoke almost directly into Aurelia's ear so the others couldn't hear. "A pistol would have made that evil man who chased you think twice."

Aurelia had to agree, though she wasn't certain she wanted anything to do with firearms. Chances were, if she possessed a pistol, she would only have an accident and shoot herself instead of her attacker.

The sharpshooting act ended with Annie Oakley breaking a series of glass balls that were thrown into the air. The show continued with a horse race between a cowboy, an Indian, a cossack, and a Mexican vaquero. Then Cody himself galloped around the arena, showing the crowd how he used to carry mail as a Pony Express rider.

Although every act was exciting and colorful, Aurelia was most impressed by the staged scenes, such as a covered-wagon train that rolled out, only to be attacked by marauding Indians. The redskins, their warbonnets, and whoops were authentic. She'd read that several Indians were Sioux war criminals from South Dakota who'd had the option of choosing to join Buffalo Bill's exhibit or be locked up in a federal prison.

At the start of a short intermission in the middle of the acts, the men of the Kincaid party rose to fetch lemonade, even Mariel's six-year old son insisting on accompanying Upton, Wesley, Sean, and Liam. Full of energy, Mariel's little girl and Fiona's three ran back and forth on the temporarily half-empty bleachers playing a giggling game of tag. Aurelia laughed and tried to pull a pigtail when any of them got close.

"This is such fun!" gushed Mariel.

Fiona agreed, "I have to admit it is a diverting entertainment." She fanned herself. "The Wild West has never been of great interest to me, but Buffalo Bill Cody has put together quite a spectacle."

"How nice that our husbands are also enjoying themselves," said Mariel.

"Our husbands and the two O'Rourkes," Fiona made haste to add. Then she asked Phaedra, "Since Theo could not attend, why did you not give his ticket to DeWitt Carlton?"

"Aurelia's beau," Mariel added, smiling sweetly at her younger sister. "You deserve an escort."

Aurelia carefully masked her irritation. "DeWitt Carlton is not my beau."

"But Fiona said—"

"You attended two social events with DeWitt, Aurelia," Fiona interrupted.

"The man only happened to be present at those events, as you well know." Aurelia's irritation was mounting. "I've never attended anything with him."

And never would if, by some chance, he turned out to be the man skulking about in Oak Park. The only person she'd shared that suspicion with was Phaedra— she hadn't even told her sisters anything of the incident.

Her aunt had at first been disturbed by the notion that the man might have been DeWitt. Then she had dismissed the possibility, had almost convinced Aurelia that she'd probably jumped to conclusions because of DeWitt's proprietary statement. No doubt Phaedra was correct in guessing some unknown scoundrel had noticed a well-off woman alone and had thought to take advantage of her purse.

Mariel sighed. "We only want you to be happy, Aura."

"Like us," added Fiona. "You should be married and raising little ones. DeWitt Carlton is prime husband material."

In other words, she should be more respectable, Aurelia thought, her anger simmering. Too often she experienced this very emotion when in the company of her sisters. As usual, she told herself that they meant the best for her.

"I am truly happy that you are satisfied with your lives," she said with more calm than she felt. "Please grant me the same courtesy. Accept my assurance that I am as satisfied with my own life."

Phaedra spoke up in her defense. "There are many

ways to be happy, darlings. Every woman has to judge for herself."

"I knew you would take Aura's side," Fiona told her aunt in disgust. "You have ruined her philosophy of life."

Her anger flaring, Aurelia turned around and glared at her older sister. "Don't you dare insult our aunt." She paid no attention to Phaedra's restraining hand on her arm or Mariel's look of alarm. She chided Fiona. "Phaedra took me in and changed her entire existence for me."

Fiona's blue eyes were icy. "Yet she encouraged a terrible attitude in you toward husbands and families—"

"That is enough!" Aurelia shook off her aunt's hand to rise and face Fiona. "As I have told you more times than I care to remember, I will marry when and whom I choose, if I marry at all. And for your information, DeWitt Carlton is a boring prig who is probably far more interested in your husband's fortune than he is in me." To her credit, Fiona looked shocked, but when she opened her mouth to protest, Aurelia cut her off, "I do not wish to hear another word!"

No matter. Her tirade had already captured an audience. Everyone within earshot was staring and her four little nieces had stopped playing and clustered about their mothers. Her face burning, Aurelia plopped back down . . . just in time to be offered a lemonade by Liam, who was helping the other men hand the drinks around. When they were finished, he slid onto the bench beside her. She was too beside herself to care, even though she knew he must have heard every word.

The second half of the show began with noisy "Cowboy Fun," an act featuring roping, bucking horses, and runaway longhorn steers.

Aurelia only wished she could wrap a rope around Fiona!

It took a few minutes for Aurelia to realize Liam was gazing at her surreptitiously, a smile hovering about the corners of his mouth.

"What is so amusing?" she finally asked, keeping her voice low. If he wanted to quibble with her, he was choosing the wrong moment.

His warm breath fanned her neck as he leaned closer to whisper, "What a tigress you are. Your sisters are fighting a losing battle if they are attempting to force convention on you."

"You overheard, of course."

"You should reassure them that I myself am husband material."

She raised her brows.

"You said so yourself." His grin made little shivers run up and down her spine. "Boring and priggish may not suit you, but you seem to tolerate sadistic and strange well enough."

Obviously teasing, he laughed softly, his green eyes sparkling. And Aurelia felt her anger draining. It was such a relief to be with someone who could look on the light side of such a deadly serious subject that she couldn't help laughing.

Now it was Phaedra who gazed inquiringly, but Aurelia avoided her aunt's eyes and concentrated on the show. After a group of cowgirls raced horses, Cody presented his own sharpshooting act, then played the part of rescuer in a scene involving the Deadwood Mail Coach and maurading Indians.

The exhibition finally ended with the two biggest and best scenes—a spectacular buffalo hunt with real bison thundering about the arena, followed by a beautifully costumed Battle of Little Big Horn featuring Custer's last charge. The audience hissed at the Indians, but Aurelia didn't think they objected to being entertained by them. When the entire ensemble came out for a final salute, the applause was deafening.

Wondering if she were going to have a second battle with Fiona or tearful reproachments from Mariel, Aurelia didn't look forward to leaving with them. She was very pleased when Cody approached Phaedra and suggested a behind-the-scenes tour before they filed out with the rest of the crowd.

Liam offered his hand to help Aurelia step down from the bleachers. He held it a bit too long and murmured, "Remember, husband material."

She wondered how long the charade was going to last, but willingly took his arm when he offered it to her. Glancing over her shoulder, Aurelia noticed Fiona frowning as she followed with Upton.

Liam's mouth was too near her ear when he whispered, "Are your sisters disapproving enough or should I kiss you for their benefit?"

"Things are going splendidly as they are, thank you." But a smile quirked her lips at his mischievous suggestion.

They followed Cody, Phaedra, and Sean along the arena's inside fencing and out through a gate that led to the livestock pens and performers' quarters. Despite her argument with Aurelia, Fiona seemed to be having a fine time with Upton and her daughters. Mariel also appeared happy enough walking along with Wesley.

To be truthful, on the surface, Aurelia wasn't sure her sisters would disapprove of Liam O'Rourke as husband material, except to the extent he hadn't been handpicked for the role by domineering Fiona. Once the two women got to know the architect, however, she thought that Mariel might distrust Liam's unconventional approach to life and that Fiona would definitely abhore his brusque outspokenness, both qualities that Aurelia admired.

"I've heard that people have come to your Wild West Exhibition and gone home satisfied, thinking they'd seen the entire Columbian Exposition," Phaedra remarked to Cody.

The famous frontiersman chuckled. "We seem to be popular—we're sold out every day, with people waiting in line."

"I am touched you were thoughtful enough to save us tickets," said Phaedra.

"I wouldn't have wanted you and your family to miss it."

"You were in Europe with the exhibition for the past several years, weren't you?" Sean asked.

"Yep, performing before the crowned heads of Europe." Cody preened at that. "The royalty seemed to like the Wild West. Why, we entertained the monarchs of England, Russia, Germany, and quite a few other countries. I even had my portrait done by some famous painter."

"Rosa Bonheur." Phaedra referred to the French-woman who was known for action and animal paintings. "He's mounted on his white horse."

Around the corner of the bison corral, they came on to an unusual sight—dressed in full regalia of feathers, loincloths, and warpaint, the show Indians were playing an intense game of table tennis across a cloth-draped table. The children of the Kincaid party grew wide-eyed and then giggled, only hushing when Cody made quite a show of addressing the Indians in their own language.

Then Cody introduced them individually, using the English translations of their names. "This is Take the Shield Away, Bring White Horse, One Star, Standing Badger, Horn Eagle, and Short Bear. Boys, say howdy to my friends."

"How do you do," a noble-looking brave said.

"You speak English?" commented a surprised-sounding Wesley.

The brave nodded. "Went to school in Oklahoma."

"Besides, lot of 'em have been traveling with me for ten years," Cody explained, leading the group on.

"Then why speak to them in the Indian tongue at all?" Wesley muttered in a low enough voice that Cody couldn't hear.

"Part of his showmanship," Aurelia whispered. "And why not? The children were delighted."

At the head of the group, Cody continued talking about Indians. "Old Sitting Bull was in the Wild West a few years back. Too bad he went back to his people and got himself killed. I miss him sometimes but I guess everything changes."

"There certainly aren't many buffalo left in the wild nowadays," said Upton.

Aurelia knew he'd had occasion to see them traveling west on his trains.

"You don't see the vast herds you once did."

"They were destroyed by marksmen for their hides." Cody sounded disapproving. "It's a damned shame, leaving all them carcasses to rot. I never shot a buffalo myself except for food. Why, the Wild West's herd may end up being the last on the face of the earth."

Cody introduced the group to other performers, including Johnny Baker, the "Cowboy Kid," and Annie Oakley. In person, the woman sharpshooter was also small and girlish of figure, though up close, her face showed her real age.

Still holding on to Liam's arm, Aurelia enjoyed the personal view of the exhibit and was only too happy to avoid talking to her sisters. She thought Buffalo Bill Cody quite a presence in his buckskins, long hair, and over-the-knee boots.

"Well, that's about it, I guess," said Cody as they headed away from the backstage area and out toward the street. "Hope you enjoyed yourselves."

Everyone expressed their gratitude and Phaedra said she planned to invite him over for a meal. She laughed when the children insisted they come, too. "Of course, darlings. Everyone is welcome."

Liam shook Cody's hand. "Indeed, thanks for the wonderful experience. I can understand how people would think they'd seen the whole exposition after coming to the Wild West. I can't imagine anything that better expresses the American spirit of pride and individualism."

"I'm honored you think so." Cody bowed. "That's why I begin every performance with the flag of the United States of America and the song 'Say Can You

See.' Of course, there are quite a few other nationalities riding with my cowboys. Some complain about that."

"Hmm, then let me amend my statement," Liam said. "Your show exemplifies the pioneering *human* spirit. If no one had the courage to take chances, try new ideas, explore the unknown, Columbus would never have discovered the country in the first place."

Seeming exceedingly pleased with that remark, Cody laughed and pounded Liam on the back. "I should hire you to write flyers for the Wild West, young man. You can be real poetic."

He certainly could, thought Aurelia. A very complex man, Liam had the courage to be critical and the heart to be sarcastic when he was dissatisfied with the world around him. Beneath his sometimes hard-edged demeanor, though, beat the heart of a romantic who passionately believed that anything was possible.

No wonder she found him so attractive.

Or rather, *could* find him attractive, if their difficulties were healed.

And if she were looking for a man. Which she wasn't, Aurelia assured herself.

Still, she surreptitiously admired Liam's profile and remained fully aware of the muscles that flexed so easily beneath his jacket as they strode along. Liam was a man of action as well as words.

Parting from her sisters and their families outside the Wild West enclosure, Aurelia gave Mariel a quick hug and hurried away without saying a word to Fiona. She was still miffed with her oldest sister, though she would no doubt wait forever if she expected an apology. Having come in Phaedra's carriage, she fully anticipated her aunt would discuss the family quarrel on their way home.

Instead, Phaedra opted to leave with Sean, saying she planned to have dinner with the elder O'Rourke.

Having work to finish up at the office, Liam started to make his own good-byes before taking off to find a streetcar. Aurelia realized she was going to be left on her own. A distinctly disappointing notion.

Liam noticed her expression. "Would you like me to see you home?"

She would if she didn't feel so awkward at the offer. "No, thank you. I shall be fine."

"I suppose you have one of your many social engagements tonight," Liam prodded.

It was really none of his business, but she could hardly say so, considering he'd been so helpful in the problem with her sisters. "Not an engagement, no, but I have some important tasks to take care of."

Liam frowned. "Errands and such? Hopefully, none that involve your traveling about the city alone."

"You need not worry about me," she assured him.

He looked around and lowered his voice. "After the incident in Oak Park, I thought you might take better care."

She stifled her irritation which was growing once more. No one would tell her where she could or could not go, especially not him.

"Thank you for your concern." The words were clipped and curt. "Now you'll have to excuse me. Good afternoon, Mr. O'Rourke."

"Liam."

Smiling, he stood watching as she climbed into the carriage and told Fred to return to Prairie Avenue. Aurelia didn't give him the satisfaction of looking back at him. While she had the chance, she told herself, she should relax and enjoy some unusual peace and solitude, something she would never have in the presence of Liam O'Rourke.

Sean took Phaedra to a small restaurant for dinner where the food was simple but good. Steak and potatoes, a real man's meal, as Sean put it. Phaedra didn't mind. Chatting about the Wild West, she enjoyed herself and tried to forget her concern over the growing tension between her nieces.

Although she fully agreed with Aurelia, Phaedra thought perhaps she herself should take action to smooth things over. She didn't want her brother's family torn apart because of ill feelings, especially when she might be partially responsible for the rift.

After the meal, Sean instructed his driver to take them on a carriage ride through the less inhabited, woodsy area of Jackson Park. Enjoying the evening air, Phaedra leaned against him and closed her eyes for a moment.

"We have a problem here."

The seriousness of his tone caused Phaedra's eyes to fly open and she sat up straight. "My heavens, what?" At the least, she expected one of the horses to have gone lame.

"You know I want to marry you, but you've been leading me around the potato patch."

Her heart fell. "Oh?"

"Don't pretend you don't know. I have told you in no uncertain terms that I love you."

Uncomfortable, she coughed delicately. "But that doesn't always mean marriage, dear."

"What do you have against marriage?" he asked, his voice rising slightly. "Am I not good enough for you?"

She had known this time would come, but she had never been ready for it. "Of course you are good enough. What would make you think otherwise?"

"I am still a poor, uneducated Irishman beneath this fancy suit. I've obtained some success, thanks to my son."

"And thanks to yourself. You don't give yourself enough credit," she insisted, though she grew nervous at the conversation. "I fully respect you, Sean. I do not care if you have a certificate from some sort of school."

But he continued to list his shortcomings. "I haven't traveled like you. I arrived in this country at the age of ten and never left it. I'm not much acquainted with fancy, famous people and I don't have a society background like you."

"You know I don't necessarily obey the rules of society."

"Is that why you will not marry me then?" He took off his hat and ran his fingers through his thick gray hair, a nervous gesture. "Is marriage too conservative for you? I wouldn't expect you to behave like a good little wife. I like you the way you are. You can paint all you want and belong to all your societies. I don't care, as long as I am the only man in your life."

His words were a heartfelt plea that threatened to bring tears to her eyes.

"You *are* the only man," she assured him.

"But I want that to be on paper. I want to honor you with my name."

She didn't know what to say. "Oh, Sean."

"Is it a problem with my son? Your niece? They are old enough to live their own lives. Why, Liam is building a house for himself."

"There are no problems with Liam or Aurelia."

"Then let us set a date."

"No."

He was silent for a moment. "Are you saying you will not marry me, then?"

"I just want some more time."

How could she tell him she *couldn't* marry him or anyone else?

"We have known each other for more than a year, Phaedra. I'm feeling well but I'm getting older. I will be fifty-eight next month. We haven't got all the time in the world." Then he said accusingly, "You must not really love me, no matter what you say."

"I love you with all my heart," she said passionately.

He nearly reached for her, then drew back. "So why won't you agree?"

"I simply can't, dear." She fidgeted, trying to find an explanation that wouldn't drive him away. "I suppose I must confess—there is a problem."

"Tell me and we shall solve it."

But no lie came easily to her lips. "I can't."

"You *won't,* you mean."

"No, I *can't.*"

Again, he was silent. But instead of turning back to Phaedra, he leaned forward to order the driver to take them to Prairie Avenue.

She felt terrible. She didn't know what she was going to do. What a tragedy, especially when she'd finally found a man she actually wanted to marry. She had never longed for a permanent union since leaving Fernando, but then perhaps her being older and more conservative made the difference. She could appreciate the idea of settling down with someone who was exciting, but also capable of keeping her company while they sat in front of a cozy fire.

Sean didn't say another word until they pulled up in front of her house. "I will see you again when you can give me a real reason why you will not consider my proposal."

Phaedra didn't respond. Thirty years was a lifetime. She'd left Fernando a lifetime ago and her impulsive, short-lived marriage to him was still haunting her. She simply had to talk to someone about this heart-breaking situation. Aurelia was the only woman who might understand.

Phaedra hoped her niece would be amenable to helping her find a way out of this mess.

10

Aurelia had been certain she'd enjoy the peace and quiet of an evening spent alone, but she soon became restless upon arriving home. Not hungry enough for dinner, she urged Mary to retire to the coach house with Fred. Then she ate some bread and cheese and went upstairs to straighten her room.

Her drawing table stood near a lovely bay window that looked out upon the lawn and porch at the rear of the house. The deep window seat, Aurelia's favorite retreat as a young girl, and cushions were covered in a ferny print of green and deep red fabric. The wallpaper, the bedspread, and the four-poster's canopy matched the cushions, but were all fading with age.

Aurelia needed to redecorate, if for no other reason than because her taste had changed. But that wasn't as important as reorganizing her belongings.

She'd already sorted through her collection of old books when she arrived in Chicago. A pile of new ones sat on the floor near the bookcase, so she began sorting through those and shelving them. She only paused when a particular novel caught her eye, one she'd intended to read long ago.

Bored, she gazed at the window seat, remembering how many hours she'd spent daydreaming and reading there in the past. Why not do so again right now? She deserved to be able to lie back and rest and perhaps start that novel.

So much for the mundane task of organizing herself.

She curled up on the cushions and opened her book. The window seat, nearly as comfortable as she remembered, faced west, so enough light still filtered in though the hour grew late. And what a setting—after reading a few paragraphs, she cast aside the book and opened one of the window's side panes to enjoy the air. Then she lay back and stared up into the branches of the big elm growing right outside. Verdant leaves moved with the slight breeze, revealing glimpses of deep blue sky.

Truly relaxing for the first time in weeks, she sighed with satisfaction and closed her eyes. . . .

She awakened later with a start, the room enveloped in darkness.

Her pulse was rapid, her breathing shallow. She felt disoriented and for some reason afraid.

Her limbs a bit stiff, Aurelia changed positions and wondered how much time had passed since she'd fallen asleep. She caught a glimpse of a star-studded sky when the elm leaves shifted. A three-quarters moon floated on high. Through the open window, she could hear the breeze still swishing through the leaves . . . and what was that other noise not caused by nature?

Listening intently, Aurelia could swear those were stealthy footpads prowling the squeaking boards of the porch below. They stopped a moment. She held her breath . . . then jumped when someone thudded to the ground!

Aurelia gasped. Who in the world could be out there? Phaedra? Fred?

But neither her aunt nor the coachman would be sneaking about or jumping off the porch. Aurelia rose on her elbow and gazed down at the moonlit lawn. It took a moment for her eyes to adjust, but then she saw the dark figure, threatening in its very anonymity. A man stood near the elm tree, his shadowed face turned upward in the direction of her window.

Aurelia ducked down, her heart pounding, her skin prickling. She forced herself to peek over the windowsill and look again. He was still there. Staring up. She would swear he looked directly at her! As in Oak Park, there was something familiar about the figure.

Familiar?

Aurelia fought back panic as she realized it was the same man—and realized he knew where she lived!

So much for Phaedra's theory about a purse snatcher.

Her heartbeat accelerated and, as if the action would protect her, she slammed the window closed. Then she scrambled to her feet, nearly falling over the drawing table in the dark. Her hand shook as she turned on the gas lamp and lit it.

The glow that filled the room should have made her feel better, but it didn't. She was all alone in the house. She wasn't even certain the front door was locked! Aurelia hurried down the stairs in the dark, wondering if she should run to the kitchen to ring the servants' bell or perhaps flee across the driveway to their quarters.

Reaching the bottom of the staircase, Aurelia faced the entry hall as footsteps skimmed toward her from the other side of the door. The handle rattled . . . and the door suddenly burst open!

Frightened out of her skin, she unsuccessfully tried to stifle a scream.

"What on earth is going on?" Phaedra sounded shocked as she entered the house and let the door slam behind her.

And Aurelia's knees went weak with relief. "Thank God it's you. Did you see that man lurking out there?"

"Where?" Phaedra sputtered, gazing about. "Who?"

"He was in the backyard," said Aurelia. "The same man who followed me in Oak Park!"

"He was in back just now?" Phaedra hurried to the kitchen to look out the window. "I shall go right out and give him a piece of my mind!"

Realizing her aunt was serious, Aurelia grabbed Phaedra's arm to stop her. "Don't! Please, Aunt Phaedra. He is dangerous. I'm certain of it."

"Well, I'm dangerous, too, after the evening I've had!"

Phaedra angrily prepared to open the door anyway. Aurelia could hardly believe her aunt was acting so foolish, if brave. Phaedra's actions bolstered her own courage.

"Then we must at least arm ourselves. And call Fred."

Nodding, Phaedra stepped away from the door to pull the cord that rang a large bell in the coach house. Three tugs signaled for the coachman. Meanwhile, Aurelia rummaged through the pantry where she confiscated two long, lethal-looking knives and a sharp pair of scissors. Then Phaedra lit a kerosene lantern.

When a loud knock came at the back door, Aurelia caught her breath.

"It's Fred," came the rumbling male voice from the other side.

Aurelia opened the door. And, as he stepped into the kitchen, she could see outside behind him—no one was moving about on the lawn. Phaedra noticed as well.

"Are you sure someone was out here?" her aunt asked as Fred turned up the wick of the lantern.

"Absolutely. I saw him with my own eyes."

Aurelia quickly related her story to Fred, who was properly indignant that a prowler had lurked around "his" house, and chagrined that he hadn't caught sight of the man. Together, the coachman and the two women searched the grounds. They even investigated the nearby alley, the neighbors' lawns, the cellar, and the crawl spaces under the porches. Aurelia was beginning to wonder if she had been imagining things, when Fred motioned them to the elm.

"Look, here's a coupla footprints." He pointed to several visible on the damp ground. "Hmm, a man, all right, though perhaps not a large one." The coachman measured his own large boot against the smaller print. "Or else his feet don't match the rest of him."

Phaedra scowled. "He may not be large-footed, but he is doubtlessly crazy, Fred, and has been following our Aurelia. Watch out for him."

"I'll do more than that. I'll take a horse whip to the scoundrel if I see him," Fred threatened.

After giving the coachman her thanks and apologizing for not being able to give him a description of the trespasser, Aurelia returned to the house with her aunt.

Sighing, Phaedra put down the scissors on the kitchen table. Something was bothering the older woman, but before Aurelia could ask her about it, Phaedra said, "Do you still suspect DeWitt Carlton?"

"I never *seriously* suspected him," Aurelia admitted, "though he is the only person who threatened to pursue me. He strikes me as closer to boring than crazy."

"And he probably meant he would pursue you in a courting manner, not chase you down deserted roads or sneak about beneath your window."

"I only know that this skulker seemed familiar."

"Could it be someone from your office?"

"Perhaps." Aurelia hadn't thought about it. "Since I've never been able to get a good look at him, he could be any number of men."

Except Liam—even if he hadn't saved her in Oak Park, Aurelia knew she would recognize his broad shoulders and proud carriage anywhere.

Phaedra poured them both heavy doses of brandy before they went into the parlor to sit down on the sofa. "My heavens, you were so distraught when I arrived! We simply must do something about this situation."

"We could add more locks to the doors and safeguard the windows."

"And we could purchase a telephone, I suppose. That new-fangled invention is expensive, but if it works properly, one could call one's neighbors."

Aurelia nodded, taking a deep sip of brandy. Warmth began to seep through her limbs.

"And then you should never go out alone."

Aurelia grew angry. "It seems I am doomed to curtail my freedom of movement whether I would or no!" That would certainly make more than one person happy, she was certain, including Liam O'Rourke. She wondered if she should tell him about this latest threat.

"He followed you in broad daylight the last time, darling," Phaedra was saying. "You want to keep yourself safe."

"But it is unfair."

"Women have always had to deal with such unfairness, I'm afraid." Phaedra gazed at Aurelia assessingly. "Did you travel about on your own in Italy?"

"Of course not." Aurelia amended, "At least not usually."

"And you never experienced danger?"

Was now the time to tell Phaedra about Rosario? Aurelia sipped some more brandy, thinking a confession could lift a burden of sorts.

"I, uh, had a bad experience in Rome that still haunts me," Aurelia admitted.

"And what was that?"

Finding it difficult to answer directly, Aurelia said, "I must admit my previous experience could be coloring this situation . . . the man who is following me here might be quite harmless."

"While some man in Italy was not?"

"The situation was a complicated one." Seeking courage, Aurelia sipped more brandy. "I was involved with a man there, Rosario Giletti. He was a relative of one of Solini's customers. He seemed intelligent, was well educated, and he sent me notes and flowers until I agreed to go driving in the country with him. Rosario was very good-looking, charming, passionate . . . and, well, one thing led to another."

Aurelia felt her face grow warm.

"You don't have to share every personal detail," Phaedra said, obviously aware her niece was embarrassed. "And you know that I of all people am open-minded."

"We went to art galleries," Aurelia went on. "We traveled the hills about the city. We became lovers." There, though Phaedra had said it was unnecessary, she wanted very much to be honest. "Rosario was my first love, really. As I wrote, you know I lived in an old convent that had been converted into ladies' quarters. He would come to me at night." Where they'd shared those delicious forbidden pleasures. "He was possessive, said he wanted me all to himself, and I naturally dreamed of marriage."

"Of course."

"I thought marriage would be wonderful, considering Rosario loved art and architecture, as well as me. But I was young and romantic . . . and deluded." Aurelia stared at her brandy glass. "He was already married."

"Oh, dear." Phaedra didn't sound in the least judgmental. "I assume he was Catholic. He couldn't get a divorce if he wanted one."

"I was heartbroken, needless to say. I felt betrayed.

A married man! I refused to see him ever again and he had the nerve to be furious with me. He demanded I continue to be his mistress."

"Such gall."

"And then comes the truly frightening part."

Phaedra leaned forward and placed her hand over Aurelia's in support.

"Rosario said he would never give me up. He would be with me whether I liked it or not. He followed me everywhere, shadowed my travel to work, threatened to kill any man in whom I showed interest."

"So that is why this pursuer frightens you so much."

"It gets worse . . . eventually, Rosario threatened to kill me. He said he'd rather I was dead than for anyone else to have me. One night I came home quite late. I walked toward the convent down a long path lined with cypress trees."

Aurelia shivered as she remembered the darkness, the sliver of a moon, the bats flying overhead. She wasn't certain she could go on.

Phaedra squeezed her hand reassuringly. "And what happened?"

Knowing she would feel better if she shared the awful truth with one who cared about her, Aurelia took a deep breath and plunged on. "Rosario was hiding and jumped out to throw me to the ground. He kissed me over and over, then tried to tear off my clothing. I fought him, weeping. Then he tried to strangle me. He would have killed me for certain if another late arrival hadn't interrupted."

Phaedra had tears in her eyes. "Oh, darling. How terrible!" She leaned forward to slide her arms about her niece. "That is the reason you left Italy so abruptly, isn't it? But the authorities—"

"Wouldn't have done a thing," stated Aurelia. "What was I going to tell them? That my married lover tried to kill me? Rosario probably could have gotten away with it even if he'd succeeded."

Phaedra grimaced in disgust. "Yes, what was I thinking? Such a primitive world we live in."

"I decided it was better to leave Rome and start all over again."

And never to become involved with anyone else who resembled Rosario. That's why Liam's strong presence and intensity sometimes frightened her.

Phaedra shook her head sadly. "I need more brandy. Love can be such an ordeal."

As her aunt fetched more liqueur from the sideboard, Aurelia thought about the other woman's odd tone. An ordeal? Phaedra had said she herself had had a bad night.

"What happened to *you* this evening?" Aurelia asked as soon as her aunt returned. "I believe I am not the only one who has been upset." She noted the sad expression on Phaedra's face. "Has something untoward occurred between you and Sean?"

"He wants to marry me."

"But that's wonderful," Aurelia said without thinking. Then she realized it wasn't at all.

"Sean loves me and I love him madly as well," said Phaedra slowly. "But I had to say I couldn't marry him and I couldn't even tell him why. I don't think he'll ever see me again. My heart is broken."

Now it was Aurelia who comforted Phaedra, holding out a handkerchief to wipe away her tears.

"Isn't there some way?" she asked. "It's been thirty years, after all. Can't you contact Fernando?" Fernando DeVarga was the grandee husband Phaedra had run away from at the age of eighteen. "Perhaps he has divorced you in the meantime and you don't even know."

"The Spanish can't divorce either, darling."

"Could he have obtained an annulment?"

"I don't see how." Phaedra blew her nose.

"But he is wealthy . . . there may be ways."

And from what Phaedra had said, Aurelia knew Fernando had been as willful and demanding as he had been charming, had expected Phaedra to hide the exciting personality he'd appreciated during courtship and fade into the background as a good Spanish wife. Surely he wouldn't have allowed himself to be saddled with a missing wife all these years.

"I see no solution," Phaedra said.

"At the very least, you should contact him and see what he is willing to do."

"Write a letter?"

"A telegram would be faster. They can be delivered anywhere these days, even to a remote area of California."

Phaedra only hesitated for a moment. "You are right. I will try it."

Aurelia was pleased to see a spark of light in her aunt's eyes. "At least there is some way to deal with your problem."

"As there is also a way to deal with yours, Aura," insisted Phaedra. "Rosario is far away. The man who is following you now is doubtlessly nothing like him.

Meanwhile, we shall take every measure to protect you. If it would make you feel safer, perhaps we should hire a guard."

"That would be very expensive and probably unnecessary." Aurelia was trying to bolster her own normally fearless nature. She hated the helpless feeling that threatened to consume her. "As we've both agreed, the man may be crazy but harmless."

"I hope so. I don't like to feel weak. I never did," said Phaedra. "In Europe, I once heard talk of a unique method of defending oneself that comes from the Orient. A sophisticated sort of fisticuffs that even women can learn. I've never encountered such an idea in this country, though."

Aurelia smiled wryly. "In times of threat, I would like to be Annie Oakley. I'm sure she wouldn't be bothered."

"Hmm, perhaps you should have a pistol," Phaedra decided. "Perhaps we both should. If we put a bullet through this man who dogs your footsteps, he would be sorry he ever tangled with the Kincaids."

On that positive note, the women decided to retire. Though Phaedra suggested she sleep in Aurelia's room, the younger woman declined the offer. Still, Aurelia checked all the door locks and lay abed for quite some time, thinking.

If she hadn't encountered Liam in Oak Park and her aunt hadn't arrived when she did this evening, what horrible thing might have happened to her?

He approached the carriage he'd left in the next alleyway and looked around furtively to make certain no one was watching him. Safe. He climbed in, his heart still pounding with excitement. She had seen him and now she must know of his secret devotion . . .

His hands trembled as he gathered the reins together. What luck he'd had. He'd thought he might get a glimpse of her, but he hadn't imagined he'd see her asleep in the window. That had set his imagination to working.

And his courage.

He'd crept onto the porch, looking for a way in. He would have liked to have climbed straight up the side of the building so he could watch over her more closely. But then she might have awakened and recognized him.

And then what would he have done? He never could have her.

Could he?

But he needed someone. The feeling was coming on him again and there wasn't any way he could stop it. He no longer wanted to stop.

If he couldn't have her, a substitute would do.

The orphan.

11

The Society for the Study of Ancient Mediterranean Cultures hosted a small private party in Liam's Egyptian temple the evening before the building was ready to open. Desserts and champagne were served in the long, dark room illuminated only by low, glimmering lights. Mummies silently watched the gathering from niches in the walls.

"My goodness, I can hardly see," complained Phaedra, holding on to both Theo and Aurelia as they stepped across the threshold.

His demeanor highly serious, Prentice Rossiter was standing just inside. "Your eyes will become used to it. Oil lamps are placed in each corner."

"And near the mummy cases, as well," remarked Aurelia. "You can easily imagine you are in a tomb." She was proud of her own contribution to the temple and aware of Dr. Rossiter's involvement. "What do you think of the borders around the niches? I feared the stencil of the scarab might be too large."

"The borders are acceptable."

The surgeon gazed at her intently before turning his back and speaking to another guest.

Aurelia was offended, both by the way the man ignored her and by his critique. But then, Dr. Rossiter hadn't seemed the friendliest of people when she and Phaedra had attended the meeting at his house, at which time he hadn't spoken to either of them. She had thought about becoming a member of the society, but decided against it since she'd have to deal with Rossiter as well as the offensive Quigley.

Aurelia joined Phaedra at the refreshment table where a waiter served them. Another oil lamp sat nearby. Flat in shape, with a wick floating in its center, the device was carved of pale stone and perched on a low stand.

"Are these lamps real antiques?" Phaedra asked Theo.

"Absolutely authentic."

"Who provided them?"

"Various members of the society . . . we all have private collections of some sort."

"They are here on loan only for tonight," added Mrs. Cunningham, who'd approached the new arrivals with her husband. "Otherwise, the regular gas sconces will be used. We can't be leaving such priceless objects out for the riffraff."

Dr. and Mrs. Cunningham made small talk for a few moments. Laughing at a droll remark from the physician, Aurelia glanced up to see Liam O'Rourke appear out of the shadows.

He grinned as if her amused expression were a

huge smile aimed directly at him. Her lips froze and a little thrill crept through her.

"I see you are once again desperately in need of an escort," he said in a low tone meant for her ears only.

Although he had spoken to her in the office several times since, he had not mentioned the Wild West outing and had been neither inappropriately friendly nor hostile, for which Aurelia was grateful.

"Luckily, I'm available," Liam continued.

The idea wasn't altogether unattractive, but she didn't want him to know he had any effect on her at all.

"I shall let you know if I am in dire straits." She kept her tone light. "Luckily tonight I don't have sisters breathing down my neck."

"Are you certain?" He gazed about, pretending threat. "The darkness in here may hide terrible dangers."

"Ghosts perhaps and frightening curses, but nothing as horrific as Fiona in a fit of bad temper."

They both laughed.

"I love my older sister," Aurelia admitted, "though we don't always see eye-to-eye."

"I understand. I may not have siblings but I have a father who is sometimes cantankerous."

Aurelia glanced about. "Where is your father anyway?"

"He said he couldn't attend . . . which is rather odd." Liam gazed over Aurelia's shoulder at Phaedra.

Who was no doubt the reason the older O'Rourke had chosen to be absent. Did Liam know about their falling out? If not, Aurelia wasn't about to bring him up to date on the older couple's problems.

She merely said, "What a shame, since this project represents your company as well as you."

"Tomorrow he'll say he's sorry for missing it and ask me for every detail."

Thinking about Phaedra's difficulties with the relationship, Aurelia fingered her empty glass.

Liam observed the subtle gesture. "Would you like more? I see they've opened another bottle."

"Thank you, yes."

As Liam fetched the drinks, Aurelia watched him, tall and handsome in his white tie and tails, and mused upon what would happen if Phaedra and Sean *were* able to marry. Then both O'Rourkes would be part of the family, which could lead to very awkward professional and personal situations. But she told herself not to worry about that. Above all, she wanted Phaedra to be happy.

When Liam returned, they strolled about the building, inspecting the mummies.

"I'm amazed at how realistic they look," commented Aurelia. She gestured toward a coffin lid that was turned outward, displaying its interior. A goddess of some sort was stretched across it. "What deity is that?"

"Nut, the sky goddess. Every good Egyptian went to his final rest with her starry body hovering over him for protection."

"A nice thought."

"Do you like the way the scarabs and lotuses turned out?" Liam asked.

"Dr. Rossiter may not agree, but I think they add to the whole display."

Liam appeared surprised. "What's this about Rossiter?"

"He said the borders were merely acceptable."

Now Liam laughed. "Don't pay any attention to the good doctor. He can be odd and moody, friendly one moment, aloof the next. The borders were an excellent idea and the credit for them is all yours."

Which made her feel much better.

He pointed to the nearest mummy. "Does that one look any different from the others?"

"I'm not sure. It seems a bit more rounded, but I'm not an expert on ancient Egypt."

"There's a skeleton inside, one of Rossiter's samples."

She didn't react, though she wondered if he thought she would blanch. "Suitably macabre."

"Though Quigley did the actual wrapping."

"Perhaps they enjoyed the collaboration," said Aurelia, who'd noticed the contentious archeologist across the room, hotly expounding on some topic— undoubtedly to some poor woman's detriment. "Aunt Phaedra told me the two men are friends."

"I would say their relationship more closely resembles friendly association. I don't think either particularly loves his fellow man."

"And Mr. Quigley specifically hates his fellow woman." It was the first time she'd brought up the topic with Liam. "Does he really have a wife?"

"No one I know has ever seen her. Sometimes I've wondered if Quigley keeps her locked up somewhere. Someone once suggested he might have her mummified in his cellar."

Though he was joking, Aurelia shivered at the suggestion. Wrapped skeletons didn't bother her, but the thought of murder did, and she suspected Jack Quigley was quite capable of violence.

"Of course, we exaggerate about Quigley because he makes himself a target," Liam added, seeming to realize she'd taken his comment seriously.

"Are you certain it's an exaggeration?"

Even in the dim light, she could tell his expression was thoughtful. "Quigley is difficult to understand and may be capable of more, or less, than he claims, but I don't think he'd go so far as murder."

Aurelia hoped he was right as she sipped more champagne, the wine she'd consumed so far already going to her head. The shadows cast by the oil lamps seemed to dance pleasantly along the walls.

"Don't tell anyone else about the skeleton, will you?" Liam leaned closer, his voice low and his lips mere inches from her ear. Memories of the kiss beneath the flowering tree flooded her mind, but she didn't move away.

"Why?"

"People could become frightened."

She nodded. "I promise to keep it secret." Phaedra came up just then. "Good evening, Liam. Who made these coffins?"

"Dr. Rossiter and Cunningham, Jack Quigley, and Theodore Mansfield. They are well executed, don't you agree?"

"The coffins' faces are particularly fascinating." Phaedra gazed at Aurelia, then glanced over her shoulder. "Some even seem familiar."

Liam frowned slightly. "In what way?"

Phaedra made a quick, dismissing gesture. "Oh, never mind. It is probably my imagination."

"This temple is the perfect environment for letting one's imagination run wild," Liam agreed.

Phaedra laughed. "It should attract curiosity seekers in droves when it opens tomorrow."

Her aunt remained at Aurelia's side as Dr. Rossiter positioned himself in the center of the room to call for quiet and a toast. "To O'Rourke and O'Rourke's Egyptian temple."

"And to you and the other members for all your help." Liam also moved to the center of the gathering and raised his glass.

"To the Society for the Study of Ancient Mediterranean Cultures!" boomed Quigley.

"And to the ancient Egyptians for leaving so many interesting artifacts to study, including their dead," Cunningham added with a chuckle.

Everyone applauded and Liam looked exceedingly pleased as he answered specific questions about the design of the temple.

Aurelia took advantage of having Phaedra all to herself. "Are you feeling all right? Sean is not here." She thought her aunt might have expected an encounter tonight.

"Unfortunately, it seems Sean O'Rourke lacks nerve." Phaedra looked tired and, for once, nearly her age. As if she were in mourning, she'd chosen to wear a black taffeta dress with a high neck.

"You still have not spoken to him?"

"No, but I sent the telegram to California. You should be proud of me."

"I am very proud, Aunt Phaedra. Let us hope the response to your inquiry will be good news."

Phaedra raised her glass. "Another toast to that." After they'd downed the wine, she asked, "What time are you planning to leave?"

"I am ready now if you wish."

Aurelia's gaze strayed to Liam, but she told herself not to be regretful. He probably wouldn't rejoin her this evening, and if he did, what more could they talk about?

"Perhaps you can be of help," Phaedra was telling Aurelia. "Fiona is dropping by tonight to give me instructions on designing a leaflet for one of her charity societies."

Aurelia nearly started in surprise. "You're helping with one of Fiona's functions when you do not get along?"

"I think it is time for me to try to be more accommodating."

"After the way she insulted you?"

Phaedra explained, "I am older, darling, and able to overlook your sister's weak points. Perhaps she doesn't know and appreciate my softer side. Fiona is a difficult person, but not impossible."

"That's very kind of you to say."

"And you are capable of being kind as well. If the two of us worked on Fiona, she would have no defense."

Aurelia sighed. "Except I do not wish to do so. Not unless Fiona apologizes." She was tired of deferring to her older sister.

"You know Fiona always thinks she is right."

"Then she will have to learn better."

Phaedra shook her head. "Oh, dear, Fiona may be at the house for several hours. What will you do with yourself in the meantime?"

"Do not be distressed." Aurelia patted Phaedra's gloved hand. "Go ahead with Theo whenever you are ready. I shall leave in an hour or so myself, perhaps hire a carriage and sneak up the servants' stairs in the kitchen."

At least that made Phaedra laugh. "Really, Aurelia."

"All right, then I shall come in the front door and go straight to my room with my nose in the air."

Phaedra laughed again. "You are incorrigible."

Liam approached, his gaze on Aurelia. "Incorrigible?"

"My niece refuses to leave with me," said Phaedra. "That is what I'm complaining about."

"You are leaving so soon?" Liam remarked politely, then offered, "I can see that Aurelia gets home, if you wish."

Phaedra raised her brows and gave Aurelia a knowing little smile. "That would be kind of you, Mr. O'Rourke."

"Please call me Liam."

Did the request mean he'd changed his mind about Phaedra? Aurelia wondered. When they'd first met, he'd complained about her aunt's influence on his father.

"You will allow me to drive you home, won't you?" Liam asked Aurelia.

She agreed. Saying good night to Phaedra then, she let Liam fetch her one last glass of champagne. The party was quickly coming to a close. Guests were drifting away.

"Would you like to take a walk on the midway?" Liam inquired when they'd finished the wine.

"At night?"

"Be daring."

"I am already daring," she said defensively.

"I forgot about your foray to Oak Park." He smiled. "That was very adventurous."

She raised her chin. "Say what you mean—very foolhardy. Though I still think women should be able to go where they wish. It was the horrible man who followed me who made the outing dangerous."

And she thought of her other, latest sighting, an incident she wasn't certain she would share with Liam.

"I wasn't trying to insult you," he assured her. "Let's not fight. I have to admit I usually enjoy it, but tonight I'd prefer a softer mood."

How soft? Aurelia fetched the wrap made necessary by her low-cut gown and hoped she wouldn't regret spending even a limited amount of time alone with Liam.

The midway was even more raucous at a later hour, which didn't surprise Liam. Aurelia securely on his arm, they passed a few drunken men and several sloe-eyed women who were obviously looking for customers.

"Are you shocked?" he asked when one of them winked and swayed her full hips at him.

"I have lived in Europe."

A nonanswer, Liam thought. Aurelia was trying to sound sophisticated, but he didn't believe she was altogether comfortable with the idea of prostitution.

"Europeans are more open about human frailty," he said, really meaning human needs.

Near the pavilion advertising Little Egypt, they watched some visitors mounting a camel outfitted in a colorful gold-and-red satin saddle blanket. The great beast made loud groaning sounds as it raised itself, front end first.

"Would you like to take a ride?" Liam asked.

"I don't believe so."

She tightened her wrap, a gauzy piece of material that covered her elegant shoulders and décolleté. Liam had appreciated the view but could understand why she'd want to cloak herself from strangers' eyes.

"Where is that daring of yours?"

She gave him a slanted, provocative look. "I would rather see Little Egypt dance."

"Now that request *does* take courage," he said with a laugh. "I heard that Mrs. Potter Palmer was highly insulted when someone said she had visited the show and suggested she approved of belly dancers."

"I'm not Mrs. Palmer."

She certainly wasn't. Aurelia was so much more unique.

After purchasing tickets, they got in line. Liam stood behind her, close enough to inhale her subtle perfume and admire the gloss of her hair. He had gotten over his resentment toward her at the Wild West Exhibition when she'd claimed to despise the idea of pairing up with a wealthy society man. He realized then that he'd made a mistake of accusing her of such. Aurelia fit his very first impression of her—a rare and unusual woman who didn't play by the rules, at least not until she'd examined them.

Inside the theater, they took their seats, two hard wooden chairs, surrounded by noisy, enthusiastic people. But the crowd hushed when the curtains were drawn. The stage was simple and shallow in depth with an exotic-printed backdrop. The musicians who filed out were even more exotic. Dark men wearing caftans, fezzes, and large black mustaches sat on the cushioned couches positioned in front of the backdrop and began to tune their instruments. As usual with Eastern music, the notes were in minor key.

The audience applauded when Little Egypt appeared, a wide-hipped dusky maiden in a bright skirt and vest worn over a body-hugging gown. The dance music began, twisting and turning like snakes in a basket, which perfectly matched Little Egypt's gyrating movements, slow and sinuous at first, then faster and faster. The long strands of beads she wore sparkled and swung back and forth around her voluptuous body.

The crowd watched, enthralled. They remained rapt even after Little Egypt had finished and other dancers filled the stage. All in all, it was an entertaining show, though not particularly shocking.

Aurelia didn't think so either. "I expected Little Egypt to be wearing much less," she complained as they filed out of the theater.

Liam laughed. "Did you imagine she'd be naked?"

"Not entirely. But surely those costumes can't be authentic. I read somewhere that the belly dance originated in the harem, where ladies often wore nothing but layers of diaphanous veils."

Liam laughed again. "Heavens above! I can see the headlines—Miss Aurelia Kincaid reveals that Little Egypt wasn't shocking enough."

Aurelia grinned at him. "I enjoy being with you when you forget to be serious."

"Do you?"

"You can tell, can't you?" She flushed slightly as if she'd suddenly turned shy, perhaps from the wine. "I'm never certain of what women think."

He'd been wrong in the past, believing a young

woman could accept him for who he was when all
she wanted was an exciting adventure without her
family knowing about him.

"I believe in being honest," she told him, "as do
you. You must admit that even when we exchange angry
comments, we manage to reach an understanding."

"Usually."

"Eventually."

He smiled. "You are truly a remarkable woman."

He valued honesty above all and found it a rare
commodity in the women he'd known.

Liam felt true camaraderie as well as a growing deep-
seated attraction for Aurelia. He insisted on taking her to
a small restaurant in Old Vienna where they ordered
sausages on rolls and sweetcakes with powdered sugar.
They also had two glasses of fruity Rhine wine.

"This is wonderful." Aurelia gazed at her glass
before taking a sip. "Though I fear I am beginning to
feel a bit woozy."

"Fresh air will sharpen your senses." The exposition was beginning to close down anyway. After they
finished eating, Liam paid the bill and led Aurelia on
a shortcut across the midway. He'd left his carriage in
a private loading area nearby and had hired a man to
watch it.

"Don't you employ a driver?" she asked when they
were underway.

"My father does. I prefer taking care of my own
transportation." He gave her a sidelong glance. "Not
that I can't afford one, husband prospect that I am. I
just like doing things myself."

She chuckled. "You'll never forget that comment I
made, will you?"

JOIN THE
TIMELESS ROMANCE READER SERVICE AND GET FOUR OF TODAY'S MOST EXCITING HISTORICAL ROMANCES FREE, WITHOUT OBLIGATION!

Imagine getting today's very best historical romances sent directly to your home – at a total savings of at least $2.00 a month. Now you can be among the first to be swept away by the latest from Candace Camp, Constance O'Banyon, Patricia Hagan, Parris Afton Bonds or Susan Wiggs. You get all that – and that's just the beginning.

PREVIEW AT HOME WITHOUT OBLIGATION AND SAVE.

Each month, you'll receive four new romances to preview without obligation for 10 days. You'll pay the low subscriber price of just $4.00 per title – a total savings of at least $2.00 a month!

Postage and handling is absolutely free and there is no minimum number of books you must buy. You may cancel your subscription at any time with no obligation.

GET YOUR FOUR FREE BOOKS TODAY ($20.49 VALUE)

FILL IN THE ORDER FORM BELOW NOW!

YES! *I want to join the Timeless Romance Reader Service. Please send me my 4 FREE HarperMonogram historical romances. Then each month send me 4 new historical romances to preview without obligation for 10 days. I'll pay the low subscription price of $4.00 for every book I choose to keep – a total savings of at least $2.00 each month – and home delivery is free! I understand that I may return any title within 10 days without obligation and I may cancel this subscription at any time without obligation. There is no minimum number of books to purchase.*

NAME_____

ADDRESS _____

CITY_____STATE_____ZIP_____

TELEPHONE_____

SIGNATURE _____

(If under 18 parent or guardian must sign. Program, price, terms, and conditions subject to cancellation and change. Orders subject to acceptance by HarperMonogram.)

GET 4 FREE BOOKS

BOOKS
(A $20.49 VALUE)

TIMELESS ROMANCE
READER SERVICE

120 Brighton Road
P.O. Box 5069
Clifton, NJ 07015-5069

AFFIX
STAMP
HERE

"Never."

Usually leery of so-called wedded bliss, the idea of marriage to Aurelia was not unappealing. Not that they had that kind of relationship, he hastened to remind himself. She worked for him and they were friends.

No courting was involved. Though the thought of it lingered in his mind.

Liam drove the carriage northward, taking a road that skirted the lake. What would be the repercussions if he acted on his instincts? Would they still be able to work together? At the moment he didn't seem to care. Probably the wine.

He was in no hurry to get her home. The moon was full, silvering the surface of the water, and the air cool but not chilly. A perfect night for romance.

Aurelia glanced behind them, then turned to stare for a moment. Her intensity interrupted his soft thoughts.

"Is something wrong?" he asked.

"When we left the midway, I noticed a carriage with small dim lanterns. It is still behind us."

"Probably someone going the same way."

"Probably." She seemed to relax.

He supposed the experience in Oak Park still haunted her. To get her mind off the subject, he commented, "Life can sometimes be difficult when you are unconventional, can't it?" How much more unconventional and difficult could life be if they got involved, for instance? Thinking of the possibilities, he amended, "If exciting."

"Are you talking about yourself or me?"

"Both. We are unusual people." As if he need remind her. "Luckily, I grew up without having society expect anything from me."

"You can certainly keep company with anyone in society now."

"When I wish to do so. I would rather avoid some people. I don't care for those who are always measuring others to see if they are worthy enough to speak to," he said truthfully. "I've met people of that ilk through our firm—they would have had nothing to do with me before I got an education and became moderately successful. I have to watch my words carefully when I deal with them."

"I understand completely. I do not care for that sort either. But I usually manage to hold my tongue."

Liam figured Aurelia had plenty of experience with judgmental people. "They project a false front and expect to see one in return."

"They live according to very rigid rules, and are especially unkind to women."

He heard the underlying anger in her calm tone. "How is it you became a rebel?"

"*Became?* I was always a rebel, always different from my sisters. I was never a perfect little girl. Fiona was my mother's lovely swan, Mariel her nightingale. I was her plain little blackbird—studious and introverted. Some considered me strange. I played by myself a lot."

"You were called Blackbird?" He gazed at her beautiful profile, the lines of her cheek and nose in the moonlight. "Well, you have grown up into an exotic species. You are certainly far from plain now."

"Do you really think so?"

"You know that I do. I've told you before."

He reached over to caress her cheek lightly and she didn't push his hand away. Her skin was wonderfully soft and he wished he could kiss her.

But he had the carriage to drive and his wits to maintain.

Nevertheless, he couldn't stop talking about her. "You enhance your looks with some of the dresses you wear. Like the one you have on right now." A deep salmon gown that flowed when she moved and plunged gently into a low neckline. "There is something ancient or classic about your taste. I like the simplicity in your clothing and jewelry." Tonight she wore only a fine gold chain at her throat and gold earrings set with matte green stone.

"I am quite complimented, considering someone else implied I had bad taste not so long ago."

"One of your sisters?"

"An acquaintance."

"Well, she or he was wrong."

Liam suspected the source of criticism to be male. While her very uniqueness appealed to him, he knew she was not for every man. Most in their circles were too conservative to appreciate her qualities properly.

They rounded a curve and Liam slowed the carriage near a shallower area of the lake. The beach gleamed pale in the moonlight and whitecaps danced to land.

"The lake is restless, even if the air is fairly calm," she noted. "There must have been a storm somewhere."

He simply admired the view, which included her. "Lovely—makes you wonder how that water feels."

"I'm sure it's quite cold, being May."

"Shall we test the temperature for ourselves?" An outrageous suggestion, of course.

"You want to go swimming?" Aurelia didn't sound astonished or disapproving.

Making Liam wonder if she felt the call of the waves and the moon as he did. "Actually, I was thinking we might wade along the shoreline."

When she didn't object, Liam drove the carriage onto the side of the road, and dismounting, they walked down toward the water. Laughing, they removed their shoes and stockings, Liam obligingly turning his back to give Aurelia some privacy. He soon caught sight of her slim bare ankles anyway when she raised the hem of her skirt to avoid getting it wet.

"Oh!" She stepped back. "It is even colder than I expected."

Wanting to see more of her legs—wanting to see more of all of her—Liam placed a steadying hand at Aurelia's waist. "Come on, you'll get used to it."

"You'll be sorry when I turn into a polar bear."

He feigned shock. "A bear? Is it midnight? And I thought that it was a pumpkin or a gypsy that a fair princess changed into."

"I'm not a princess."

"Pardon me, I meant goddess."

She laughed softly.

Perhaps it was the wine they'd been drinking all evening, but the moon and the water . . . and Aurelia all seemed to call to him at an elemental level. He could see her rising from the Mediterranean— Venus, the classical goddess of love, born of foam and yearning.

"Large bodies of water sing an ancient rhythm," he said. "They draw forth your soul and your emotions like the moon draws the tides."

"Very poetic. You should write verse."

"I'd rather dance, with you."

She turned her face toward him, and he took her in his arms as if they were in a ballroom. She placed her hand on his shoulder and they turned slowly, took several steps and turned again, this time faster. Another few steps and he twirled her about, water splashing around their feet.

"How do you feel?" he asked.

She was smiling, if slightly breathless. "Wonderful! As if I could obtain my very heart's desire. Dance, swim, fly, be free!"

"That's the way life should be."

He pulled her closer, once again wanting a kiss, but she managed to extricate herself. Half-running, she fled down the beach, only pausing to stoop and splash water at him. Laughing with delight, he gave chase and soon caught her. His arms snaked around her waist and she froze as he lowered his head to touch her lips with his.

At the same moment, a waist-high wall of water came in to hit them hard and square, nearly knocking them both off their feet.

"Ahh-h!" cried Aurelia, thoroughly drenched as she fell against his chest. The splash from the impact had even reached her hair. Tendrils sticking to her face, her skirt sodden, she struggled out of his arms and the water's range. "Now look what happened! Is this the way life should be?" But she was laughing.

Liam felt responsible for her discomfort. "You will catch your death," he said, slipping his arm around her. Beneath her thin garments, she was shivering.

"Actually, I haven't had such a good time in years," she assured him.

Liam realized how chilly the wind had turned. "Nevertheless, we must bring you inside and get you warm and dry."

"Bring me where? I can't arrive at home this way. Fiona is with Aunt Phaedra," she told him, sounding distressed. "Even so, I wouldn't care if my aunt hadn't told me she was attempting to make peace with my sister. My coming home this way would start an argument between them, I'm certain. Fiona would blame Phaedra for my actions, as usual."

"Then I know of another place that is much closer."

Leading her to the carriage, Liam wondered how exactly this special night would end. Like the water, he would flow with the tide. For the moment, he could think of nothing he wanted more than to be with Aurelia.

He *wanted* Aurelia, he amended, desired her so intensely she made him burn like fire. And feeding the flames, Lord help him, was the knowledge he might even love her.

12

"*This is my house,*" Liam announced as the carriage turned into the gravel drive of a lot a little north of the fair.

While the outer structure seemed complete, the materials sitting around it indicated the building was still under construction.

"*Your* house?" Huddled in a lap robe, Aurelia pulled down a fold to see. "I thought you lived with your father."

"My lodgings are there at the moment, north of the business district, but I plan to move south as soon as this place is habitable."

With the eye of an architect, Aurelia took in the lines of the brick building, which were longer and lower than those of most modern domestic buildings. "A unique design," she said approvingly.

"What did you expect after all that talk about how unusual we both are?"

Indeed, Aurelia felt they had established a deep

bond. She had been as charmed by Liam as by the moonlight. Stopping the carriage, he jumped down and offered his arms to help her to the ground. She hesitated, reminded of the kiss that he'd instigated.

If it hadn't been for the lake . . .

"Don't worry, I won't let you fall," he assured her, no doubt thinking she was leery of her sopping skirt.

But falling from the carriage was the last thing Aurelia was concerned about. Placing a hand on Liam's shoulder, she allowed him to lift her down and felt the warmth of his hands through her clothing. A thrill shot through her and ended too soon when he let go.

While Liam tied the horse to a post, Aurelia thought to clear her mind, which was still fuzzy with wine. She took a few steps, breathed deeply of the now chill night air, and switched her focus to her surroundings. But the night remained enchanted. The lights lining the quiet street seemed to be low-hanging stars . . . until two of those stars moved.

Aurelia stiffened. Another carriage was visible a block away—a lone vehicle with small, dim lanterns. Could it be the same one she'd seen following them before, or was she imagining things now?

"I began building last year."   Liam continued on the subject of the house, interrupting her brooding. "But only the first floor is habitable, I'm afraid. There's plumbing, but no electricity yet."

She looked again but the lanterns had vanished, and her unease over the carriage fled. Besides which, Aurelia knew she was safe with Liam.

"I shall be most happy if I can find a way to dry my clothing," she said.

"I'll start a fire immediately."

Liam unlocked the door and left Aurelia standing in the entryway while he rummaged in a closet for a candle. The knowledge that they were completely alone slowly sank in. Again, a perverse doubt made her hesitate when he lit the candle and indicated she should come with him.

"There's hardly any furniture," he told her. "Nothing to stumble over."

A great fireplace dominated the main room into which he led her. Shades covered a wall of windows, but only a small table and a straight-backed chair sat beneath them. Liam dragged the chair toward the fireplace for Aurelia where she watched as he piled in logs and lit a match to some kindling.

"I stay here sometimes when I'm working on the house." When flames began to flicker, he gazed at her, the gold and crimson a reflected glimmer in his eyes. "This should dry your clothing and warm you up as well."

She smiled but lowered her own eyes and stared at the fire. "It must be nice to have a house of one's own. Not that Aunt Phaedra doesn't allow me privacy."

He stoked the fire and the flames leapt higher. "Are you going to take off your clothing now?"

She started, warmth spreading throughout her body. "Pardon me?"

"To *dry* it. You can hang your things by the fire."

"And wear what?" she objected. "I can dry my dress while I am inside it."

"You'll be more comfortable if you undress. There are sheets and an old blanket on the bed in the next room. You can wrap yourself in one of those."

"I don't think that is a good idea."

He leaned back against the fireplace, one elbow propped on the mantel. "You have nothing to fear. Despite my unconventionality, I am basically a well-behaved gentleman with ladies. I would never take liberties unless the woman was willing."

She raised one brow. "Oh? Like that day at the fair?"

That silenced him for a moment. His eyes darkened with the memory. "All right, perhaps I did become a little carried away. I won't kiss you tonight . . . unless you ask me to."

Though he'd already tried.

And the real problem wasn't Liam—Aurelia wasn't certain she could trust herself.

He continued to coax her. "It shouldn't take that long to dry your dress since the material isn't heavy."

True. And her clothing was very uncomfortable.

"As soon as your garments are ready, you can put them on again and I'll take you home."

With that promise, she rose, reluctantly giving in. "Where's the blanket?"

"In there." Liam indicated a doorway. He took the robe and gave her the candle.

A small bed and a trunk were the room's only furnishings. Quickly unbuttoning her dress, Aurelia inspected the threadbare blanket but deemed it too small. She'd have to wear a sheet instead.

Exactly how long would it take her clothing to dry? she wondered, still thinking about the situation in which she'd gotten herself. Highly attracted to Liam already, she'd only compounded her desire by dancing with him in the moonlight. He tempted her to shed all her inhibitions and indulge her greatest passions.

Passions.

Rosario had awakened them and now she couldn't put them to rest. Was that natural for a twenty-five-year-old woman? Aurelia wished she felt comfortable enough to discuss it with Phaedra. When Liam had started to kiss her on the beach, she'd wanted him with every fiber of her being. She'd longed for him to place his mouth on hers, to touch her, to draw forth her soul. The longing hadn't subsided.

She sighed as she took off her petticoat and corset. Perhaps her senses were askew, but she didn't think she'd ever had such an exciting evening before. Not even Rosario could match Liam's wit and robust approach to life. She knew her former lover would never have waded through waves at night while wearing evening clothes.

And it seemed Liam thought she was equally exciting. He wasn't the sort of man to offer empty praise. They shared interests, experiences, and proclivities.

Though that didn't mean they should go any further than they already had, she told herself.

Tightening her resolve along with her sheet, she came back out into the main room and stopped short, flustered. Liam had spread the lap robe in front of the fire and was now stretched out before it, bare-chested, bare-footed . . . probably bare everywhere, if the piece of checkered fabric wrapped around his middle were any indication.

He stared at her admiringly. "Venus in a toga."

Adonis lying by the fire, she thought as she complained, "I did not know that you planned to undress as well."

"Surely you wouldn't want me to stay in wet things while you dried. I found an old tablecloth in the kitchen."

How could she object? she wondered, her skin warming up beneath the sheet. She turned away, but not before her breasts had tightened at the sight of his well-made physique. His skin was browned slightly, obviously from working shirtless in the sun at construction sites.

She drew the chair closer to the fireplace and began hanging clothing on it. "Look away, please. I have ladies unmentionables to dry."

"I don't find underthings that fascinating unless a lady is actually wearing them."

Heat coiled through her. She could easily imagine that experience, his hands seeking warm flesh through a thin layer of lace and silk. She swallowed and hung her things along the mantel.

"Your dress is probably ruined," he pointed out. "I'll buy you another, if you like. The damage was my fault."

She kept her tone light and refused to look at him directly. "Really? Do you control the waves?"

"If I did, I would have told them to warm up and merely caress you to your lovely ankles."

What an image that aroused. "Mentioning a woman's body parts is a questionable thing for a man to do," she said, thinking she sounded like a prig.

"If I always talked like a gentleman, you'd be bored."

True, though Aurelia sensed it would be dangerous to admit so right at this moment. She turned only to glance at Liam, but her eyes lingered on his sun-kissed torso gleaming in the firelight.

"Are you going to join me?" His expression was unreadable as he patted the floor beside him.

She attempted humor. "My ensemble hardly lends itself to such athletic ventures."

"I can be of service."

Liam started to rise, the tablecloth slipping to reveal that the red-gold hairs on his chest spiraled downward toward his belly.

"Never mind!"

Aurelia held out a cautioning hand and quickly plopped down, managing to keep her sheet intact and making sure there was adequate space between them.

"I won't bite," he teased.

Her own belly tightened. "I'm not sure about that."

"Not hard, anyway."

Incapable of ignoring his innuendo, she nevertheless concentrated on smoothing her hair, much of which had loosened from its knot and spread about her shoulders.

He stretched out again and watched her. "Your feathers are dark and pretty, Blackbird."

"They are all atangle."

"Do you have a brush?"

"In my evening bag."

Though she started to retrieve the item herself, he reached over and fetched it for her, getting too close by far in the process. He held out the bag and their fingers touched as she took it from him. A spark of something forbidden traveled up her arm, making her turn her face away.

"Thank you." She took out the brush and began to remove pins.

"I don't think you can do that by yourself."

Before she could object, in one fluid movement, he sat up and knelt beside her. His hand closing over hers, he gently took away the brush.

Now she could object, but her voice sounded feeble. "My hair is not that important."

But he was already disentangling her long tresses. He'd promised he wouldn't do anything untoward, though she supposed brushing hair didn't fall into that category.

Besides . . . she had already given in to the sensuality that made her glow from the inside out.

The brush plied through her hair in a wonderful rhythm. She leaned back and closed her eyes, all the more aware because of her nakedness. The fabric caressed her skin with the slightest movement. Her nipples hardened to tight little buds, and her upper thighs grew moist.

Pausing for a moment, Liam ran his finger down her cheek. "You have beautiful bone structure."

She gazed into his eyes, smoky green pools. Spirals of warmth crept outward from her middle as he cupped her chin. Lord help her, she wanted him so!

"Such lush lips. I am very attracted to you, you know."

"Umm," she managed to murmur.

"And I think you are attracted in return."

"Umm, hmm."

"To be honest, though, I have to admit I am more likely besotted with you."

"Besotted?" she echoed softly.

"I have been head over heels since the first moment we met." Liam's expression was intense. "I am not exaggerating, Aurelia. You know I speak my mind. I have always felt a special sort of bond with you. At first, I thought it must only be physical longing, but as I grow to know you, I realize we are much alike in mind and spirit. Do you feel the same?" he demanded. "Tell me."

"I am very attracted," she admitted. An understatement. Liam was tantalizing, overwhelming.

"I want you." He caressed her with his fingertips, spreading a path of fire from her throat downward along her collarbone and then across the upper swell of her breasts. "We are not children who do not know their own minds."

"No." Shaken, she gazed at him silently, wanting him as well.

"You are not objecting to my touch, but neither are you asking me to take further liberties. I said I would not do so, but at your request."

She struggled with her emotions and her desire. "I-I can't. That's something a lady doesn't do."

Especially not make the initial move. Suddenly, in the midst of her longing, she felt distinct panic. What if they did come together? She was not a virgin and she couldn't tell him. She couldn't make love with him even if they both wanted to. Could she? What would he think? She had no idea of how a woman handled such a situation as this, neither could she imagine how they would deal with each other at work afterward.

Aurelia knew she felt more for Liam than physical longing. Losing his respect would devastate her. Thinking she had more to lose than to gain, she drew away, but he grasped her arm and pulled her back.

Every callus on his palm sent a quiver issuing through her flesh.

"A *conventional* lady may not give out invitations," Liam said softly. "You yourself admit that you don't go by convention, unless you wish to. Besides, society's view of morality is stifling."

"Easy enough for a man to say."

"I believe the same rules should apply to both sexes when it comes to matters of the heart."

He sounded so sincere and his touch was so erotic, she couldn't help but lean closer. If the truth be known, her heart was pounding madly. He took a deep breath, obviously holding himself back. Intoxicated by the idea of having such power over him, she touched his lips with hers.

His grasp tightened. "My God, Aurelia, don't toy with me!"

"I am not toying."

Her assurance was all he needed. Taking her in his arms, he angled his head to find her mouth. At first, the kiss was more feverish than sweet. He was a starving man, ravening for her deepest mysteries. His tongue plundered, his hands explored, his body shifted closer.

Corsetless, she easily arched against him, glorying in the path of each fingertip. She loved the taste and feel and smell of him.

"Ah, Aurelia!"

The words were an invocation which she couldn't deny. She wound her arms about his neck, pressing herself against him tightly. The movement dislodged the sheet, exposing a breast. As if it were a precious offering, he cupped it gently, his thumb moving over the sensitive crest. She moaned, lost to sensation.

His breath came ragged as he pulled the sheet down farther, letting it lie in folds about her waist. "Stop me now, if you will. It will be unbearable to do so if we continue."

"I don't want to stop." She had never desired anyone more. "Please, don't stop."

The tablecloth had fallen away as well. She saw his arousal and the heat rose to scorching temperatures within her. Exciting, so exciting. Her insides trembled as she imagined him disappearing inside her soft, wet folds.

"I want you." He lowered her to the floor.

Looming over her, he suckled at one breast, then the other, all the while stroking and kneading her flesh. Wanton little cries escaped her lips as he laved her aching nipples with his tongue.

He placed a knee between her legs and spread them rather roughly. Reminded for a moment of Rosario's attack, Aurelia panicked. Her eyes flew open and she pushed at him, but he grasped her arms and held them over her head. Her heartbeat thudded in her ears. His masterfulness frightened her, but then he released her and she forgot about everything but what he was doing to her. He paid detailed homage to every inch of her body, stroking, caressing, demanding response.

Gladly she gave it, everything she had.

When Liam's hand found her tender inner thighs, they quaked, then spread of their own accord. Fingers moving to the thatch of hair between her legs, he stroked her hot, sweet center until she thought she would die of painful desire.

"Please!" she cried.

"Please what?"

"Please take me!"

His eyes burned like green fire as he spread her legs even farther and exposed her secrets to his gaze. Aurelia grew even hotter and more desperate for relief. She tugged at his arms.

"Now!"

Positioning himself above her, he bit her lips and rubbed himself against her. She ran her hands over his hair-roughened chest, trembled as his organ ignited fire where it probed against her belly. Then he moved his distended flesh lower, teasing her nether lips with the tip. She nearly writhed as she repositioned herself to take him in.

Finally, when she thought she could stand it no longer, he ended her frustration by thrusting into her soft tight folds, plunging hard and long until he filled her.

He gasped, "Oh, Lord!"

Aurelia cried out as well, from need and satisfaction and because the pressure was a bit painful. It had been so long since she was privy to such pleasures.

Quieting for a moment, Liam kissed her lips, her throat, her breasts. Hand between their bodies, he began stroking her again until she writhed in truth, shattered by tiny contractions, while he held himself frozen inside her. She had never felt anything so wonderful.

"You are so passionate," he told her. "And beautiful. I believe I might love you."

Love?

She had no time to respond as he withdrew, only

to thrust into her again. This time she experienced an even deeper pleasure. Arching, she wrapped her legs around his hips and clung tightly, hands gripping his muscular back. His arms trembled as he began moving, rocking back and forth, taking her with him.

The pressure within her began to build again as the rhythm picked up. She undulated her hips as he plunged harder and faster.

Skin slid over sweat-slicked skin. She ran her fingers through his thick red-brown hair. He groaned and lifted her hips, more and more urgent. Her head thrashed, her need spiraling into fiery rapture.

"Liam!"

At the sound of his name on her lips, he stiffened, then shuddered with his own intense release. They collapsed together, their bodies quieting gradually. Resting on his elbows, he laid his face against the curve of her neck and let his breathing slow.

Only then did she wonder what he had thought about his easy entry. But it was far too late for that worry. What was done was done.

Besides, Liam was sweetly stroking her into a delicious state.

"Aurelia," he whispered, rolling over, cradling her against him. "I was serious when I said I might love you."

He loved her. Then she need not worry at all.

Or did she? Her mind struggled to consider the repercussions of acting without first giving the situation proper thought. Only when he gave her a little shake was she startled into giving him her full attention.

"Do you think you might love me in return?" he demanded.

She did, indeed. "Y-yes."

"Does saying so scare you that much?" Not waiting for her answer, he said, "Then you will have to learn better." He stroked her hip, nibbled her ear, finally kissed her mouth. "Remember to listen to your heart, dance to its rhythm. You can make your greatest desires come true."

She only hoped he was correct.

But she didn't think about anything. Lying before the crackling fire, they were completely content in each other's company. She stroked the forearm that lay across her, enjoying the rough texture of its hair. He sighed and gently bit the back of her neck.

The gesture was highly sensual, yet struck her as funny, and she smiled. "I thought you said you wouldn't bite."

"I said, 'not hard,'" he corrected.

"So, are you practicing at being an animal? Perhaps it is you who will change at midnight."

"Animal?" He rolled over her and tried to look threatening. "Is that the game you want to play?"

She giggled. "I didn't say I wanted a game of any sort."

But the games were only beginning, she discovered, aware of the growing tumescence that lay against her thigh.

He rose to his elbow, drawing her up as well. "Let's try the bed this time."

Outside, the full moon shone brightly, so brightly he hid himself carefully beneath the window. The shade was drawn but, at times, he could see moving shadows against the flickering orange light within. They were obviously using the fireplace. He listened carefully, catching murmuring noises, imagining what was going on. Only when a cry rent the air could he identify their activities for certain.

And he was repulsed. So much so, his stomach roiled. A suitor was one thing, a lover another.

How could Liam O'Rourke defile her?

Liam deserved to die or at least be tortured in a terrible way. But the man wouldn't die, of course, unless he came up with a very creative idea.

And neither would she.

Both straining, sweating bodies inside were hurtling down the road toward sickness and age and decay of the flesh, their activity speeding the process.

He shivered, thinking he simply *had* to do something, anything. The orphan was his only solution. He could no longer draw out the anticipation that was part of the pleasure. It was time to implement his plans.

Then another cry split the air, the kind creatures make when mating.

His stomach clenched and he leaned over and retched.

13

"*You'll let Fred* drive you," Phaedra insisted the next morning as she and Aurelia took their last sips of breakfast tea.

"It's only a short walk to Mariel's—"

"One that you will not be making alone, not when some man with wicked intentions toward you might be lurking about the grounds." When Aurelia merely clenched her jaw, Phaedra went on, "If you insist on walking, I shall accompany you myself. Fresh air and exercise would do me good."

Aurelia sighed. Phaedra could be as stubborn as she. "But readying the carriage is too much fuss for such a short drive."

"I have a few errands to run, so I'll be needing the carriage this afternoon anyway."

Although she hadn't meant to add to her aunt's worries—Phaedra was still estranged from Sean—Aurelia knew she had caused the older woman some unease the night before by being so late. Phaedra had not, however, questioned her about her activities. When Aurelia had crossed the threshold in the wee hours of the morning, Phaedra had been awake and staring into the fire. Upon seeing her niece, she had sighed with relief, and kissing Aurelia's cheek, she had made her way upstairs.

Aurelia hadn't even considered telling Phaedra that she'd feared someone might have been following her and Liam in another carriage. Feeling a bit guilty about keeping the suspicion to herself, she acquiesced. "I'll summon Fred, then."

"Thank you, my darling. I am glad you have the good grace to be sensible."

"But I do not like it," Aurelia insisted. "I hate the idea of feeling that someone must always watch over me."

But she said no more about the matter as she pulled the bell for the coachman and met him at the back door where she gave him instructions.

Earlier, Mariel had sent Aurelia a note via the housekeeper's son, begging her to come for a visit. Certain that soft-hearted Mariel was disturbed because the sisters hadn't all made peace after the argument at the Wild West Exhibition, Aurelia was in a generous mood after her night with Liam. At least toward her middle sister, that is.

She swept back into the dining room and began clearing her breakfast dishes. The housekeeper was busy on the upper floor, tidying bedrooms. It was taking Mary longer to complete even the simplest tasks these days, but neither Phaedra nor Aurelia would insult the older woman by suggesting she might need a young, energetic assistant. Instead, they did what they could to ease Mary's burden surreptitiously.

"Do you think Fiona will be at Mariel's?" she asked, taking Phaedra's empty cup and saucer. Her older sister had spent the last evening with their aunt, after all, and might have said something about the rift.

But Phaedra was noncommittal. "I know nothing of Fiona's plans."

"She didn't mention anything last night?"

"Sorry, darling, but your name did not so much as pass Fiona's lips once."

Aurelia was inexplicably disappointed. Fiona's ignoring her was almost worse than her complaints. In a way, she was glad to be free of her oldest sister's overbearing presence, but at heart, she wanted peace between them.

Picking up the tea tray, Aurelia said, "At least I have one sister who cares about me," as she made her way back to the kitchen.

Phaedra followed, assuring her, "You have two . . . but, alas, it is only natural you and Fiona fight since you are quite alike."

The cups and silver spoons rattled as the tea tray banged to the counter. "Why, we're nothing alike!"

"Hmm."

"What does that signify? Fiona and I couldn't have taken more different paths in life—"

"I was referring to the strength of your personalities," Phaedra interrupted. "You both firmly believe that the path you chose is the right one. You are both correct, you know."

Aurelia was shocked. "What?"

"Fiona is as happy being a wife and mother and society leader as you are being a freethinker and an architect. You each put all your energies into whatever task you tackle, and you are equally outspoken in your beliefs. Who is to say which is better?"

"This from you?" Aurelia was truly shocked at her aunt's turnaround. "The woman who challenged me to dare to be different? I don't believe it!"

Is this what came of falling in love? Had her aunt's tender feelings for Sean changed her very thinking?

"I didn't say *I* would want to lead Fiona's life any more than you would, but she does believe in it, darling. And if she's truly happy, as I am convinced she is, what more could we ask for one we love?"

True enough. Aurelia had no quarrel with her aunt's logic and was comforted that the older woman hadn't really changed.

But she grumbled, "I could ask something *from* Fiona. Primarily an apology. And a promise to stop trying to foist her standards on me wouldn't be amiss, either."

"One has to recognize a tiny victory when one sees one," Phaedra warned. "It may not come in the form we most desire."

"You mean if she speaks to me pleasantly, I should pretend nothing has passed between us?"

"Well . . . if you can."

"Do you think I'm so rigid, then?"

"I think you're a wonderful, loving human being who is also quick to anger and sometimes a bit slow to forget."

Before Aurelia could comment, Fred knocked at the back door and opened it. "Miss Aurelia, Harry and me, we're ready." Harry was the coachman's nickname for Harold the Bold, a once-spirited black who now seemed nearly as old and graying as his driver.

"Coming, Fred."

Aurelia went in search of her purse and checked the hall mirror to make certain her hair was still in place. She smoothed a stray curl back from her temple, planted a swift kiss on her aunt's cheek, and left.

She had barely seated herself in the carriage before she started brooding about Phaedra's theory that she and Fiona were alike. While Aurelia had never thought it possible, she was actually beginning to envy her oldest sister just a tad. There was nothing wrong with having a husband if he were loving and supportive—and there was definitely everything right with having children to nurture and to watch grow up.

Hadn't Phaedra, the staunchest supporter of woman's rights she knew, given up practically everything of her old life to do right by her? Aurelia sometimes felt she was to blame for the sacrifice Phaedra had made in her behalf, but she knew her aunt didn't regret the decision one whit. And, as she'd thought before, Phaedra loved Sean desperately and would marry him if she could.

Thinking of marriage and the possibility of raising children led Aurelia back to the question of a potential father and husband who would suit her. Only one man came readily to mind. As Fred stopped the carriage in front of the Sheridan residence and alighted to help her out, Liam O'Rourke filled her thoughts.

And those thoughts frightened her as much as they appealed to her. Used to leading her own life and making her own decisions, Aurelia wasn't certain she wanted to sacrifice that independence. No matter how loving and supportive a man might be, a married woman was still answerable to her husband both by society's standards and by law. And perhaps even by her own heart.

All that she would have to give up was driven home to her quite clearly a few moments later.

The butler let her in, and after he informed her the Sheridans were in the solarium, Aurelia dismissed him. Entering the south wing of the house, she realized Mariel was in the midst of a marital disagreement, if her husband's raised voice were any indication.

"Where do these crazy notions come from?" Wesley was demanding.

"They're not crazy notions. Albert Drury stopped by yesterday afternoon."

"Drury? The conductor? Here?"

Reluctant to intrude, Aurelia stopped short in the hallway, wondering if she should have Fred take her for a short drive and return later.

"Mr. Drury asked me to reconsider performing with the orchestra."

Mariel's voice shook and Aurelia immediately made up her mind to remain nearby in case her sister needed her. She slipped closer to a potted palm stationed at the solarium's entrance so neither husband nor wife would see her unless she chose to announce herself.

"My wife has no need of employment. We met that Drury man at the Palmer's reception on opening night of the fair. That pushy Bertha Palmer put him up to this—"

"Mrs. Palmer did no such thing!" Mariel protested. "And I wouldn't be an employee of anyone, Wesley, merely a guest artist."

But the subtlety didn't budge her husband. "You told him no, of course."

"I said I needed time to think about the offer."

"Why ever for?"

"Because it's the opportunity to fulfill a dream I've had since I was a child and realized I had a talent that went beyond the ordinary."

"Of course you have talent. And I allow you to use it, don't I? You entertain our guests. And, if it will make you happy, you may teach music to our children. But performing in public?"

Aurelia grew more tense with each word Wesley uttered.

"I only want to play a few times, to experience the thrill of sharing something I love with other musicians and a large appreciative audience."

"Absolutely not! You perform in public, and the next thing I know you'll be leaving me and the children and running off to Europe like your scandalous aunt! Will that woman's influence in this family never end?"

Appalled at the ridiculous accusation, angered by his unkind reference to Phaedra, Aurelia had to hold herself in check so she wouldn't march into the room and give the man what for herself. Though she had no business interfering in her sister's marriage, she couldn't help glaring at Wesley through the fronds of the potted palm and wondered that he didn't feel the heat of her anger on his neck.

"I would never run away," Mariel was saying. She was

pacing the tiled floor, wringing her hands. "I love you and the children more than anything. But I love music, as well, and I would give anything for the opportunity to be part of something larger, to share my talent—"

He cut her off again. "Sharing your talent publicly will make you forget your values. You'll become addicted and won't be able to handle such feelings."

"Other people who perform in public don't run away from their families!"

Mariel's heart-wrenching tone got to Aurelia, who had never before realized how much she and her middle sister had in common the need to explore and challenge their own talent.

But Wesley Sheridan was not to be budged from his narrow point of view. "You are speaking of men who are used to providing for their families. You are a woman, Mariel. An emotional creature. You couldn't possibly handle such a situation. I've said my last word on the subject. Is that clear?"

Mariel's brief flare of defiance withered before Aurelia's eyes.

"Yes, Wesley," she whispered, bowing her head like the dutiful wife. "Of course."

"Good!"

With that exclamation of primal satisfaction, he stalked out of the room, passing Aurelia without ever seeing her. Looking lost amid the cheerful blooming plants, Mariel sank to a cushioned wrought-iron bench, face in her hands, quietly crying.

Aurelia saw red as she stared at the man's retreating back. Quickly she hurried into the sun-lit solarium, smelling of fresh earth and vegetation.

"Do you need someone to talk to?" she asked softly.

"Aura!" Startled, Mariel jerked and furtively tried to dry her tears.

"Do not bother trying to hide your feelings from me," Aurelia told her sister. "I didn't mean to eavesdrop, but I seemed to have arrived at an inauspicious time."

Mariel turned her head away, angering Aurelia even more.

"It was nothing. Nothing for you to worry about."

But the slump of Mariel's shoulders, the hopeless tone, the fingers that tightened around one another in her lap belied the assurance.

Aurelia couldn't tolerate seeing her sister beaten into submission this way. But what good would her counsel in the matter do? Mariel didn't seem to have enough backbone to stand up for herself, no matter her wishes, not when her husband put his foot down—or rather ground it down upon her.

But then marriage to a man of strength and conviction might do that to any woman, even to herself, Aurelia realized.

Thinking about the ride over to the Sheridans' home and her silly musings about marriage, Aurelia shuddered. What had she been thinking of? One night of ecstasy did not promise a lifetime of happiness. Rather than take the chance of putting herself into her sister's shoes, which must pinch at every step, she resolved to remain single for the rest of her days.

More's the pity that she got no satisfaction from that conclusion.

Phaedra was mooning over Sean while waiting for Aurelia to return when she heard the *clop-clop* of shod hooves, a neigh and a snort, and a familiar booming voice.

"Whoa, Chief. We have arrived at our destination!"

"Bill?"

Phaedra rose and peered out the window in time to see her old friend dismount without his usual panache. Cody took a few steps toward the nearest maple tree where he secured his mount's reins. He patted the horse on the neck.

"Be on the lookout for any larcenous characters, old boy," he said in a theatrical stage whisper nearly loud enough for the whole neighborhood to hear. "Anyone tries to steal you, just neigh and I'll come a-runnin'."

And then he swept toward the house, his steps a little too careful, his back a little too straight. Why, the showman was foxed, Phaedra thought, her lips curling in amusement. Always a charming and entertaining companion, he outdid even himself when he'd had a few whiskeys. He was exactly what she needed to chase away her gloomy pall.

She threw open the door before he had a chance to knock. "Hello, Bill."

"I didn't know you were expecting me," Cody said in surprise. He scratched his goatee. "Did I forget an engagement?"

Phaedra laughed. "If you want to create a sneak attack, you'll need to advance more quietly."

Cody laughed, too, and gave her a quick hug. "I've missed you, Phaedra. You do have a sense of humor, one of the things I most appreciate about you."

"Come on in, you old rascal."

Sweeping off his white Stetson, he crossed the threshold and entered the parlor. "Ah, a real home. I so seldom have the opportunity to feel like I'm part of something so nice and solid." Tossing his hat on the couch, he made himself comfortable on the wingback chair near the fireplace and plopped his booted feet up on a hassock.

"Real would bore you to death, Bill."

"Not if *you* were part of the deal."

Phaedra couldn't help herself. She smiled broadly at the compliment, even though she knew it was part of Cody's natural patter when with an attractive woman.

"I don't think your wife would approve."

"Louisa doesn't approve of much," he grumbled. "That's why she stays put in Rochester."

Phaedra noted his apparel, a white buckskin jacket decorated with beaded red, white, and blue flags and wondered if he'd worn it especially to impress her. He certainly was a ladies' man, wife or no wife.

"Can I offer you"—She was going to suggest a drink, but he'd undoubtedly reached his limit, considering he had two performances to give later that day—"some tea?"

He made a face. "Something a little more potent would be more in order."

"Whiskey, then?" Phaedra figured he was the judge of his own capabilities.

Cody winked at her. "Straight."

Crossing to the liquor cabinet, she poured a generous whiskey for him and a very small brandy for herself. Not that she usually drank spirits during the day. Somehow not joining Cody would seem inhospitable.

She'd barely settled into the chair across from him before he asked, "Did I ever tell you about the time I was driving stage in my youth and had to outwit some holdup men?"

"I don't believe so."

Cody was always one for a tall tale, so Phaedra quickly settled in, prepared to be entertained. He took a large swig of whiskey and began.

"Well, you see, this particular day, I was carrying a package containing a large sum of money. Two of my passengers looked like ne'er-do-wells and het up my suspicions. So, before they could surprise me, I decided to turn the tables on 'em. I pulled the horses to a quick stop, jumped off the driver's seat, opened the door and asked the men to hand me a rope I'd left under the seat."

Phaedra was already grinning. "And did they fall for your ploy?"

"You bet." He took another sip and savored the liquor as much as he did his tale. "While their hands were busy, I pulled out my revolvers. They raised their hands skyward, whining about what was wrong and such. Well, I ordered one of the men to tie the other one's hands behind his back. Then I got rid of their weapons and finished trussing up the first."

"So you saved the money."

"That was merely the first time. One of these rapscallions warned me there was more trouble down the road, and I believed him. I turned the pair over to the stocktenders at the next relay station, then I cut out one of the seat cushions and hid the money under it. When I ran into the second bunch, they couldn't find nothing."

"Very clever."

Cody chuckled. "I even showed 'em my strongbox. Empty. And I sent 'em on a wild goose chase after the first pair, saying they'd gotten the money and were a half-dozen miles back down the road on foot!"

"You didn't!"

"I did! Can you imagine them grumbling and cursing to each other when they didn't find nothing and realized they were outsmarted?"

Phaedra could indeed. They began laughing so hard that she didn't hear Aurelia return until the front door opened and her niece found them in the parlor. Only a bit unsteady, Cody rose to his feet.

"Mr. Cody, how nice to see you again." Aurelia's eyes swept over him but she didn't sound enthused. "Fred is waiting on you, Aunt Phaedra. I'll tell him you have company. Do you have any idea when you might need him?"

She'd uttered all in a desultory tone that sobered Phaedra immediately. "Aurelia, what is it? You haven't spotted that horrible man?"

"No," Aurelia was quick to assure her. "Please, there's no cause for concern."

"What horrible man?" Cody asked.

The two women exchanged glances. Phaedra thought Cody might offer some sound advice, but she hadn't meant to violate her niece's confidence.

"Some man seems to be interested in me . . . from afar," Aurelia explained.

"You mean someone's been tagging after you?"

"Once anyway," Aurelia said. "And maybe last night . . ."

Phaedra's heart fluttered. "Last night? You didn't say anything about last night." And she'd had to fight to make Aurelia let Fred escort her this morning.

"I thought a carriage was following us. It might have been anyone actually."

Phaedra informed Cody, "A few days ago, the man was lurking outside this very house."

"Where? Let me at the varmint!" His expression threatening, Cody pushed aside his jacket and reached for the gun holstered on his hip.

"Bill, calm down. I've already established that the man in question is not here now," Phaedra reminded him.

Appearing not in the least embarrassed, Cody relaxed and sank back into his chair. "A shame when a pretty woman has to be worried about some ruffian trailing her." He frowned at Aurelia, who'd also sat down. "You know how to shoot?"

"You mean a gun? No. I don't like weapons. I gladly leave them to the men."

"What if there's no man around to protect you? We can't have that. I'm gonna teach you to shoot myself."

"I'm not sure—"

"No arguments, now. I'm awfully fond of Phaedra here, and she would be right unhappy if something happened to her favorite niece. Today I'll ask Little Missy if she's got anything smaller than the pistols she uses in the show—you know, something that would fit in your purse."

"Little Missy?" Phaedra asked.

"My nickname for Annie Oakley. Now there's a woman who knows how to defend herself."

"I doubt that I could ever be as good as she is," Aurelia protested.

"Don't have to be. A man's chest is a sight bigger than a cigar or a pack of cards, and if you ever have to use the gun it'll be 'cause you're a lot closer to your target than she is to hers."

Aurelia's face went white. And the thought of her

niece shooting a man made Phaedra shudder. But the alternative could be far worse.

"I think you ought to consider Bill's offer, darling."

"Well, perhaps."

Phaedra could tell Aurelia was tempted. "Just because you know how to use a gun doesn't mean you will ever have to use it. But you'll feel safer."

"And it'll take a load off your aunt's mind," Cody added. "Think of her." Brow furrowed, dark eyes serious, Aurelia finally nodded in agreement. "All right. I'll do it. When?"

"I got two shows today, but I'm free first thing in the morning."

"Thank you, Bill," Phaedra said. "You don't know how much this will ease my mind."

Now if only someone could come up with a solution to fix her relationship with Sean so easily, she would be a completely happy woman.

Easy. So easy. She had barely objected when he'd lured her into the carriage. She'd wanted a friend so badly, someone who could speak to her in her own tongue, that she hadn't even struggled. Now she was properly sedated with the specially mixed wine and the time was at hand.

"What's happening to me?" she mumbled, relaxed from the laudanum, as well as a bit confused by the additional pinch of belladonna.

In the same language, he answered, "Don't worry, little orphan, you will no longer be alone in the world. Gods and goddesses will be your companions."

She stared at him uncomprehendingly, and her

hand fell listlessly into the wine chalice, knocking it to its side. A ribbon of red liquid that reminded him of her life's blood spilled across the table.

But he had difficulty concentrating on the little orphan as he stroked the dark hair so like hers. He touched her cheek gently as he helped her stumble to the chaise on the dais, imagining the skin belonged to another. Her dark eyes fluttered and she moaned as she lay back. She would moan louder if she suspected.

"I must leave you for a moment to prepare myself," he said gently.

"Prepare?"

He didn't answer as he slipped behind a screen that separated the feast table and chaise from the work area of the room. The panels were covered with images of the gods and goddesses who sat in judgment of the dead, their names spelled out below each in hieroglyphics: Thoth, Horus, Anubis, Geb, Hathor, Isis, and others.

As he slid on the protective clothing, all oiled so none of the poison could get to him, his pants tightened over the start of his erection. He set the mask in place and fetched the basket, heavy with the weight of death. He shook the basket until he could hear it stirring inside. Slithering and writhing. Waiting for its moment.

He neared the reclining woman whose eyes barely opened to slits.

"What's that?"

"A present. The gift of eternal life."

Before she could question him again, he shook the basket even more briskly, then opened the lid just wide enough to allow the narrow, deep-hooded snake partial exit. With an angry hiss that sent chills of excitement up his spine, the Egyptian cobra struck and made contact with her exposed neck.

"Aah!" Her eyes flashed open, her breath thickened into a wheezing gasp.

"Now, that wasn't so bad, was it?" he cooed, knowing there wasn't much pain involved in the bite.

Besides, she'd had the belladonna to dull her senses and to speed up the injected poison's spread. Thankfully, there would be no hemorrhaging or swelling near the bitten area. He wouldn't approve of such sacrilege to her person.

"It will only be a few more moments of discomfort," he assured her kindly.

Even now she was struggling to hold on to life. And he tried to take in every nuance as he wrangled the three-foot-long asp back into the basket with a gloved hand. This was the hardest part, staying in control without missing anything—not the fright fixed in the eyes that were even now going blank, not the struggle for air, not the involuntary tensing of the body. He secured the serpent so it could not escape and set the basket on the table.

His eager gaze never left the orphan.

"The darkness," she gasped. "Closing in on the light."

Within moments, the venom had totally paralyzed her.

A final harsh sound escaped her mouth as it went slack. Her eyes stared.

Then he undressed her, taking delight in each new revelation. Her body was young. Fresh. Undefiled.

"'You are mine, my love,'" he said, quoting poetry. "'You are perfume a-wing, a shower of myrrh./ See, sweet, the bird trap set with my own hand—'"

But, for some reason, probably because he so longed for the lady to be *her,* he wasn't as thrilled by the poetry as usual.

He lifted the orphan and carried her to the recessed area of the room behind the screen where he placed her on a work slab. This was covered with another oiled cloth that would contain the tainted blood so there would be no chance of accidental poisoning later, for the cobra was an even more deadly creature than he.

His tools were ready.

"'Anubis, guide my hands.'" He intoned the prayer to the jackal-headed god of embalmers.

After which he inserted a long metal hook up one nostril and began slowly and carefully removing her brain. Of no value now, he discarded that pale, oozy material into an urn of no consequence.

Then, with a surgeon's finesse, he made a precise incision several inches in length in the left side of the body where he would similarly remove the liver, lungs, stomach, and intestines. Stopping between each organ, he cleaned her blood-stained flesh with linens and tossed the blood-soaked material into the urn holding the brain. He hated to see her beauty marred by bodily fluids even for a moment.

Rivulets of blood oozed down the oiled tarp as he set each of these organs carefully on a tray. Each would be embalmed and placed in its own canopic jar, the lid of which bore the image of one of the gods of the dead. The heart he left in place as was traditional for the ancient Egyptians.

After filling her body cavity with bundles of

natron wrapped in linen, he placed her corpse on a special slanted embalming bed with a groove at the bottom. Then he covered her with more natron—a grainy chemical found in deposits in the Nile River. The salt would dry and preserve her outer shell while her fluids dripped into a container below.

"'Oh, Osiris, Prince of the Dead, God of the Underworld, watch over her while she sleeps between earth and heaven. May a place be made for her in the boat of the sun. May a seat be given to her in the hall of judgment. . . .'"

He paused in reciting the poetic spell from *The Book of the Dead* and glanced back at the painted screen, at the deities who quietly watched there. His neck prickled.

Judgment?

But the Egyptians had had a much more open view of the universe, he reasoned quickly. Their gods wouldn't fault him for sending them another lovely lady.

If only he'd been able to send them the *right* lady.

That was what was causing his slight discomfort.

Pushing aside any uneasiness, he concentrated on his task. Using a crank, he lowered the orphan into the sarcophagus where she would ripen. A twist of another crank, and the lid closed over her still form.

Here she would remain for forty days, awaiting the next step toward paradise.

14

Learning to shoot a gun—one that under the circumstances might wound or even kill a man—somehow seemed sacrilegious on a beautiful Sunday morning graced by a blue sky, a few perfect fluffy clouds, and a brilliant sun. But resigned to the task, Aurelia led the way to a vacant lot across the street from the house.

Phaedra was the one who seemed to be having second thoughts. "I hope we don't scare the wits out of our neighbors with the noise."

"*Hearing* a few gunshots never hurt anyone," Cody said with a chuckle. He hefted the long case he was carrying to the other hand. "Besides, there's plenty of room. Probably no one's likely to notice."

"I thought you said you were going to get a *small* gun," Aurelia protested. "That case looks big enough to store an entire arsenal."

Cody laughed. "That it is, though the contents are

less lethal. I got your weapon right here," he said, patting the pocket of his fringed buckskin jacket. "Small enough to tuck in your purse or even under a garter. But you needed something to shoot *at,* and I figured on providing such."

For emphasis, he set down the case with a flourish in the knee-high grass. Then he dug out a three-legged wooden contraption to which he attached a heavy paper target of colored concentric rings.

"Not the same as shooting at a man, of course, but it'll give you some idea of accuracy."

Shooting at a man.

Aurelia could hardly believe things would come to such a pass. The world was supposed to be civilized now, wasn't it? Then she remembered Rosario. He had seemed utterly civilized until that last encounter. Having the means to protect herself would make her feel more at ease when she was alone. Plus, she was counting on Phaedra's willingness to let her travel unescorted.

Cody pulled a palm-sized gun out of his pocket. "This here's a Colt 2.5 derringer-type pistol. Weighs only seven ounces. A gift from Little Missy."

"That's not necessary. I can pay—"

Cody raised his hand and rode roughshod over her protest. "Now, she insists. Annie just said to tell you to do her proud and shoot that varmint right between the eyes if he so much as comes near you again."

He handed the weapon over to Aurelia. Heart thudding at the cold touch of metal, she carefully inspected the small piece. It was quite pretty, actually. The walnut grip was carved into the shape of a hawk's head, and the frame was intricately etched nickel plate.

"Something so small and fancy can be lethal?" Phaedra asked, echoing Aurelia's very thought.

"Up close, you bet. Short-range firearms are large-bored and designed for self-defense. That little piece takes .41-caliber shot."

Cody pulled a bullet out of another pocket and proceeded to talk Aurelia through the proper loading routine. Releasing a button enabled her to break open the pistol by swinging the barrel to the right. Then she dropped the bullet, which was nearly a half-inch in diameter, in place before resetting and locking the barrel.

"That looked easy enough," Phaedra said.

Aurelia nodded. "The difficult part would be using it."

"You'll be an expert in no time," Cody assured her, obviously not catching her meaning.

She wondered how many men Buffalo Bill Cody had killed. If she asked, he would no doubt exaggerate as he had with his Indian-rescue of Phaedra. Then, again, maybe she didn't want to know the truth.

"You want to use two hands, the left to steady the right," Cody said, getting behind her and adjusting her arms. "Look right down that barrel. See the little notch and the rise at the tip? That's the sight. Line those up so's they're aimed at the center of the target, then release the hammer spur with your thumb." Because she was nervous and clumsy, he helped her cock the gun before stepping back. "Now take a breath and hold it while you gently sque-e-e-eze the trigger."

Aurelia did as instructed, but as it fired, the little

weapon jerked up and surprised her into taking an awkward step back. Immediately, Cody's hands were on her shoulders steadying her.

"Good."

Checking the target, Aurelia couldn't see a hole anywhere. "But I missed."

"Not uncommon for a first try," Cody assured her.

She tried again and again, her third shot hitting the corner of the target, her fifth the outer ring. Both Cody and Phaedra continued to issue encouraging remarks each time she loaded a bullet into the pistol. A few neighbors or their servants did step outside nearby houses to see what was afoot, but no one came to complain.

Growing tired of the tension in her arms, Aurelia tried her best to ignore everything but the target. She imagined it to be the stalker as she took aim. She lost count of how much ammunition she wasted, but eventually she got closer to the center, though she never quite hit the bull's-eye.

"Impossible." Discouraged, Aurelia sighed.

"The varmint who's been following you is not gonna be wearin' a target. Besides, you're doing real good," Cody assured her. "Even waving that thing around at a body will be effective." He cleared his throat dramatically. "I once had a sobering experience at the wrong end of a derringer myself!"

"But a derringer is usually a lady's weapon, isn't it?" Phaedra asked. "I can imagine a woman wanting to kill you with attention, but with a gun?"

"I couldn't imagine that either," Cody said, easily swinging into his storytelling mode, "especially not Lil. Now there was a woman of the world. Reminded me of you, Phaedra."

Phaedra's eyebrows shot up at that. "Oh?"

He hastened to explain. "I meant beautiful and intelligent and possessing a rip-snortin' zest for life."

"Oh." Phaedra relaxed and smiled.

Knowing the showman liked to tell stories, Aurelia smiled, too. She could use a respite from the tension that had been building with each shot.

"We, uh, got to know each other quite well," Cody was saying. He cleared his throat again and wiggled his silvered brows. "Then one morning, Lil brought up the subject of marriage."

"Marriage?" Phaedra echoed. "What in the world was she thinking of?"

Cody appeared sheepish. "Well, I had somehow forgotten to tell her about Louisa."

"Convenient memory lapse."

"When she found out I already had a wife, Lil was, shall we say, indignant."

"As well she should be," Aurelia murmured. Rosario hadn't told her about his wife, either, and look how that had turned out.

Paying no attention to her disapproval, Cody continued. "After a short if heated argument over the matter, I decided it would be best if I made a hasty retreat. That's when Lil pulled the pistol from under her pillow."

Aurelia relaxed as she realized he was probably telling one of his tall tales not meant to be taken as gospel at all.

"So," Phaedra mused, "she scared the pants off you, did she?"

"More than that. She put a hole in them."

"She actually fired on you?" Aurelia asked.

"Oh, yes, ma'am. She grazed, uh, an unmentionable

part of my person. As I limped away while trying to stem the flow of blood, I thanked God *I* hadn't taught her to shoot or I might have been in real trouble."

"Bill, will you never behave yourself?" Phaedra said, pinching his cheek.

They were all laughing over Cody's exaggerated misfortune when a neigh of protest caught their attention. Aurelia turned and saw a carriage in front of their house, the driver pulling on his horse's mouth. The big bay pranced in place and protested once more.

And Aurelia noted the driver was Sean O'Rourke.

She was jubilant for her aunt until she realized Sean was staring their way with a huge frown on his face. She glanced at Phaedra who hadn't yet spotted her lover and realized how close her aunt was standing to Cody. Phaedra had just touched Cody's cheek in what must have looked like an intimate gesture. Surely Sean wasn't misinterpreting the innocent scenario.

Finally Phaedra turned and saw the carriage. "Sean!" she cried, pleasure lighting her face as she gathered her skirts to go to him.

But she was too late, for the older O'Rourke cracked his whip and ordered his horse to move on. Phaedra stopped dead, her shoulders drooping. Aurelia wanted to run to her aunt and comfort her, but she was certain that would embarrass Phaedra all the more.

Hurting for her aunt, angry with Sean, Aurelia announced, "One more shot and then we shall go inside for some tea."

How could Sean be jealous of a fly-by-night like Buffalo Bill Cody? Surely he knew how much

Phaedra loved *him*. He must realize that she would marry him if she could. Why couldn't he give her the benefit of the doubt? Men! What in the world was wrong with them all?

She loaded, took aim, and quickly dispatched the image she had of the one who had been following her.

And Cody shouted, "Bull's-eye!"

"Turn your shoulders a little more to the right," Phaedra instructed Aurelia as she sketched her niece's outline on a drawing pad. When she had the perfect view of Aurelia's profile against the draped pale turquoise cloth behind her, Phaedra said, "That's it. Now hold the position."

They'd spent late morning and the entire afternoon working on the book project for the Society for the Study of Ancient Mediterranean Cultures. Aurelia had already struck several poses in her pseudo-Egyptian garb.

A sheath of white linen clung to her full breasts and hips in a most shocking way since she couldn't wear the normal undergarments below. Afraid a seamstress might be scandalized, Phaedra had bought the costume from an actress she knew and had altered it for her niece. Parted in the middle and tucked behind her ears, Aurelia's heavy dark hair hung loose from the thin gold band circling her forehead. Her only other adornments were a collar and earrings of turquoise, lapis, and carnelian beads—conservative but beautiful imitations of ancient jewelry—treasures Phaedra had received from a lover in Paris many years before.

"You know, the Egyptian look suits you, darling. You are even more striking than usual."

Though she didn't break her pose, Aurelia lifted a derisive brow. "If you want your sketch in proper form, you'd best not make me giggle."

"I am serious. You are the past brought to life. I couldn't ask for a better subject."

Phaedra meant to have several sketches and one oil as samples to show at the meeting later in the week. As a working woman, Aurelia's time was limited, so they had to take advantage of every moment she was able to spare. Phaedra only wished that fact inspired her pencil to work faster, but alas, thoughts of Sean kept interrupting and distracting her at the most inopportune times.

As if her niece could read her mind, Aurelia asked, "Aunt Phaedra, do you think a man and a woman can have a successful personal relationship without marriage?"

Remembering the way she had been abandoned and abused, Phaedra said, "I used to think so, but now I am not certain."

"Because of Sean."

"He did walk out on me because I refused to marry him." The lead tip angrily met the drawing paper and she had to smooth out the ragged line.

"Though he did not know your circumstances."

"Nevertheless, Sean could not have trusted that I loved him or he would never have broken off our liaison."

Aurelia was silent for a moment. Then she said, "About this morning . . . I'm sorry."

"Whatever for?"

"If your friend Bill hadn't been teaching me to

shoot . . . well, it's my fault that you and Sean are not back in each other's arms."

"Nonsense!" Phaedra stated. "The fault belongs to that stubborn old fool for being so blind about some things and jumping to conclusions about others."

Whereas before she had simply been heartbroken, now Phaedra was angry to boot. How dare Sean jump to conclusions about her and Bill! How dare he assume that she was a light-skirt, ready to go from one man's arms to another within the space of days, and after she'd made uncounted assurances that she loved him! Then something occurred to her—what if he thought Bill was the reason she wouldn't marry him? If only she had been able to tell him about Fernando. . . .

"And it's my fault, too, for impetuously marrying in my youth," she admitted with a sigh. But one could not turn back the clock. "Aurelia, when you asked me about marriage, were you referring to Sean and me?"

"Uh, yes," her niece said, looking away, but not before Phaedra saw the blush on her cheek.

"You were not." Setting down the drawing pad, she rose to face the young woman. "You were speaking of yourself, weren't you? Of you and Liam. Has he asked you to marry him?"

Aurelia's cheeks were even ruddier when she broke her pose and met Phaedra's gaze. "No, of course not. I mean, we don't know each other well enough to . . . I mean . . ."

Phaedra smiled for the first time since Sean's unexpected appearance and disappearance that morning. "No explanations are necessary, darling. Certainly none to me."

"I've been thinking of the future lately, that's all."

"You're not considering marrying Liam out of practicality, are you? Fear of being labeled a spinster?" For that would be the worst of reasons.

"No. I'm afraid I'm in love with the man."

"Darling, how wonderful." A relieved Phaedra hugged Aurelia, but when her niece didn't respond in kind, the older woman stepped back and frowned up at her. "It is wonderful, isn't it?"

Aurelia looked decidedly unhappy as if she thought herself in a fix. But the shine in her eyes told Phaedra of her true feelings—she was in love!

"I thought it was wonderful," Aurelia agreed. "But then yesterday morning, I was thinking about how much Mariel loves Wesley. Look how miserable he makes her."

"Liam is not Wesley."

"He does not seem to be of the same ilk," Aurelia admitted. "Though sometimes he does frighten me a little with his forceful nature."

Phaedra was reminded of Sean once more. "Sounds as if the O'Rourke men are more alike than I'd even guessed."

"Doesn't that quality in Sean alarm you?"

Having tested her own will against her lover's to no ill effect until this last quarrel, Phaedra admitted, "It excites me. Then, again, I have more years of experience than you. I know who I am and what I want. Perhaps you are not equally certain."

Aurelia approached the window and stood looking out. "Sometimes I want to remain independent and pursue my talent to the extreme." Then she paced the room like a lioness Phaedra had once seen in a French count's private animal park. "Other times I want a family also, but I'm afraid I can't have both. Am I irrational because I'm not content to be like other women, giving over my will to a man? If I were forced to choose, I fear it would be in favor of my independence. Did you ever find yourself in that quandary?"

"If I hadn't, I would never have married Fernando," Phaedra assured her. "My problem was that I was so blinded by passion that I didn't take a good look beneath the surface. If I had, I would have recognized the dictatorial, humorless man he really was. Sean doesn't have Fernando's polish, but he does have a wonderful heart and a giving nature beneath his rough exterior. He loves me for who I am and has no desire to change me."

"It's no wonder you want to marry him."

"I did. Now I'm not certain." And with Aurelia and Liam involved, Phaedra realized, things between her and Sean would be even more complicated.

"That's anger and disappointment speaking," Aurelia said wisely. "You still want him, I know, just as I want Liam. If we both get our heart's desire, won't we scandalize Fiona?" she asked with a laugh.

Cheered by the suggestion, Phaedra smiled. "Amazing that Fiona is the oldest, yet she doesn't know you at all. Imagine thinking DeWitt was good enough for you! I knew you needed someone stronger, a man who could match your own temperament while giving you the room to be yourself. I think you've found your match in Liam."

She was about to go on reassuring Aurelia when she heard a shuffle at the open door. Realizing they weren't alone, she whirled around and caught Theodore Mansfield standing frozen in the doorway and staring at Aurelia most peculiarly.

"Theo. I wasn't expecting you."

He quickly looked away from Aurelia to concentrate on the floor. "Mary let me in. Sorry if I am interrupting. I stopped by because I need your help."

"Of course," Phaedra said. "What is it?"

"The next meeting of the society is to be at my residence."

"Yes, Thursday night."

"I'm not much for entertaining." He pulled out a linen square and mopped the perspiration off his brow. "I thought you might be agreeable to helping me with details . . . refreshments and such."

Phaedra could tell he'd worked himself up into a knot over what to anyone else would be a simple decision. He was hardly comfortable in a group situation anywhere, so he never entertained. Knowing he was fastidious about whatever he did, Phaedra realized how important this was to him.

"I can consult with you now, if you like. We were just finishing up, weren't we, darling?"

Theo raised his eyes from the floor and once more fixed them on Aurelia. "You plan to attend the society's meeting, as well, do you not?"

Aurelia shrugged. "Actually, I hadn't decided."

"You indicated you were interested in joining at the last meeting!"

Shocked by his demanding tone, the likes of which she'd never before heard from Theo, Phaedra stared closely at him and realized he seemed absolutely mesmerized by her niece. His eyes glinted brightly. Glancing at Aurelia, she recognized the problem. What thoughts must be going through his head seeing Aurelia in what she herself considered a shocking costume.

"Aurelia will come if she has the time and energy after a long day at work," Phaedra said soothingly. "I'm afraid I've tired her out myself today. Aurelia, perhaps you'd like to refresh yourself before dinner."

Seemingly unaware of the stir she'd caused in Theo, Aurelia headed for the door. "Yes, my back is beginning to ache. Theo, nice to see you again."

Phaedra didn't relax until Aurelia was safely out of the room and the glint out of Theo's eyes.

How odd—he'd always seemed so nonsexual, and she was certain the glitter had been lust. Then she supposed any man would have difficulty repressing even deeply buried longings when confronted by a woman who appeared to be half-clothed by modern standards.

Thinking no more of it, Phaedra got down to business. "Now, to your refreshments."

"You went off and delivered the contract without the accompanying prospectus!" Sean yelled at the messenger who had just returned to the office.

Aurelia turned and stared as did every other worker in the office. Sean had been ranting and raving all morning, and the young man named Timothy who was at the moment his object of derision looked as if he wanted to sink right through the floor.

"But Mr. O'Rourke," Timothy protested weakly, "you handed me the envelope yourself. You said nothing about another."

"Of course I did!" Sean roared. "It's obvious that you weren't listening. That's the problem with you young men these days. Heads in the clouds. Fool romantic notions. Always dreaming!"

Romantic notions? Aurelia wondered if that was the problem. Was Sean as irritable as an old bear because of what he thought he saw between Phaedra and Cody the day before? No doubt the same reason he'd avoided *her* the entire morning, because she reminded him of her aunt.

The front door opened with unusual force and Liam entered. "What's all the commotion, Father? I could hear you all the way down the hall, in the elevator."

"This ninny has the audacity to tell me I'm wrong!" Sean waved a large envelope for emphasis. "He was supposed to deliver this as well as the contracts—"

"If there's been a mistake," Liam interrupted smoothly, "then Timothy will be glad to correct it." He took the envelope from his father's hand and gave it to the messenger. "Here you go. Hurry now."

"Thank you, Mr. O'Rourke." The relieved young man made a hasty escape.

Liam's gaze strayed around the office, landing directly on her. Aurelia could feel a blush starting below her collar. She concentrated furiously on her rendering lest he later criticize her for not having the appropriately professional manner.

"Come, Father, let's go into your office. We have a few things to discuss."

A grumbling Sean preceded his son. The door closed behind them. A murmur started and Aurelia glanced up to see eyebrows lift across the room. And no wonder! Usually Sean was the good-natured one, having to calm down Liam for some reason or other. How odd to see the roles reversed.

Aurelia took her eyes from the glass-enclosed office and the breadth of Liam's shoulders. She did her best to concentrate on her work, but all she could think about was Liam being in the next room. He'd been at a site that morning, and this was the first time she'd caught a glance of him since the wee hours when he'd brought her home after their orgiastic night together. Though she was nervous, she was determined to act as if nothing had happened between them—at least not while here in the workplace.

Aurelia planned to give Liam no cause to think they'd made a mistake.

When he left Sean's office a few moments later, her grip tightened on the pencil and the page blurred before her eyes. Liam drew closer, then paused behind her.

"Good afternoon, Miss Kincaid."

Simple words that sent a thrill up her spine. "Mr. O'Rourke," she mumbled, staring hard at her drawing and suddenly realizing she'd made a mistake because of the distraction he'd caused.

As he leaned in to take a closer look, Aurelia swallowed hard, not looking forward to his criticism—she'd sketched in an extra window instead of the door. She felt heat on the back of her neck as he peered over her shoulder and prepared herself for his sarcastic wit.

"Very nice," he murmured. "Keep up the good work, Miss Kincaid."

He was smiling at her in the manner of a man who was utterly besotted. Now she did blush. Surely no one could miss that silly grin crooking his lips. She sneaked a look at her co-workers—more lifted eyebrows—and a sinking feeling tilted her stomach.

"Do you think you could step into my office for a moment with the Gray renderings?" he asked. "I would like to go over them with you."

"Yes, Mr. O'Rourke. Of course. I'll be but a moment."

Aurelia wanted to correct the mistake before someone else caught sight of it. He hesitated, then nodded and turned toward his own office. While she concentrated on hurriedly remedying her blunder, she was certain she felt his gaze and that of the other draftsmen on her back.

The second she finished, she pulled the portfolio for the Gray house. The last thing she wanted was for Liam to come looking for her. She would bask in his undivided attention if they had the opportunity to be alone again, but certainly not here at the office. What in the world had gotten into him to act so blatantly personal in front of the other employees?

"Ah, there you are," he said glancing up from his desk as she entered his office.

He was all smiles, and as much as part of her wanted to beam at him in return, she kept her expression neutral. Professional.

"The Gray portfolio," she said, handing it over.

He spread her renderings on his own drawing table. "Excellent work," he said before even taking the time to get a proper look at them. "It's important to lay a good foundation for any relationship. Don't you agree?"

"Building project," she corrected.

"Taking care with each step in the process is important. We want to make sure that all parties concerned are satisfied."

"Are you satisfied?" she asked, meaning the drawings.

"Very."

He wasn't looking at them but at her, and his statements weren't professional, but personal. She couldn't believe it—he'd been worried about a woman working with an office of men and here he was the one who couldn't keep himself in professional order! Thinking about Sean's mood that morning, she agreed with Phaedra that father and son were quite alike.

Suddenly, Aurelia realized Liam was staring fiercely over her shoulder. She turned and swallowed a gasp. Everyone including Sean was watching them through the windowed wall from various parts of the other room.

Determined to escape gracefully, she gathered the sketches. "I'm glad you are pleased with my work. I hope the Grays will be as well. Can I get back to my current project now?"

"After you answer one very important question," he said, before she could move to the door. "Will you agree to share a quiet supper with me tonight?"

15

"*This color doesn't* suit me. I don't know what made me buy this dress," Aurelia complained as she frowned at her image in the parlor mirror.

"It's a beautiful gown," Phaedra said soothingly, though it was indeed unusual for her niece. The moss green silk taffeta with drapey, elbow-length sleeves was trimmed with a wide white lacy collar, no doubt the object of Aurelia's uncertainty. "And the color does set off your skin and hair quite wonderfully, so stop fretting."

"I look more like a schoolgirl than a professional woman. Liam will laugh at me."

"He will be enchanted."

"I'm going to change back into the black and salmon."

Phaedra bit her lip so she wouldn't laugh. She'd never seen Aurelia in such a state. And over a man, no less.

"Wear whatever makes you feel most comfortable, my darling." Her niece started for the steps when Phaedra thought of something she'd been meaning to ask her. "Aurelia, wait. You do remember Fiona's maid, Gina?"

"The pretty young woman from Italy? Of course."

"When you spoke to her in Italian, did she by any chance say anything about plans to leave Fiona's service?"

"No. We merely exchanged a few pleasantries. She quit, then?"

"Disappeared without saying a word. Fiona is beside herself."

And, remembering that some man had been stalking Aurelia, Phaedra couldn't help feeling concerned. It was clear that a woman simply wasn't safe on the streets anymore.

"Fiona's quite fond of little Gina," she went on. "Your sister is very worried that some harm has come to her maid."

Her expression immediately sympathetic, Aurelia asked, "Does Fiona know where Gina's family lives?"

Phaedra sighed. "She doesn't have a family, poor child. She's an orphan."

"Oh. Then perhaps she met a man. We women have been known to do some impulsive things in the name of love."

Aurelia was obviously thinking of herself. Not wanting to ruin her niece's evening, Phaedra said, "Yes, that must be it," though her instincts argued otherwise. Something about the maid's disappearance chilled her.

"I'd best be getting upstairs if I'm to change," Aurelia said. But the sound of a carriage pulling up to the house made her freeze halfway up the stairs. "He has arrived. Oh, dear, now what?"

"I can take care of Liam while you change. It doesn't hurt a man to wait just a little while anyway."

Aurelia didn't try to hide her shocked expression. If anything, she exaggerated it, no doubt to tease.

"Aunt Phaedra, I would never have guessed *you* would use such a ploy."

"I may be unconventional in many ways, but I know and appreciate the power of anticipation. Now go!"

Her niece flew up the steps, and, trying to put the conversation about Gina behind her, Phaedra crossed to the entrance. She hoped her niece would be luckier in love than she. Opening the front door, therefore, she was nearly startled out of her mind when she saw Sean, not Liam, approaching.

"Phaedra, you and I have some talking to do!" he thundered as he ascended the last few steps.

"Sean!" Then she quickly regained her wits. "Inside."

But he hardly waited until he'd crossed the threshold before demanding, "What is it between you and that cowboy fop?"

His tone effectively countered her shock at seeing him. And, indignant that he'd denigrate Bill Cody, she said stiffly, "Bill and I are old friends as I've told you several times before."

"You were looking like more than friends to me when I saw the two of you."

"That's jealousy speaking if I ever heard it." She flounced by him into the parlor and was aware that he followed practically on her heels. Though she suspected Sean had come to reclaim her heart, the frustration and anger of the past few days kept her from throwing herself into his arms as she longed to. "And I don't know why you would be jealous—it was you who walked out on me!"

"Because you wouldn't marry me."

"I have a good reason."

"One you refuse to share!"

Guilt flooded Phaedra. She should be honest with the man she loved, and yet she was in a hopeless situation. If she didn't tell him the truth, he would no doubt storm out of the house never to darken her doorstep again. And if she told him she was married, he would no doubt do the same.

"Phaedra, please," Sean begged, "if you have a care for me, tell me what is standing in your way of becoming my wife."

"Another man." The words flew from her mouth before she could think.

"Damn Cody!"

"I told you it wasn't Bill!" All the anger she'd felt the morning before came flooding back. "His name is Fernando DeVarga."

"I never heard of any DeVarga in Chicago. Who in Hades is he?"

"I met him in California and he is my . . . my husband."

Sean went ashen and silent and grabbed his chest. Phaedra almost panicked. Dear God, if he had a heart attack . . .

"When would you have been marrying this man?" Sean asked too calmly.

"Thirty years ago. I was blinded by foolish youthful passion. When I got to know the real man, I couldn't tolerate the thought of being tied to him forever. I ran away and never looked back."

"And how long ago would that have been?"

"The same year I married him."

Sean remained silent so long Phaedra started to get very nervous. Though he didn't say a word, his face looked like a thundercloud and the glint in his eyes accused her. Just as she'd thought, she'd lost Sean. She fought back tears. He couldn't see her cry.

But when he asked, "Why didn't you tell me?" in an almost gentle tone, she almost allowed the tears to fall.

Instead, she stared down at the worn pattern in the carpet. "It's not an easy thing to tell."

"But I'm the man who loves you!"

"Exactly." Phaedra met his heated gaze pleadingly. "Sean, I only hope you can find it in your heart to forgive me. It was just that I loved you so, and I didn't want to lose you."

"You were afraid you'd lose me if you told me the truth?"

Phaedra nodded and Sean took her in his arms. "Foolish woman, indeed," he muttered. "Is there no getting out of this marriage, then?"

Conceding that he'd suffered as well as she, Phaedra held on to Sean for all she was worth. Maybe, just maybe there was still hope for them if her efforts went rewarded.

"I've sent a telegram asking Fernando if he could

see his way to having our marriage annulled." Being in Sean's arms felt so right and she would spend the rest of her life there if she could. "After all, I did not do my Catholic duty and give him children. I am afraid he has not yet responded to my plea. Perhaps he never will."

Sean pushed her away from him and gripped her upper arms. "Marry me anyway! Who would know the difference?"

"And become a bigamist? Sean, that's the talk of a desperate man." Which to some extent pleased Phaedra, because it told her she hadn't lost his love. "But my nieces know that I'm married, so bigamy is out of the question." As if she would do that to the man she loved under any circumstances.

"Then we can go on as we have been . . . or live together in sin. I don't care which as long as I can have your love and devotion."

"That you do," she assured him. "Never doubt it. Though I would have flaunted convention to live with you in the past, I can't do that to my family. I hope you understand. Would it be so terrible if we went on as we have?"

"It'll likely be killing me, but I'll agree to anything to keep you in my life."

Sean sealed that concession with a kiss at once sweet and passionate and filled with promise, one Phaedra wished they could fulfill immediately. She broke free with a gasp.

"We're not alone," she whispered. "Aurelia's upstairs getting ready to have a quiet supper with your son. We'll have to wait until they leave."

"I'll not be waiting any longer," Sean stated,

pulling her toward the door. "And I intend to hold you until daybreak. Liam will be spending the night at his new house. You can come home with me."

Though Phaedra hesitated to leave Aurelia alone, it wouldn't be for long, she knew. And though she would spend them in the arms of the man she loved, there weren't enough hours in the night to satisfy her.

It was nearly dark by the time he arrived to pick up Aurelia, but Liam recognized his father's horse and buggy on the Kincaid premises. Not wanting to disturb Sean and Phaedra's peace—for he'd realized some argument or other between them had been tormenting his father—Liam pulled his carriage into an empty lot on the other side of the street where he secured his horse under an old elm tree. He suspected that if all went well, Sean's temper would improve considerably by morning. The problem was how to get Aurelia away from the house without interrupting the older couple.

Maybe he could catch her attention by throwing pebbles at her window and luring her down the back way. The thought made Liam smile. At the moment, he was feeling every inch the silly schoolboy.

He approached the house cautiously, thinking to scout around. Perhaps Aurelia was downstairs with Sean and Phaedra and his skulking would be for naught. He was in the shelter of a large maple, about to peer in the windows, when the front door opened.

"Sean, not here," Phaedra said breathlessly. "Someone might see."

"And who's to be seeing in the dark?" his father demanded.

The moment of silence that followed made Liam avert his gaze and silently slide around the side of the house. He didn't want to embarrass Phaedra or his father.

"Come, my love, so we can finally make my house a home."

Their footsteps were quick as they descended the stairs and crossed to the buggy. "I can't believe we'll be able to spend the entire night together."

Liam's brows shot up. Quite a reunion, indeed. He fell farther back into the shadows as the horse and buggy pulled around front and onto the street. He waited until they were out of sight. About to make his approach, he hesitated when he heard a noise toward the rear of the house—a rustle of leaves and the crunch of twigs, as if someone other than he were skulking in the shadows.

Frowning, he went to investigate, hoping it would only be one of the staff. Though moonlight threw a soft glow over the path, he saw nothing and wondered if he'd merely heard some animal, a raccoon or coyote. Then he saw movement, a silhouette stealing along the carriage house. But a glance at the windows told him Fred and Mary were both inside eating their evening meal.

Liam decided to investigate further.

Another sound around back made him slip toward the alley where a shadowy form lurked near the cement incinerator. Whoever it was had no business being there if the furtive movements were any indication.

He approached with stealth, his footsteps muffled by the cinder-covered alley, fully prepared to give the trespasser a scare.

Since the alley was not lit, Liam was within yards of the figure bending over and half-buried in the incinerator before realizing how slight it was. He could have sworn he'd seen the silhouette of a full-grown man come this way.

"What are you up to?" he demanded.

The figure straightened with a start and garbage went flying in every direction. A boy who looked to be thirteen or so gave Liam a wild look before bolting. Liam was right behind him, with a long reach that made up for the boy's quickness. He grabbed the lad by the scruff of the neck, then fought to encase his flailing arms.

"I asked you a question."

"I didn't do nothing wrong!"

"You don't live in this neighborhood, do you? Where are your people?" Liam looked around cautiously, wondering if the others were nearby and it had been the boy's father he'd first seen.

"I don't live nowhere and I don't got no people. I was hungry was all."

"Hungry."

So the boy had been digging through the garbage for scraps of discarded food. He weighed next to nothing and the light of the moon revealed gaunt features that hadn't seen a trace of soap in weeks. How had things come to such a pass that children weren't taken care of? he wondered.

"You gonna turn me over to the coppers?"

Liam sighed. Homeless and hungry and barely

more than a child. "No, I won't turn you over to anyone. I'm going to make sure you have something to eat. Something substantial." Hanging on to the indigent boy with one hand, he pulled out his wallet with the other. Only when he saw the leather did the boy go still and focused. "And don't get any ideas."

"I'm no thief!"

Liam grunted and let go so he could shake out some change. "What's your name?" The boy's eyes went round when Liam handed him a silver Liberty-head quarter, two nickels, and a half-dozen copper Indian-head pennies, which added up to nearly a day's wage for a child laborer.

"Name's Frankie." The lad sounded disbelieving when he asked, "You're giving me all that?"

"For food and tram fare," Liam told him. "If you want a job."

"Doing what?" Frankie asked suspiciously. "I told you I ain't no thief."

"Whatever errands my head gardener wants you to run. I'm an architect. My father and I build houses."

Liam quickly gave Frankie directions to the site of his new house where landscaping materials would be delivered early the next morning. He wasn't convinced the lad would ever show, though Frankie promised to be there. At least if he was able to hang on to it, the money would keep the boy well fed for several days. Liam shook his head as he made his way back toward the house. The poverty that lay beyond the splendor of the White City of the fair was appalling. Not that he could fix things. He could only offer as many jobs as his business afforded.

Immersed in thoughts of the seemingly insurmountable problem that faced so many, Liam rounded the front of the house only to be jerked out of his reverie by a shrill demand issued in a familiar female voice.

"Stop right there!"

Halfway down the steps, Aurelia was illuminated by the gaslight spilling from the front porch. And to Liam's horror, he noted she was pointing a small gun at his chest. She couldn't see him clearly—he was still in the shadows!

"Aurelia, it's me, Liam," he said quickly to avert disaster.

"Liam! Oh, my God." Her hands dropped and her voice quivered just a tad. "I-I thought . . . I'm so sorry."

"What's going on?"

"I thought you were the man from Oak Park. The one who followed me."

Liam frowned. "Whatever gave you such an idea?" His arm lightly circling her back, he led Aurelia up the front steps. "Why would you think he was here?"

"I saw him outside the house last week." She peered over her shoulder, her manner nervous. "When I heard noises, I thought he'd come back."

"There was someone out there," Liam admitted. "I investigated myself."

She stiffened and gave him a stricken look that he longed to soothe immediately. "I was correct, then?"

"Only if your stalker was around the age of thirteen or so."

"A boy?"

"He was going through the incinerator, looking for food. Are you sure he mightn't be the one you saw here before?"

"Maybe." She sounded uncertain as she entered the house and closed the door behind him. "I would have sworn it was the same person, but the footprints we found weren't very large—they could have belonged to a boy. Maybe I never saw the man from Oak Park again, after all."

Aurelia sounded relieved. Liam only wished he felt equally at ease. He'd thought the silhouette had belonged to a grown man, had even considered the boy's father might be around. What if there *had* been two of them? He considered admitting such to Aurelia, but he didn't want to frighten her. His imagination might have added size to Frankie. Then, again, it wouldn't do to let Aurelia get careless, either.

"It's good you have that gun," he said, stepping closer to her. "Just in case the man does come around. I trust you know how to shoot it?"

She was staring down at the weapon, which fit her hand perfectly. "Bill Cody taught me what he could in a short time. I-I don't know if I could actually use it on another human being, though."

"Anyone who might consider attacking you has lost his humanity," Liam said, caressing Aurelia's cheek and tilting her head up so he could look into her dark eyes. "A woman should be able and willing to protect herself unless there's a man to do it for her."

Liam bit back the urge to volunteer. He couldn't protect her unless they were together all the time.

Unless they were married, he amended. And they had only known each other for a short time, too short for such a commitment.

Or was it?

"Have I told you how beautiful you look tonight?" Liam asked as they finished their meal.

"Twice," Aurelia said, attributing her growing warmth to compliments heaped atop too much wine.

Somewhere between the first course and the dessert, they had gone from topics of general interest to those of a more personal nature. Liam had listened attentively as she talked about her time in Italy, and if he had noticed that she'd left out parts of the story, he hadn't challenged her. She was glad, for she did not want Rosario to intrude tonight.

They sat in a quiet corner of a discreet supper club whose gas wall sconces and table candelabra created a romantic ambience that made her long to be alone with Liam. He looked so handsome in his black-and-white dinner clothes, and his initialed gold cuff links and shirt studs winked with tiny emeralds the exact color of his eyes.

When he slipped his hand over hers, his thumb curled around her flesh and did unspeakable things to her palm without being obvious to any possible prying eyes. As he leaned closer across the table toward her, his features were intense, his gaze positively erotic.

"I wish we were alone this very moment," he said softly.

The fine hairs along her arms and neck rose, and her spine tingled. She wanted to be alone, too. "You could give me another tour of your new home, point out the improvements since I was last there."

Liam chuckled. "As you very well know, not enough time has elapsed for me to have made any substantial progress. You have seen everything I have," he added, his tone a tad wicked, making her breasts and belly tighten deliciously. "Now it's my turn to see yours."

Aurelia's ears burned and her toes curled in her satin slippers. "My what?"

"Your home, of course," he said smoothly. "It would be of great interest architecturally."

Because she wasn't certain whether or not he was teasing, she said, "My family's home is simple compared to its neighbors. Now you might consider touring Glessner House or the Marshall Field residence a better use of your time."

"Anything to do with you is worth far more than what a mere mansion has to offer."

Aurelia couldn't temper her smile. Only one other man had made her such outrageous claims. Only one other man had tempted her to forget virtue in favor of sensual satisfaction. But the two men were nothing alike.

She could trust Liam.

Even so, she was unexpectedly nervous, perhaps because he'd never questioned her about the other man in her past. She pulled her hand away and fiddled with the linen square protecting her skirts.

"Aunt Phaedra did not say what time she might return. She feared it would be late."

"If at all," Liam corrected. "When I arrived, I

overheard your aunt and my father making plans for an all-night tryst."

Aurelia's breath caught in her throat. "You mean . . ."

"Your house is waiting for my further exploration."

She stifled a giggle at his expense. Not voicing her exultation was difficult. Alone with Liam. Again. And so soon. Perhaps Sean was the best thing to happen to Phaedra for both her aunt's sake *and* her own!

But it wasn't Phaedra she was thinking of on the ride home when Liam found ways to tease and taunt her both verbally and physically. A risqué suggestion here . . . an accidental touch there . . . and she was ready for anything by the time they arrived at the Prairie Street address.

And so she was startled when Liam walked her to the front porch and in a slightly raised voice said, "Thank you for the honor of your company, Miss Kincaid."

"What?"

His finger on her lips shushed further questions. He whispered, "We mustn't put your reputation under scrutiny. Wait five minutes, then meet me at the back door."

She thought to protest that Fred and Mary were long abed, their quarters dark, but Liam was already gone, and a moment later, his carriage was smoothly rolling down the block. Wondering where he meant to leave his horse and rig, Aurelia closed and bolted the front door. The gas lamp near the stairs glowed softly. She looked up toward the bedrooms longingly, then thought of Phaedra's claim that it did not hurt to make a man wait a bit.

Smothering a laugh, she hurried to the parlor

where she lit a table lamp, turned it down low, then set out two brandy glasses and a crystal decanter of the amber liquid. Checking her shadowed image in the mirror, she frowned. The offensive white collar glowed back at her. Why hadn't she worn the salmon and black as she'd meant to? Then again, she probably wouldn't be wearing anything much longer, so she had no need for dissatisfaction.

Nervous with anticipation, she drew the drapes, then headed for the unlit kitchen where she unbolted the door and opened it in time to hear the porch boards creak—stealthily it seemed. An uneasy feeling filling her, she hesitated, then decided she was being ridiculous. She threw the door open wide.

"Liam?" she softly called into the night.

A whisper of warm summer air was the only sound that returned, shooting a chill through her. Certain she had heard something else a moment ago, she was about to close and relock the door when a scuffle on the footpath made her jump. Her hand hit the metal bolt and she cried out.

"Aurelia, are you all right?" came a low voice.

Liam! He was there, after all. She took a deep breath. "Fine. Hurry."

Hurry he did. And if she had thought to make him wait, she was mistaken, for the moment he entered the kitchen he had her in his arms, masterfully bending her to his will. A kiss . . . a caress . . . the promise of more . . .

How could she resist?

She tried. Pushing herself out of his arms, she breathlessly said, "I broke out Aunt Phaedra's favorite brandy. You do like brandy?"

"I'm ready to sample whatever you have to offer."

She heard the laughter tempering the urgency in his voice even as he gave over to her whim. And as he followed her to the dimly lit parlor, he couldn't keep his hands off her. One slid around her back from the curve of her waist to the fullness of her breast. The other brushed an imaginary hair away from her cheek. She slid a glance up at him and read the impatience he was doing his level best to contain.

She had to give her aunt credit—Phaedra knew a thing or two about men!

While her hands were busy pouring the brandy, Liam's were busier unfastening the buttons of her dress. She turned in his arms and offered him a glass.

"To the most desirable woman it's been my pleasure to know."

They touched glasses and he downed the contents, while Aurelia stared, breath caught in her throat. He was the most desirable man she'd ever known, yet she dared not say that, considering what lay unspoken between them.

Liam set down his glass and noted her full one. "I thought you wanted to fortify yourself."

"You speak as if I find entertaining you a harsh task when I merely thought to draw out the pleasure we've shared this evening."

"You've done your job well, then." He took the glass from her and set it next to his. "But now it's time for other delights to take us through the night." And without further preamble, he demanded, "Undress me."

Startled by the command, Aurelia blinked up into his hooded eyes. Therein lay a sensual challenge, one

she was compelled to meet. Hoping her hands wouldn't
shake, she stripped him of his jacket and threw it to the
wingback chair. As he unhooked the remainder of her
buttons, she began removing the studs from his
shirtfront, dropping the gold-and-emerald jewels on
the table next to the brandy decanter.

Within minutes their outer clothing lay strewn
around the room. A few minutes more and they were
as nature intended, Liam backing to the sofa and
drawing her with him. Mesmerized, Aurelia followed
without protest. He sat and wedged his knees
between hers as she stood before him.

"Let down your hair."

She freed the pins from her Psyche knot and the
dark tresses tumbled around her shoulders. Liam
captured her hips and urged her toward him, teasing
a breast with his tongue as he pulled her onto the
sofa. On her knees, she straddled him, thighs wide,
vulnerable to whatever he would do to her. She was
aware that he was heavy with need, though he didn't
move to join with her just yet.

For a moment, their surroundings intruded.
They were in the parlor, for heaven's sake! Should
her aunt return home earlier than expected, they
could be discovered. The thought shot an urgency
through Aurelia and she looked around, almost
feeling as if someone were watching her now. But
she'd already drawn the drapes and the front door
was bolted. And she realized she was merely anxious
for Liam.

"You have the most beautiful body," he murmured,
his hands making her forget everything but him.

His palms smoothed her skin from her thighs to

her belly to her breasts where her hair lay. She attempted to move the tangles out of the way, but he caught her hands and stayed them. Unsure of what he wanted her to do, Aurelia frowned down at him. He didn't speak, merely thumbed her hands open and pressed her palms against her own breasts.

"Touch yourself," he whispered in a low vibrant tone. She hadn't expected such a request, and so her first instinct was to whip her hands away and back off the couch, but he caught her hips, staying her and urging, "Please. For me. I want to watch your pleasure."

Embarrassment flamed through her. She'd never touched herself before . . . not in front of a man.

Her fingers trembled and she quaked inside, but the strength of Liam's silent will forced her to do as he asked. Her hands returned to her breasts. His eyes intently followed every movement as she cupped the heavy flesh and flicked the nipples hard with the pad of her thumbs. When she tugged at the distended nipples, his breathing deepened and she felt a stirring against her inner thigh where he lay full and hot and expectant. A flood of warmth that was excitement rather than embarrassment filled her, too, traveled to her extremities, wet the flesh that awaited his.

Gently, he circled one wrist, guided her hand down her belly and didn't stop until her fingers touched the thatch of hair between her thighs.

"There, as well," he whispered.

Their gazes locked and Aurelia gave in more readily to Liam's will this time, her tentative fingers finding herself wet and silky and burning. She wanted to please him because she loved him. Spreading the fluid with a fingertip, slipping it up inside herself and then forward to the source of her pleasure, she shuddered and began a natural rhythm, wondering how long it would be before he took over.

His hand dipped lower under her and she knew he was touching himself, running his hand along his shaft in an imitation of her own movements. She looked down, mesmerized by what she could see and what she could not. Her undulations grew stronger with her desire, and pressure quickly built within her.

"Liam," she gasped when she could stand the pleasure no longer. "Now, please!"

His hands flashed out to her hips and he impaled her, his penis easily snaking along her well-prepared inner flesh. With a moan, she sank down onto him and grabbed his shoulders with both hands as she rode him hard.

"I love you," she murmured.

"As I love you."

Hooking a hand behind her neck, he pulled her face down, found her mouth, and drew from her a kiss of as much depth as the quake that shuddered through them both.

His anger and repulsion were so overwhelming that he almost revealed himself. But then caution overtook him and he slid farther back into the dark passageway between kitchen and parlor. They had been so intent on violating each other that neither had thought to secure the back door. He had slipped in, had watched every disgusting thing they had done.

He could still see them from his hidey-hole, naked and wet with perspiration and other liquids. And she was laughing softly, as if with delight, as if she enjoyed it! That was no way for his queen to act!

How could she betray him so?

He felt like an animal. Trapped. Thwarted. Filled with rage. He had to do something. Had to relieve his own frustrations. Unfortunately, the orphan wasn't nearly ready. What then?

If he could not obtain the kind of gratification he craved, he would do the next best thing. He would make sure this sacrilege didn't happen again.

Not to her!

She didn't understand now. But soon. Then she would accept her lot like they all did. Of course, she would be the most precious among his collection. An honor. All he had to do was stop her from further defilement.

He waited until O'Rourke carried her naked up the stairs. His stomach churned at the thought of what would go on in secret chambers, probably for the rest of the night.

He couldn't stop it now, couldn't even try without revealing his identity! But as his gaze swept over the room, at the evidence of their betrayal, a plan formed in his mind and he knew what he must do. He picked up her stocking, inhaled its fragrance, and tucked it close to his heart.

If he eliminated the competition . . . then she would be his alone, just as it should be.

*   *   *

Swathed in a silk dressing gown, sated from hours of luxurious and slightly decadent lovemaking, Aurelia padded barefoot around the parlor, picking up discarded garments, totally aware of the man who drew on his own clothing.

"It's almost dawn," she said, wishing the night would last forever. She would feel the imprint of him inside and out for days, she was certain, but it was not the same as being close to the one she loved.

"Don't remind me. I don't like leaving you after making love. I wouldn't if I didn't have to."

There was only one way that he wouldn't have to leave that Aurelia could think of. But while Liam had professed his love several times during the night, he had not once mentioned further commitment, certainly not marriage. Perhaps, considering her previous experience, he didn't consider her worthy of that institution.

Aurelia had never dwelled on the idea of being someone's wife—quite the opposite, actually—yet the thought of Liam as potential spouse did not displease her. Although he could be a difficult man, he was not usually an impossible one. Certainly nothing like Mariel's Wesley.

She tried not to think in negative terms—Liam had given her no grounds to do so. Looking down at the bundle of clothes she'd collected, she realized she was missing something.

"I've somehow managed to lose a stocking."

"Is that an accusation?"

Liam's teasing tone made her look up and challenge

him. "Mr. O'Rourke, are you the kind of man who would steal a lady's stocking?"

"A perfect souvenir of a memorable evening."

His very agreeableness made Aurelia uneasy again. Is that all their lovemaking had meant to Liam? She hid her distress by peering under various items of furniture. He didn't stop her, didn't try to ease her mind.

As a matter of fact, Liam seemed to think nothing more of the exchange, for he continued dressing and complained, "And I am missing two shirt studs."

In her own search, Aurelia spotted one of them. "There. Under the table."

He stooped to pick it up. "Hmm, now where could the other little devil be hiding?"

"It's so tiny it could be anywhere and impossible to find in this light," Aurelia said. Then, "Oh, dear. I'd better make a complete search at first full light before Mary cleans. It wouldn't do to let her discover it."

"Then we would be found out."

His tone was again teasing, yet Aurelia couldn't help but take the words to heart. Though she tried to fight it, when Liam left her with a hasty kiss and a promise to see her later at work, she was left with a chilling uncertainty that he perhaps considered her a loose woman, someone not worthy of anything more than a clandestine affair.

16

"Anything I can do for you, sir?"

To Liam's satisfaction, the boy named Frankie had indeed shown up at the construction site of his new house and had even made an attempt to clean his hands and face of grime before arriving. Dark smears on cheeks and chin and on clothing that should be burned rather than washed were testimony enough to the filth in which the boy had been living.

"You stick by Old Will," Liam said of the elderly gardener who was in charge of executing the landscaper's plans for O'Rourke and O'Rourke's residential sites. "He can teach you a trade. He knows everything there is about planting and nurturing trees and bushes and grass and flowers."

Even as the electricians worked inside the building installing wires and fixtures, Will was beginning to cultivate the grounds.

About to run off, Frankie hesitated. "Old Will—he

said he's got an extra mat on his back porch the right
size for a boy like me." He stared down at his torn
shoes and swallowed hard as if filled with emotion he
was trying to hide. "Guess I gotta thank—"

"No need for thanks," Liam said gruffly to avoid
the lad further discomfort. He was simply pleased
that in this particular instance, he had been able to
help someone less fortunate than he. "Just don't disappoint me. Or Will. You do right by him and he'll
do right by you."

"Yes, sir!"

Frankie ran off, leaving Liam staring at the vacant
house that would soon be his home. But would it
really be a *home* without a woman to add the small
special touches and the warmth of her presence?

There he went, thinking of marriage again. Yet
how could he not after the night he'd spent with
Aurelia? Perhaps the enchantment would wear thin,
but he feared he was besotted, truly and deeply. And
she had said she loved him. He should be content,
happy to look to the future.

If only she would be honest with him.

He wasn't a stupid man. A woman wasn't so passionate and easy to seduce and even easier to please without
experience. That first time, he had realized there had been
someone else. He hadn't thought her lack of innocence
would bother him, but it did increasingly. He didn't like
the idea of another man holding her, touching her, filling
her as he had done so thoroughly. He didn't like the truth,
but he could accept it if only she would reassure him that
whoever it was had long ago been forgotten.

He refused to be one of many.

Even as he formed the demand in his mind, Liam

knew he was being unreasonable. Aurelia wasn't a loose woman. He was intelligent enough to realize that. She wouldn't succumb to passion with simply anyone. She would have to care for the man. That was the real problem—deep down, he feared her affections might not be for him alone.

Absorbed in thought, he wasn't aware of the approaching carriage until he was hailed by a familiar voice. He turned to find Rossiter at the reins, Mansfield next to him.

Surprised at their unexpected appearance, he asked, "Has something urgent come up, gentlemen?"

"We were out for an early morning drive," Rossiter said, "discussing the society's book project." The physician pulled his team to a stop mere feet from where Liam stood on the gravel path. "Since we were nearby, we decided to fill you in if you were to be found."

Liam indicated the grounds around the house. Everywhere one looked there were piles of materials for the inside as well as trays and buckets of vegetation Old Will would see to on the outside. A dray filled with more supplies had arrived a short while ago, as well.

"I can spare a few minutes, though I'm not exactly in a position to receive callers yet," Liam said. "Sorry I can't offer you the amenities."

"A walk around the grounds would do us good," Rossiter stated. "Could use a leg stretch."

"As you like."

The thin man alighted from the carriage, followed by Mansfield. Liam taking the lead, they circled the house, avoiding several workers who were busy unloading supplies from the dray, others who were carrying their wares into the building.

Not having shown off his house to anyone other than tradesmen, Liam was pleased when neither of his colleagues found fault with his design.

"Very advanced, very modern," Rossiter stated. "Though a touch of the classical wouldn't be amiss."

"I have some modest plans for the interior, having included built-in niches and shelving in the main rooms," Liam admitted as they rounded a corner and headed toward the rear of the house. "For I hope to have a growing collection of ancient artifacts to display."

Satisfied, Rossiter nodded. "A good design is important to the skeleton whether in a building or an educational tome," he said, getting around to the subject he'd come to discuss. "So far, we've chosen several historical essays and a dozen or so poems."

"Cunningham, Rossiter, and I have taken a crack at a few of the poems in Latin," Mansfield added.

"Though Quigley is responsible for the majority of the translations since he is the most adept both with ancient Greek and especially with hieroglyphics." Rossiter's expression tightened and his eyes grew cold and angry behind his spectacles. "Now if only the infernal man can keep himself out of any more trouble until we finish the translations . . ."

The physician let the sentence dangle.

"What's Quigley been up to now?" Liam asked with a sense of foreboding.

The three men stopped under the shade of an old elm Liam had insisted on saving, and Mansfield mumbled, "Got himself arrested."

"Appears he has a penchant for other people's maids." Rossiter ran his hand over his balding pate.

"Unfortunately, he doesn't seem to care whether or not they're agreeable. He roughed up a little Greek girl, and her father brought in the police quick as you could blink. When Quigley was questioned, he said it was all a mistake, that he'd thought she was someone else when he approached her, a young woman amenable to a tumble for a price."

"So he's in jail?" Liam asked.

Mansfield shook his silver head. "No jail cell can hold a man with his money—not unless the crime were of high consequence, of course."

"What is the man coming to?" Liam muttered. "Quigley has always *sounded* volatile, but this? Attacking maids and bribing city officials." Thinking the man must have an even more perverted relationship toward women than he'd guessed, Liam shook his head. "One can never know the true person without looking beneath the surface."

The men remained silent for a moment, all undoubtedly thinking of the very real manifestation of Quigley's mercurial temperament. Liam wondered what, if anything, the mysterious Mrs. Quigley might have to say about the incident.

Not that he would ask should he ever have the opportunity to meet her, which seemed doubtful if Quigley had anything to say about it.

Finally, Rossiter cleared his throat and brought them back to the subject of the society's project. "At any rate, the hunt for words of wisdom and beauty will continue until Phaedra is done with her paintings."

"Any idea how those are going?" Liam asked, not having thought to question Aurelia herself.

"Coming along spendidly," Mansfield responded.

"Phaedra's niece is an admirable model. She perfectly fits the part of a Mediterranean beauty of antiquity."

Liam noticed the physician's disapproving expression. He hadn't seemed pleased when Aurelia had agreed to pose for the paintings, either. "You don't think she's right for the project, Dr. Rossiter?"

"Phaedra should have chosen an actress used to exposing herself in public," the physician stated frankly. "I don't believe a woman of Miss Kincaid's class should put herself in such a position."

He adjusted his spectacles, but not before Liam noted yet another spark of passion behind the glass. Dr. Prentice Rossiter's likes and dislikes obviously went deeper than he'd ever suspected.

Mansfield cleared his throat nervously. "Carlton probably won't care for it, either."

"DeWitt Carlton?" When the silver-haired man nodded, Liam subdued his immediate rise to calmly ask, "What in the world does Carlton have to say about the issue? He is not, after all, a member of the society."

"He is, however, planning to marry Aurelia Kincaid."

"What!" Liam thundered so loudly his exclamation left shocked expressions on the faces not only of his colleagues, but on those of the surrounding workers as well. "Where do you get your information, man?" he demanded.

Mansfield appeared to shrink into himself, but not so Rossiter.

"Carlton has not kept his intentions secret," the physician stated. "And he has been Miss Kincaid's only escort since she returned to Chicago."

What was *he*, then, if not an escort? Liam wondered, both confused and angered by the topic. Merely a convenient dalliance? The thought outraged him, though he did not protest further. He would not embarrass himself by allowing his innermost feelings to be dissected by the other members of the society.

Aurelia had sworn she loved *him*, and Liam desperately wanted her to love him and him alone. And though he'd convinced himself he could accept the fact that she'd been with another man as long as she assured him he was now the only one in her life, he couldn't tolerate the thought that the other man might be DeWitt Carlton, especially not after she'd stated for all to hear she thought Carlton a boor and a prig.

But had that been the truth? Or could Carlton have been the first to take Aurelia? If she had committed herself to another man, then was she dallying with *him* in order to make comparisons? Or worse, to ingratiate herself professionally, so that she could skip the usual apprenticeship to be promoted based on his feelings for her? He'd almost forgotten about the way she'd been hired, through her aunt's influence on his father.

The very idea of Aurelia's using him raised Liam's blood. He wouldn't be made a fool of a second time!

"I'm sorry, gentlemen," Liam said tightly, "but I must get back to supervising the work here. I still need to make it into the office for a very important meeting this morning."

The two men nodded and shook his hand before going off to Rossiter's carriage. In a cold fury, Liam stared after their receding backs.

He hadn't clarified that his meeting would be with one Aurelia Kincaid.

* * *

Rather than being hard at work in her usual no-nonsense fashion, Aurelia sat dreamily sketching at her drafting table. The rendering she was completing denoted the exterior of a mansion scheduled for Millionaire's Row, one commissioned by a wealthy Southside meatpacker, another Irish immigrant and an old friend of the O'Rourkes named Patrick Shaunessy.

The facade of the structure was primarily accurate . . . except for a few imaginative embellishments she hadn't been able to stop herself from adding.

The strips of decoration—the basic motif of which came from the free-flowing asymmetrical forms of plants, shells, and garlands—was so common in Europe that the images had arisen from her subconscious. She sighed at the way her pencil had been carried away. Rococo did not reflect her personal taste so much as it did her current state of mind. Having tempered her negativity of early morning, she was unashamedly basking in the glow of being in love.

So she beamed when Liam made his late entrance.

Aurelia checked the watch pinned to her bodice, which was a single piece but had the appearance of being a vest and shirt. Amazed that the hour was half-past ten, she realized the morning had gotten away from her. Oh, dear! She had completed no more than this single rendering, one she would have to alter drastically before showing it to the client. Thank goodness, she was still working in lead.

Remembering that Liam had been so besotted that he hadn't noticed the error when she'd sketched the window in place of a door, she didn't bother to hide the sketch when he approached her drawing table directly.

Like a hunter stalking a deer, his gaze focused solely on her as he ignored the greetings of other draftsmen. A sensual thrill shot through Aurelia . . . until she noticed something akin to a thundercloud enveloping his beloved visage. Her smile waned and a trickle of fear oozed through her, but she told herself not to imagine things.

Who knew what might have gone wrong at the site this morning? Something unsettling must have happened to him after they parted, for Liam had no reason to be angry with *her,* she decided.

"How is your work going, Miss Kincaid?" he asked so smoothly that she was almost lulled.

"Fairly well. I have some refining to do," she hedged, not wanting to lie outright.

He cast his gaze on the rendering and she shifted uneasily, barely stopping herself from throwing her body over the sketch so he couldn't see it.

After eyeing her morning's work for a moment, he said, "Patrick Shaunessy is a simple man, no matter the size of his wallet." His tone was low, but cool and precise and sent a shiver of foreboding coursing through her. "I thought my father made that clear to you."

"Y-yes, he did."

"This won't do." He tapped the drawing with his fingers. "It won't do at all."

Aurelia had the distinct feeling that all eyes in the room immediately turned to them, no matter Liam's low voice. She tried to explain. "I have not finished with my—"

"Plot to humiliate the name O'Rourke?" he supplied.

Aurelia blinked and frowned at Liam. What in the

world was wrong with the man? He had to know she meant to correct her fanciful adornment of the Shaunessy mansion.

But what else could he mean?

"I don't understand," she said in a small voice.

He picked up a pencil and stared down at the rendering, his expression openly hostile. "That is obvious." He leaned closer and carefully drew a half-dozen thick black slashes through the proof of her daydream. His grip was so heavy, the lead even ripped the paper in a couple of places. "Maybe I shall explain it to you. In my office!"

Throwing down the pencil, he stalked off, evidently expecting her to follow immediately. She stared at the ruined rendering—he'd made certain she could not modify it, but would have to start from a blank page.

Without warning, a searing sensation attacked the back of her eyelids, for she felt betrayed somehow.

No, no! She couldn't, she *wouldn't* cry!

Arming herself with anger, she stalked after the wretched man, determined to get to the bottom of his foul temper. Stepping into his office, however, she was careful to close the door softly rather than slam it as she desired.

Liam was already sitting behind his desk, scrutinizing a prospectus for a new client's project. Aurelia waited for him to look up, to recognize her presence, since he had so rudely demanded it, but he continued to ignore her, to page through the damned folder.

Arms crossed over her chest, foot tapping, she waited. And waited. Then chose to wait no longer.

Furious, she snatched the proposal out of his hand and slapped it down on the desk. "What was the meaning of that . . . that horrid display?"

"Mine?" he asked, his visage grim, his green eyes flat like jade. "Or yours?"

Mine? she wondered. "What is wrong with you?" Aurelia wasn't certain they were discussing the same issue. "So I added a few embellishments to a rendering—"

"And what other kinds of *embellishments* have you been prone to in the past weeks?"

Having the feeling that he was angry at something other than her professional gaffe, she took a deep breath and backed off. "All right, let's stop this verbal dance, please. Tell me what is wrong. What has you in such a state?"

He stared at her coldly and a terrible suspicion made her stomach knot. His anger must have something to do with their personal relationship.

"I thought we were being honest with each other," Liam said.

She was certain of it. She should have told him about Rosario before she ever allowed him to touch her.

Squirming inside, she said, "I wasn't trying to be dishonest with you."

"So you admit it, then?"

Shamefaced, she asked, "Liam, do you really think this is the place to discuss our personal relationship?"

She didn't have to look over her shoulder to know every eye in the office was trained on them through the glass. She could only hope he wouldn't raise his voice so her colleagues could hear, as well.

He dashed that hope by shouting, "It may be the best place, the most appropriate place!"

"Liam—"

"Don't give me that shocked innocent look." Liam bounded out of his chair, used his greater height to threaten her. "I told you not to toy with my affections, Aurelia, but you couldn't resist, could you? You couldn't wait until you were married to DeWitt Carlton to get what you wanted. Surely a man with his money and influence could buy you a partnership in some architectural firm."

Realizing her mouth was hanging open, she snapped it shut. Where had he gotten the idea she wanted anything from DeWitt? Or that she would consider marrying him? How could he believe such utter nonsense?

"Well, say something, damn it!" he thundered.

"Is that what you really think of me?" she asked in a controlled voice.

"Should I think any differently? Give me cause."

She'd already given him cause. She'd spent two nights with him, had shared her troubled childhood with him, had been open with him about who she was. She'd never given him reason to believe she had designs on DeWitt. On the contrary, Liam knew what she thought of the merchant. And she'd told Liam she loved *him* several times.

Obviously he did not believe her. But why?

She could only figure that Liam couldn't live with the fact that he wasn't her first and only lover. And maybe his dissatisfaction went deeper, to some twisted sense of guilt at having her both as an employee and as a lover. Well, if he was looking for a way to get rid of her, she would make it easy for him!

"I have the distinct impression that you are not happy with me," she said far more calmly than she was feeling.

He barked a laugh. "That's an understatement."

She lifted her chin. "Then you will no longer be needing my services."

Professional or personal, she thought, her heart breaking. If he felt any differently, now was the time for him to speak.

But his accusatory, "You're resigning?" weren't the words she wanted to hear.

"I think it's best."

Now he became argumentative. "You'll have a hell of a time getting another job from a reputable firm."

As if he cared.

Or perhaps he meant he would try to ruin her!

Furious, Aurelia said, "But I've already had an offer. I intend to work for Mr. Frank Lloyd Wright."

"You'll be lucky to see a penny out of that parasite!"

If anything, he was angrier. She didn't understand him at all. Perhaps she had made a mistake . . . but no, the mistake was his. She would not join her sisters in examining her every move as to how it would affect a man's ego.

"I don't have to worry about money, do I," she stated, "not being engaged to DeWitt Carlton and all."

With that rejoinder, she slammed the door so hard the windows shook. She stopped at her drafting area long enough to throw off her sleeve protectors, gather her jacket, purse, and a few personal articles.

Storming out of the office, she both hoped and feared that she would never see Liam O'Rourke again.

The weight of the rolled carpet was exhausting him even though he stood on a wooden crate to give himself better leverage. Impossible to get into the Midway Plaisance while balancing the burden at the top of the fence. Reluctantly he released it, let it slide, then winced when it hit the mucky earth on the other side with a distinctive plop.

"A sacrilege, I know," he whispered into the night.

His eyes skimmed the deserted area behind the Streets of Cairo. The fair and midway had been closed for hours and all was quiet and dark but for the bluish moonglow cast along the white buildings.

"But sometimes we must do what is necessary," he muttered. He had already thrown a second wooden crate over the fence to make his quick escape possible. He'd also hidden his horse and carriage in a copse of trees down the road so they wouldn't be spotted. Because he was a bit shaky from carrying the bundle so far, he lifted himself with difficulty over the fence and dropped to the ground on the other side.

There he waited until he was certain . . .

No night watchman around, thank the gods. And he was barely a hundred yards away from the temple, though it seemed like a thousand by the time he delivered his charge to the darkened entrance.

Breathing more easily now, he pulled the key from his vest pocket, and fumbling in the dark for the lock, fitted the iron skeleton with a hand that trembled from a combination of fright and excitement. He barely had the door open and the rolled carpet inside before hearing faint voices from too short a distance for his ease.

"I thought I saw something move over there."

He began to sweat inside his suit. Quickly dragging the carpet through the dark, he groped his way to one of the niches holding a coffin.

"Why'n't you check it out, while I go this way?" came a second voice. "If someone broke into the grounds, one of us'll find 'im."

"I think we should stick together," the first one muttered.

He found the coffin he was seeking and quickly removed the contents.

"Wha's'a matter, Pete? Not afraid of them mummies, are you?" the second nightman asked with a guffaw.

" 'Course not," Pete answered indignantly. "Everyone knows they ain't real anyway."

He could hear them clearly now. He'd left the door open a crack, hoping for a bit of moonlight, since he hadn't been able to manage a lantern. He unrolled the carpet even as the nightman approached. The dolt was coming to the temple!

His heart pounded as loudly as the footsteps sounded. Had Anubis decided to punish him? Had the gods sent a mortal fool after him for tampering with one of his sacrifices to them? Silently, he mouthed a prayer, assuring Anubis that the god should be proud that he was displaying such a nice piece of perfectly executed handiwork.

He hurried desperately, but he wasn't fast enough to make the switch. A silhouette carrying a lantern filled the doorway. He backed up farther into the dark, wildly thinking of what he could do other than dispatch the guard who was armed with a club and a gun. Then it came to him.

"Someone in here?" Pete demanded, though he didn't move from the doorway.

He slid along another wall . . . found another coffin . . .

"Come out now and you won't get hurt!"

Tucking himself into his hiding place, he never took his eyes from the glow at the doorway. The lantern moved closer now, illuminating the nightman, who cautiously lifted it and peered all around into the dark. Pete was a big brute with a mean-looking face. His nose was set weirdly, probably from a distasteful round of fisticuffs.

He barely breathed as Pete stumbled and muttered, "Here, what's this." And looked down.

The brutish face went blank for a moment and the eyes widened, then seemed to bulge from their sockets. The nightman quickly looked up at the empty coffin and back down at the two bundles on the floor.

"O-o-o-h, n-o-o!" Pete cried, backing away while looking around wildly. His shoulder hit the door. The lamp swung wildly and the light went out. "Alfie!" Pounding footsteps on the walk quickly led away from the temple and the voice grew fainter. "Alfie, get your arse over here, now!"

From his shelter, he took a deep breath of relief. The gods were still with him! He had a few minutes to make good his disappearance. He danced around the fake mummy as he slid out of the coffin. About to leave, he remembered his exact purpose.

Taking the tiny souvenir from his empty watch pocket, he hooked it into the fringe of the Turkish rug, then slipped silently into the night.

"Open up!"
Bam, bam, bam.
Liam sat straight up in bed, his naked torso wet

with sweat, his head filled with Aurelia's image, his heart pounding. He must have been having a nightmare about losing her for good . . .

Bam, bam, bam.

. . . or not.

Someone was at his front door. His father, no doubt. Liam checked his watch and grumbled to himself, but he lit a lantern, wrapped a sheet around himself, and left the bedroom as the infernal pounding continued.

Bam, bam, bam.

"I'm coming, I'm coming!" he shouted to make the racket stop.

Though he was in no mood to soothe the elder O'Rourke if Sean had had another row with Phaedra. He had his own woman troubles. Damn, Aurelia, anyway! Why couldn't she have reassured him and thrown herself into his arms rather than agreeing with everything he'd said about her and Carlton? And then she'd quit to boot!

Jerking open the door, he was surprised to see two men, neither of whom was his father, on the other side. The younger one was dressed in a familiar dark uniform, the polished star-shaped badge on his chest catching the lantern's glow.

"Are you Liam O'Rourke?" the older man in civilian clothes asked.

"Yes. What is it?"

"I'm Lieutenant Anthony Frigo." He flipped back his jacket. A badge flashed from his vest, as well. "I need to know your whereabouts of the past several hours."

Shaking away the last of his sleep, Liam stated, "I've been right here all night."

"Alone?"

"Yes. Why?" He looked from Frigo's poker face to that of his back-up man. "Has there been some problem in the neighborhood?" It had better be something important considering it was nearly dawn.

"I'm afraid you'll have to come with us down to the station for questioning."

"About what?"

"Murder, Mr. O'Rourke. Murder."

17

Dawn was breaking as Liam entered the station house. The main room was narrow and depressing, with graying walls and worn bare wood floors. Frigo indicated Liam should sit on one of the two uncomfortable-looking benches across from the desk, but Liam didn't bother. He stood while the lieutenant conferred in low tones with the burly desk sergeant, a man whose double row of polished buttons looked ready to burst free from his broad shoulders to his bulging waistline.

A *real* mummy found on the midway—Liam could hardly believe such a wild tale. He still had hopes the whole incident was a ridiculous mistake, that the mummy in question was the one the men had made from Rossiter's office skeleton. All the male members of the society who had anything to do with assembling that aspect of the temple exhibit had been called in for questioning. At least the police would leave Mrs. Cunningham and associates like Phaedra Kincaid alone for the present.

"Your friends are already here."

Frigo indicated Liam should follow him. They were halfway across the room when the front door opened and a small middle-aged man in a threadbare plaid suit burst in.

"Is it true?" he demanded eagerly, patting his pockets. "A nightman found a real mummy on the midway?" He triumphantly pulled a pad of paper and a pencil from his left pocket. "Give me his name and lead me to the evidence!"

"Hold it, Miller, you're not going anywhere," the desk sergeant stated.

"But they're holding the presses for the story!"

Liam realized this must be Jeremy Miller, notorious reporter for the *Chicago Evening Post*.

The sergeant cleared his throat and made a particularly large deposit of tobacco in the brass spittoon at the foot of his desk. "Well, they can hold for a while longer." He indicated a bench with a beefy hand. "Sit and maybe someone will talk to you if you behave yourself."

"Haven't you ever heard of freedom of the press, man?" But Miller sat.

Lieutenant Frigo steered Liam into the inner room—the lockup. The two cells were sparsely decorated. A couple of uncomfortable-looking metal frames with inch thin pads passed for beds.

Only one cell was occupied.

Liam began to sweat as he envisioned the other filled with members of the society, himself included. For a moment, he wondered if Aurelia would take pity on him and visit should he be incarcerated, then realized how ridiculously melodramatic that sounded. He hadn't committed any crime, certainly not murder. Of course he wouldn't be arrested.

He would have to find some other way to get to the woman he loved. Surely he could win her away from DeWitt Carlton, the boorish snob. He promised himself that he would formulate a plan as soon as he was done with this nonsense.

Frigo was leading him through yet another room where several uniformed men were getting ready to go on shift. They were discussing a case involving a lurid stabbing that brought all sorts of gruesome images to mind.

Finally, they reached the windowless back room where Rossiter, Cunningham, and Mansfield gathered around the table with a stranger who was dressed in a protective duster. On a table in their midst lay the mummy.

Heart pounding with a combination of excitement and dread, Liam drew closer, then took in every detail. The form undeniably human . . . the binding of long, narrow strips of linen . . . the hieroglyphics inked on the top layer meant to identify the corpse for the gods. He knew that if the person inside really had been mummified, beneath the layers of shroud and binding they would find a dried and shrunken form on the skeleton.

"It is real, isn't it?"

The fine quality bandages and the hieroglyphics alone proved it wasn't one of the fake mummies the committee had constructed. Liam couldn't help wondering if one or more of his colleagues had been lunatic enough to steal a fresh body from the morgue to practice on as had been suggested. If so, there would be hell to pay!

"It's real enough," Cunningham said, eyes alight, mouth turned up in a mocking smile. "Can you imagine the poor guard's shock when he discovered it? Even he could tell the difference between this and the ones we made for display. Poor man believes a mummy came to life."

"Have you gotten any more information?" Frigo asked the other official who Liam figured was the coroner.

"We've given the, uh, deceased a thorough inspection. Dr. Rossiter here thinks the mummy is fairly new."

"Probably not much more than the required seventy days for the pickling," Rossiter confirmed.

Not a theft from the morgue, then. Liam grew uneasy with the implication—possibly they really were looking at a murder victim.

"Smell the residue salts mixed with the more fragrant odors of oils, ointments, spices, and resins," Rossiter demanded. "The scent is strong, the mummy fresh." Gaslight washed over his zealous expression and reflected off his spectacles, hiding for a moment the intensity of his gaze. "Perfect, perfect," he mumbled, his trembling fingers smoothing the bandages with the care of a lover. "Such exquisite work. Don't you agree, gentlemen?"

Frigo and the coroner gave each other questioning looks as if trying to decide if the exquisite work might have been done by a maniacal Rossiter himself. Being a physician—not to mention a man obsessed with the idea of mummification—he had the skills and appetite to have done it, Liam thought. Then, again, Cunningham was a physician, as well.

Liam glanced from face to face. Rossiter was enthralled, no other way to describe it. Cunningham wore his usual sardonic expression as if he were sitting back watching the scene with a warped sense of fun. Mansfield looked like he wanted to crawl into the woodwork.

Liam finally realized someone was missing. "Quigley, where is he?"

Mansfield shrugged and averted his eyes from the table. "No one knows."

"He wasn't at home. Spooky place. And the batty old housekeeper don't seem to know where the wife is, either," Frigo stated. "Seems your friend's taken a powder on us."

Liam remembered all of Quigley's disparaging comments about women, his assertion that they were better off mummified, their mouths wrapped in bandages . . . and no one present had ever seen his wife, not since Liam had joined the society.

"So you think Quigley's guilty?" Liam asked the lieutenant.

"Or knows who is." As he dug into his pocket, Frigo's expression became crafty.

Making Liam uncomfortable. "And who might that be?"

"For starters, how about you?"

"*Me?*" Though Liam knew he shouldn't be shocked, he was. "Why would you suspect me?"

"Ever seen this before?"

Liam stared at Frigo's open palm, at the bit of gold decorated with his initials and emerald chips. "My shirt stud. Where'd you find it?"

Frigo's immediate smile was triumphant. "With the corpse, Mr. O'Rourke. With the corpse."

MUMMY FOUND ON MIDWAY PLAISANCE
CASE OF MISSING LOCAL WOMAN
ALL WRAPPED UP!

"Can you believe this, Aunt Phaedra?" Aurelia asked, showing her aunt the lurid headline. "Our friends plastered on the front page of a tabloid?"

They'd already heard about the mummy being found and about certain members of the society being brought in for questioning. But Fred had just hand-delivered the paper with its sensational details. Aurelia sat at the dining room table and stared at the *Chicago Evening Post* article.

Phaedra swallowed a bite of chicken. "Not exactly an appetizing subject when one is trying to eat one's midday meal. But I admit I am equally anxious to find out what happened."

Aurelia read, "'The dead woman has been identified from the hieroglyphics, translated by Dr. Cunningham on the linen bandages. Her name was Hallie Pappas, a scullery maid who was in the employ of Mr. Samuel Ayers of Ayers Northside Shipping. Officer Paddy O'Brien confirmed that the young woman had been missing for nearly three months." She scanned the next paragraph and the breath caught in her throat. "Aunt Phaedra, this says she was an immigrant and an orphan . . . an orphan who disappeared like Fiona's maid Gina."

"You don't think . . ."

The women sat staring at each other for a moment, and Aurelia knew her aunt and she were of a mind. They both feared Gina had met a similar fate.

"Let's hope not," Phaedra said quietly.

Aurelia nodded, her heart going out to the poor young woman. She went back to reading, and this time, her blood ran cold. "Oh, dear Lord! Liam is the chief suspect!" she told Phaedra indignantly.

"They've arrested him?"

"No, but he's been questioned and told not to leave town."

"On what do they base this claim?"

"It says . . . there's evidence." Heart pounding, Aurelia read further and tried to stay calm. "'One of O'Rourke's shirt studs was found on the carpet that held the mummy. Being of gold, engraved with his initials, and decorated with tiny emeralds, there can be no mistake that this distinctive item belongs to O'Rourke.'"

Aurelia clearly remembered Liam missing a stud after they'd made love. Later, she'd searched for it herself, to no avail. Surely it couldn't be the very same item. Had he lost a second one, then? Perhaps he had made an unexpected trip to the exhibit before going home to change that morning. But even if he had innocently lost a second stud, how had it come to be attached to the rug?

"How ridiculous," Phaedra was muttering. She took a bracing sip of tea. "Oh, poor Sean. He must be sick with worry."

"As am I."

Aurelia was also feeling sick about the accusations against Liam and her inability to deal calmly with his silly jealousy. But he was no murderer, even if he could be unreasonable and very definitely volatile.

Was she herself any better tempered? she wondered, remembering the conversation with her aunt several days before concerning her estrangement from Fiona. Phaedra thought she was too quick to anger and too slow to forget. Aurelia feared her aunt's reasoning had validity.

If Fiona hadn't given an inch, neither had she.

Now Aurelia put aside her own worries to wonder how her eldest sister would feel upon seeing this article. What if she made the same comparison between the disappearance of little Gina to that of poor Hallie Pappas?

On impulse, Aurelia asked Phaedra, "Didn't you tell me you were finished with the illustrations you did for Fiona's charity event?"

"Yesterday," Phaedra agreed.

"I'm going out this afternoon. Perhaps you'd like me to deliver them for you."

Perceptive as usual, Phaedra gave her a knowing look. "I think that would be very charitable of you, my darling. This estrangement between you and Fiona has gone on long enough."

"Yes, it has."

And by the time she saw Liam that night at the next meeting of the society—assuming he hadn't been arrested—she hoped to have a plan to set things right between them, as well.

When Aurelia arrived at the Millionaire's Row mansion barely an hour later, Fiona was ensconced on the rear sun porch reading the *Chicago Daily*

News. Dressed in a tea gown of buttercup yellow, she glowed among bright baskets of flowers and print cushions piled high on the settees and chairs of woven reed. Glancing up, she set the tabloid on a table, allowing Aurelia to see the headline: "MURDER MOST FOUL—ANCIENT ART PRACTICED ON CITY'S POOR."

"Aurelia." The greeting was passive, neither cool nor warm, as if Fiona were waiting for an explanation of her sister's presence.

Bravery fleeing her, Aurelia held out the portfolio she'd used as her excuse to come. "From Aunt Phaedra. Your illustrations."

Fiona took the packet and set it on a flowered cushion next to her. "She asked you to deliver these to me?"

"I volunteered."

"Why?"

Aurelia knew that if she were to be honest, the time was at hand. "Because you're my sister and for all our differences—and according to Aunt Phaedra, for all our similarities—I do love you."

"Oh, Aura." Losing some of her dignity, Fiona launched herself at Aurelia and enveloped her in an affectionate hug. "Of course I love you, too." After a moment, she said, "Do you think we inherited our stubbornness from Mother or from Father?"

"As well as I can remember, they both had their fair share of the trait."

Fiona nodded in agreement and stepped back. "I'm sorry if you do not appreciate what you call my meddling in your life, but I only want the best for you."

Not exactly an apology, Aurelia thought, but

undoubtedly as close to one as she could expect. "Let us agree to disagree then, and not to hold a grudge about our differences."

"Done." Fiona sighed and looked back at her tabloid. "We have enough problems plaguing us. You *have* read about the members of Aunt Phaedra's society being involved in that horrible murder investigation, I assume."

Thinking Fiona was about to criticize their aunt, Aurelia tensed. "The police merely have to question people connected to the temple." Which included her, she suddenly realized.

"And your employer is the chief suspect."

Despite her conciliatory mood, the statement sparked her ire. "Liam is *not* a murderer!"

"Liam, is it? And defending him with such passion."

Aurelia damned her instant response. She felt her face suffuse with color. Fiona's brows shot up.

"Don't entertain ideas that are very well untrue," Aurelia said quickly. "Anything that might have been between us may now be destroyed, though I sincerely hope not. We had a disagreement of the first magnitude, and then . . . I left his employ." The import of the situation dragged at her, deflating her already tenuous spirits. "And I may never see him again." Especially if he were arrested before that night's meeting.

"I don't believe it. You *are* in love."

"Don't start, Fiona! If you utter one word about Liam's appropriateness —"

"But whyever not? He's obviously the perfect match for you," Fiona stated, stunning Aurelia to silence. "And I am certain his name will be cleared upon investigation. Liam O'Rourke is a good man."

"Then you approve?"

"He wouldn't have been my first choice . . ."

An outright endorsement would have been too much to expect, Aurelia supposed. "No, that was DeWitt Carlton."

"I hear my name and from such precious lips!"

To Aurelia's dismay, the last man in the world she wanted to see now stepped from the hallway to join them on the sun porch. Fiona's husband followed.

"Upton, old man, I must be dreaming," DeWitt said heartily, as if his last meeting with Aurelia had been to both their satisfactions. "Why didn't you tell me your fair sister-in-law was to visit today."

"Probably because I didn't know."

DeWitt stepped closer to take her hands. "Aurelia, enchanting as always."

She hardly thought she could enchant anyone wearing a jacketed suit of brown ticked material, but she forced a polite smile to her lips and murmured, "DeWitt."

Unable to believe her bad luck, Aurelia felt her heart sink even lower. Once she realized Fiona approved of Liam, she had been considering asking her sister for advice on how to fix things between them.

DeWitt asserted, "It's been too long, Aurelia, hasn't it?"

Not about to agree merely to avoid an unpleasantry, she pulled away from the man and gave her sister a pleading look. Fiona for once seemed amused by the situation and remained silent.

Catching sight of the newspaper, Upton asked his cousin, "Did you see today's headlines?" as he picked it up for a closer inspection.

"Positively grisly." DeWitt shook his head. "I don't know what the police are thinking, arresting men of our class."

"They weren't arrested," Aurelia clarified. "They were merely brought in for questioning."

"Even so, it's unseemly. O'Rourke could be imprisoned next."

The concern DeWitt expressed made Aurelia soften a bit. "Not seemly at all," she agreed. For she couldn't imagine anyone thinking Liam could commit such a nefarious deed.

"All this fuss over a girl of no consequence."

"DeWitt Carlton!" Fiona's tone was shocked. "She was a human being, just like you or me!"

Aurelia closed her gaping mouth. Before she could give DeWitt a good dressing down herself, Upton made a strange noise and waved the tabloid at his wife.

"Fiona, dear, have you read this entire article?"

"Well, no. As a matter of fact, I had just begun the piece when Aurelia arrived."

"You didn't get to the part about the young woman's identity, then."

Fiona stiffened. "Who was it?"

Upton rushed to assure her, "No one we know, my dear, but there is a disturbing similarity . . . "

"Upton, you're making my heart palpitate. What is it?"

He shook his head. "The victim was an immigrant who worked as a maid, an orphan who disappeared under mysterious circumstances without having given her notice."

Fiona blanched and wavered. The hand she put to her lips trembled. "Just like Gina."

"Now, now, maybe not," Upton said hurriedly. "I never should have mentioned it."

Fiona's eyes shone with tears. "How could I have been so careless with someone entrusted to me?"

Aurelia felt her eyes sting, too. "Fiona, whatever happened to Gina . . . it isn't your fault."

"But she was alone in the world," Fiona mourned, "with no one to look after her but me."

Upton put his arms around his wife. "Us, my dear, she had us. But how could we have suspected?"

Fiona began softly crying, upsetting Aurelia further. "Fiona, would you like me to get you something? Some tea, perhaps?"

"No, nothing. I-I think I might like to lie down."

"Then I'll take you to your room," Upton said, leading her toward the hall. "Hush now. Gina's *disappearance*"—he emphasized the word—"isn't your fault. Believe that."

As they left the room, DeWitt cleared his throat. "Such devotion."

Devotion that released a few tears from Aurelia's eyes, as well. Under her brisk, authoritarian guise, Fiona had a soft heart and a tender conscience. It had been years since Aurelia had seen this side of her sister. And Upton's feelings for his wife were very clear. Though he might not be present every moment due to his work, he loved her dearly. Only a fool would fail to see that.

She fumbled in her purse for a handkerchief to dry her tears, but the little pistol she always carried with her now was in the way.

DeWitt cleared his throat uncomfortably. "I cannot stand to see a woman cry," he said, presenting her with a linen square.

Which she refused. She snapped her purse shut before he could see the weapon.

"I am not going to cry," Aurelia stated more to convince herself than him. Considering his unconscionable comment about the murdered young woman, she didn't even want to be alone with DeWitt, yet she found herself explaining, "It's just that so many things have been going wrong lately, and I no longer have my work to busy my mind."

"You were fired?"

"I resigned."

"Wonderful!" DeWitt said, then grew sober. "O'Rourke didn't try to take advantage of *you*, did he?" When all Aurelia could do was gape at that assumption, he said, "You can confide in me, you know."

"You . . . you . . ."

"Oh, my dear Aurelia," DeWitt said, his tone tender as he took her in his arms.

Aurelia stiffened, wanting to stomp on his toe when she spotted a familiar if thunderous visage over DeWitt's shoulder. She froze and locked gazes with Liam O'Rourke, who stood stock-still in the doorway.

"I would take care of all your problems if only you would allow me the honor," DeWitt continued, apparently unaware that they were being observed.

Through gritted teeth, she said, "I can take care of my own problems."

Her gaze still locked with Liam's, she surreptitiously pushed at DeWitt's chest to no avail.

Liam finally unfroze, his mouth turning up into a shallow smile. "Now isn't this a cozy scene?"

"What are you doing here?" Aurelia demanded, grateful when DeWitt finally released her.

"Phaedra told me where to find you."

Though he turned toward Liam, DeWitt didn't move from Aurelia's side. "Miss Kincaid doesn't work for you anymore, O'Rourke, so she doesn't answer to you."

"It's not our professional relationship that I want to speak to her about!" Temper slipping, Liam nearly shouted, "Would you give us some privacy, man?"

"And leave her alone with you, a *murder* suspect?" DeWitt placed a protective arm around Aurelia's shoulder which she tried to shake off gracefully. "Certainly not!"

Liam stepped closer, his green eyes darkening, and bellowed, "Take your hands off her!"

"Don't the two of you speak about me as if I were not present!" she demanded, increasing her struggle at the same time DeWitt asked Liam, "To whom do you think you're giving orders?"

Totally ignoring her, Liam went after DeWitt. "A boorish snob who doesn't deserve to touch Aurelia Kincaid, much less marry her."

Before Aurelia knew what was happening, Liam stepped closer to grab DeWitt's shirtfront. He lifted the merchant to his toes and shook him like a terrier with a rat until he let go of Aurelia and began flailing his arms.

"Step back so we can fight like men!" DeWitt insisted.

"Is that what you think you are?"

Liam let go and, before Aurelia's amazed eyes, drew back his arm and let his fist rip into DeWitt's jaw.

Crack.

The smaller man went reeling. Catching the back of a settee to save himself from falling, he shook his head and drew himself together quickly. Then, with fists and body in the boxing posture, he danced forward.

"Stop it!" Aurelia cried.

But the men paid no attention. With a wolfish grin, Liam waited until DeWitt got within arm's length and let go with a double punch that knocked the merchant out cold. His lifeless body sprawled against the settee, then slid to the floor.

"My God, have you killed him?" Aurelia went to DeWitt's side immediately.

Liam's tone was wounded when he said, "You sound as if you really care."

"Of course I do."

She didn't want to see any physical harm come to DeWitt, no matter that she didn't like him. And she didn't want to see Liam on trial for his murder. Breathing a sigh of relief when she found DeWitt's pulse, she rose and stalked the man who was both the love of her life and the bane of her existence.

"What do you think you are about, breaking into my sister's home, and to what purpose?" she asked, punching him in the chest with an angry finger. "So you can issue more orders? So you can commit violence?"

"I came for you!"

Had he qualified that statement with some loving words, Aurelia might have thrown herself into his arms. Instead, she bristled. She would never, *ever* be like Mariel, though she didn't think Liam would want her to be. Still, she determined to make that point clear. "I am not a lapdog to be brought to heel!"

"Not for me, perhaps," Liam said, giving the senseless DeWitt a look of utter loathing. "I see that I've made yet another mistake."

"You certainly have!" Aurelia planned on setting him straight on the truth once and for all with a lecture that would make his ears burn.

But before she could utter another word, Liam said, "Then you, my dear, can go to the devil!"

Turning on his heel, he stormed off the sun porch, Aurelia staring daggers into his back, cursing his vile temper, feeling indeed as if she'd descended into Hades. Liam had misinterpreted her meaning altogether. The only thing that kept her from bursting into tears was the knowledge that she had the power to make the man act like a mad fool.

He *must* love her!

Now if only she could find a way to make him trust her . . . and his own feelings.

18

Liam would have sworn Aurelia had been truthful when she'd declared her love for him. Then, when she'd confirmed that she was going to marry Carlton, he'd thought her confused by her own emotions or perhaps even unwillingly bound by some silly obligation to her sisters. He'd lost his senses when he'd seen the wretch's arms about her. And after he'd had the satisfaction of putting Carlton down for the count and she had raced to his side, Liam's hopes for a future with Aurelia had flown.

Wrong again. He hadn't been this stupid since he'd attained manhood and the wealthy daughter of his father's client had dallied with him only to spurn him once he'd fallen in love with her. It was a mistake he'd vowed never to repeat after figuring out how things stood—that women generally found breeding and old money worth more than a man who worked hard to better himself—and he'd been on his guard ever since.

How had he allowed himself to be convinced Aurelia was different?

Now she irked him by appearing at Mansfield's Grand Boulevard residence when she might have had the good grace to stay away. Not that she acknowledged him. Her gaze never met his, had skipped over him several times. She sat on the opposite side of the parlor on a blood-red velvet sofa with her aunt and Mrs. Cunningham and acted as if he didn't exist.

The walls were closing in on Liam. The Victorian mansion was dismal with its mahogany-paneled walls and dark, tasteless furniture like many other stately homes of the period. Normally that didn't bother him, but tonight he felt oppressed.

"This meeting must by circumstances be quite different than any of us imagined," Rossiter stated as he began. "Rather than getting on with plans for our book, we must direct our attention to the police investigation, since the temple was our project, therefore making us suspect."

"Pretty obvious who's the guilty party." Ernest Williamson, the new member, clarified, "I knew something was not quite right with Quigley at our last official meeting."

Rossiter stated, "While Quigley is wanted for questioning, the police have no—"

"But Quigley fled," Mansfield cut in.

"And the police have O'Rourke's shirt stud," Cunningham interrupted with a smirk.

"The shirt stud," Rossiter echoed. "O'Rourke, are you quite certain you can't place where you lost it?"

He'd only lost one, and that at the Kincaid residence. All the matching studs were accounted for.

He'd checked. He still couldn't figure out how the thing had turned up where it had. The thought was interrupted when he suddenly realized that Aurelia was staring at him, her eyes wide, and he knew that telling the truth would ruin her reputation.

"I have no idea how it escaped me," he hedged. He was as much a gentleman as her soon-to-be fiancé, breeding or no breeding. "And as I told the police, I wore them *two* nights ago, and found it to be missing then."

"Curious," Cunningham said. "Can anyone corroborate this?"

Aurelia could if she chose to speak up, Liam thought even as he asked, "Am I on trial here?"

"Of course not," Mrs. Cunningham said. "We want to clear your good name, not help the authorities hang you." Aurelia choked and turned pale. Phaedra took her hand and patted it while they whispered together. Everyone stared at the two women, especially Mansfield who wore an expression that was at once distressed and oddly fixated, making Liam wonder if he didn't have a secret regard for Phaedra.

When Aurelia settled back in her seat, her features were blank, her posture stiff, her hand safely tucked under that of her aunt.

"Why don't we try to think of who else might be suspect?" Phaedra suggested. "Perhaps one of us here might know someone outside our circle with extensive knowledge of the ancient world."

"Knowledge is one thing," Rossiter said. "Those of you who were not privileged to be at the station house cannot imagine the skill and experience it took to mummify Hallie Pappas. Quite an extraordinary accomplishment."

Rossiter's zeal remained undiminished, Liam

noted. But no one else in the room looked as enthusiastic. The general tone of the group was as somber as the surroundings. And so the meeting droned on with suppositions being traded back and forth without any real results.

All the while, Liam waited and wondered. Waited for Aurelia to look his way with a soft expression. Wondered if she would offer to speak, to offer the truth about his shirt stud . . . at least to the police. When the meeting ended, he was curiously disappointed when she didn't approach him, though he didn't know what he had expected.

Her telling the truth might ruin her chances with Carlton, who would surely not want a soiled dove for his wife.

But Liam swore he would not be the one to speak out. He would hold his silence and take his chances. He was innocent. Surely he could find some way to point a finger at the guilty party without pointing a finger at the woman he loved.

Aurelia exited the house to the imposing side porte cochere in time to see Liam fling himself into his saddle and ride his horse away without looking back. Her spirits sank. Not that she'd had a plan of any sort. Rather, instinct had bade her follow him outside after the meeting broke up.

The canopied side drive was dark and quiet but for the soft nicker of beasts waiting for their owners. Phaedra was still inside, saying her good-byes. Not wanting old Fred to work a longer day than necessary, Phaedra had insisted she drive them herself, and so they had taken a smaller rig than usual.

Aurelia guessed Theo's groom must be about somewhere. But for the moment, she was alone and relieved to be free of the oppressiveness of Theo's house.

Wondering how she and Liam had come to such a pass after the joy they'd shared, Aurelia intended to give Harold the Bold a pat and a few words of cheer. The old horse was always agreeable to extra attention, and at the moment an appreciative nudge or two from a friendly nose seemed just the thing to perk up her own spirits.

She'd barely stepped between two carriages when something caught on her foot, however, almost tripping her. She looked down. Though the porte cochere was lit with two lanterns, the pool of yellow light barely invaded the ground. She stooped to better see what bound her foot to a carriage wheel—some sort of material.

As she removed it from her boot with a gloved hand, a shiver of apprehension shot through her. She whipped up and around, her eyes searching every direction. She had that feeling again, as if someone were watching her. When she saw no one, she ordered herself to relax. After all, she was carrying a weapon and knew how to use it.

Taking a deep breath, she looked down at her hand, at the substance that had pulled free from the wheel. A piece of narrow, finely woven cloth with a strange scent. A bandage? Realizing the carriage was the one belonging to Dr. Cunningham, Aurelia dropped the material and thought no more of it as her aunt and the Cunninghams left the house.

A moment later, she and Phaedra were in their

carriage, and Aurelia was determined to pick up the furtive discussion they had started inside.

"I must do it," Aurelia maintained. "I must clear Liam."

"You intend to clear O'Rourke?"

At hearing the male voice, Aurelia jumped and turned to meet their host. "Theo, you startled me." For a moment, his eyes seemed to burn through her.

He quickly stared down at the ground. "How will you clear him?"

Not wanting to announce a relationship to the world that was for all practical purposes over, she merely said, "I have certain information." Information she would give the authorities first thing in the morning.

Reins in hand, Phaedra said, "Good night, Theo," and moved Harold the Bold off into the street.

Though Phaedra approved the plan they discussed during the ride, Aurelia was left with an unsettling feeling all the way home.

The next morning, Aurelia was quite certain that, while she didn't in the least care for Lieutenant Anthony Frigo with his dozens of personal questions and suspicious attitude, he believed her. She left the station house with a much lighter heart. Outside, the carriage was waiting; this morning, Fred was doing the driving. He helped her inside, then took his position behind the reins.

"C'mon, Harry, get it moving," Fred urged.

"It went well?" asked Phaedra, who had accompanied her niece, but who had waited outside at Aurelia's insistence.

"I hope so."

"And will the police be discreet?" Phaedra's voice was low against the *clop-clop* of hooves.

"The lieutenant promised he would do his best to keep my name out of the tabloids."

"Thank goodness." Phaedra sat back and relaxed. "We do not need another scandal in this family."

"Aunt Phaedra, you are sounding positively stuffy," Aurelia noted.

"My concern is for you, my darling. I enjoyed shocking people in my youth. I do not think you are of the same temperament."

"No, I think not."

"Though it is very brave of you to risk yourself."

"Any decent person would have done the same," Aurelia argued.

"I only hope Liam appreciates your sacrifice."

"Liam is a stubborn fool."

"But, since he is so much like his father, I'm certain he's worth fighting for," Phaedra said.

"Perhaps. Are you certain you don't want me to come with you to the telegraph office?"

A messenger had tried to deliver a missive from California, but Phaedra hadn't been home, and the boy had had strict instructions that it be left with no one else. Aurelia knew how nervous her aunt was now that she was to have Fernando's answer.

"I think I would prefer facing this alone," Phaedra said. "You'll know the contents soon enough."

And Phaedra and Sean's fate, as well.

Fighting her growing despondency, Aurelia thought of Mariel, with whom she would visit this morning. At least she could brighten her sister's day with the news that she and Fiona were on speaking terms, which made her feel a tiny bit better. In the course of trouble, having family for support lightened the load.

Only after Phaedra dropped her off at the Sheridans' with the promise of returning for her within the hour, did Aurelia's mood change. She'd barely stepped foot in the hallway despite the butler's not-too-subtle hint that this morning might not be the best time for a visit when she heard a crash coming from the music room.

"Wesley, you can't mean to do this."

"Does this look like an idle threat?"

More odd squeaky noises brought Aurelia rushing to see what could possibly be wrong. Upon reaching the music room, the sight before her eyes amazed her. Two burly men in workmen's clothing were wrestling Mariel's piano across the room while Mariel herself was desperately hanging onto it, as if her slight strength was their match.

"You're being childish, Mariel." Wesley's voice was harsh.

"It's *my* piano! My father bought it for me when I was but a girl!"

"Your marrying me gave me the right to do what I would with what you think of as your possessions."

"How dare you!" Aurelia interrupted, stepping in the way of the rolling piano.

"Whoa!" called one of the two men. He planted his feet and said, "Mike, hang on, now."

The piano rolled to a stop barely a foot from Aurelia. And Wesley shouted, "Aurelia Kincaid, what do you think you are about?"

"I'm about to stop this travesty."

"The hell you say!" Wesley was livid, his complexion mottled. "Men, move that piano."

"But sir, the lady —"

"She's no lady. If she resists, run her over!"

"Wesley!" Mariel cried.

But her husband ignored her plea. He spoke to the men, "You heard me. You want your money, move the damnable piano out of this house!"

"Sorry, ma'am," the first man said. "Please take yourself out of the way. Mike."

He signaled his companion and the piano came inching toward Aurelia. She stared past them to Wesley, but he stood firm.

"Aura, please, I don't want to see you hurt," Mariel said, breaking into tears.

Furious at the situation and that Mariel had forsaken her unexpected bravery and had once more caved in to her husband, Aurelia stepped out of the way not a moment too soon.

"And you can go with the piano," Wesley told her.

"Not until I am certain my sister is all right."

"*You* are the reason this is happening!" Wesley pointed an accusing finger at Aurelia. "Until you came back from Italy, Mariel was a well-behaved, obedient wife. You've been a bad influence on her. But no more! I order you to leave this house at once and never to step foot across my threshold again!"

"Aura, I am sorry, but you must do as he says," Mariel choked out through her tears. "We'll talk later, after I straighten out this mess."

"You'll do no such thing." Wesley was triumphant with his power. "I forbid you ever to see or to communicate with your sister until I feel that you are properly repentant for neglecting your duties as my wife."

With that, Mariel pressed her knuckles to her mouth and ran from the room.

Aurelia could hold back no longer. "You, sir, are the most ill-tempered, the most selfish, the most close-minded, the most petty man I have ever had the displeasure to meet. With you for a husband, my sister is cursed."

Aurelia spun on her heel and marched for the door. Wesley was babbling something inane behind her, but she wouldn't give him the satisfaction of stopping to listen. She was outside and starting for home before realizing Phaedra would soon be arriving to collect her. Her aunt would be walking into a snakepit unprepared.

She stopped short. Perhaps she should wait outside the Sheridan residence in the shade of a tree. That way she could catch Phaedra and warn her. The plan appeared sound, and so she took a spot from which she could watch the struggle to get the piano out the side entrance and to the dray that waited. Suddenly she realized there was one thing she *could* do.

Aurelia hurried to the side entrance, checking behind the men to make certain Wesley was not there. "Excuse me." She kept her tone low so her voice would not carry inside. "Is there somewhere in particular you are taking that piano?"

The workman in charge said, "Mr. Sheridan gave us leave to get rid of it anyways we see fit."

"Then I want the piano delivered to my home."

He looked doubtful. "Don't know, ma'am."

"I'll pay a fair price."

That's all it took to make up his mind. Aurelia dug through her purse for the money, glad she had removed the pistol and had tucked it in her garter. Not that she had need for a weapon. The man who'd stalked her seemed to have given up. She found her cache, gave the money and the address to the workers, and ordered them to find the housekeeper when they arrived. Mary would let them bring the piano into Mariel's old music room.

She'd barely returned to her vigil at the front of the house before a carriage drew up, but not the one she was expecting. Theodore Mansfield was at the reins.

"Theo. Why are you in the neighborhood?"

He didn't meet her eyes directly. "Your aunt asked me to come by for you."

Startled, she asked, "Has something happened to her?" Bad news from California?

"No, no. Phaedra is quite all right. She was merely delayed and wanted to make certain you would not be walking home by yourself."

"Oh, bother." But if she took the ride, Aurelia realized, she would beat the dray home and could supervise the moving in of the piano herself. "All right. Thank you."

Theo helped her up into the carriage, and because she'd forgotten her gloves that morning, the clamminess of his hand bothered her. As he took the front seat, she surreptitiously wiped her palm on her skirt.

The carriage moved out and Aurelia thought about the irony of Fiona's being the happiest of the Kincaid women. Mariel's life was certainly a disaster, and she and her aunt were both in questionable situations.

If only she could think of a way to undo the last

two days, Aurelia was certain she and Liam would be happy together. Not normally given to violence, she nearly felt angry enough to shoot whomever had led Liam to believe she was attached to DeWitt Carlton. And while Phaedra and Sean were in the renewed throes of love, she only hoped the telegram from California held the news Phaedra dreamed of.

Aurelia was so immersed in her troubled thoughts that it took a while for her to realize that they were going at a crisp pace south down Grand Boulevard.

"Where are you taking me?"

"To my home. I have something of utmost importance to show you."

"This is not the time —"

"Yes, it must be now," he said firmly. "It has to do with the society's project. I have a special costume for you to wear. Phaedra will take a look at it, too. She'll be joining us shortly."

Her aunt was coming to Theo's house? Aurelia felt a bit confused, but they were halfway to the man's mansion already. "All right, but my aunt didn't tell me anything about this."

"We arranged it when I just saw her. She agreed that it's very important."

Important? After the murder and turmoil of late? But Aurelia had so much on her mind already, she put aside her doubts. She'd do as Theo asked, get it over with, then leave as soon as Phaedra could be coaxed to do so. She only prayed her aunt would have good news about California.

Little more than a half hour later, Aurelia stared at her mirrored reflection in the bedroom where she had changed. Theo had insisted she try on the new costume to be certain it didn't need alteration. The pale yellow linen shift fit so perfectly she might have been embarrassed if unaccompanied by the overlaying turquoise and carnelian cape whose trim was shot with real gold. That garment and the elaborate headpiece decorated with a hooded cobra made her feel as if she had stepped out of some ancient kingdom.

A tentative knock at the door made her start and pull the cape tightly around her person.

"Aurelia?" Theo called softly. "May I take a look?"

Though uneasy, Aurelia opened the door. Theo stared at her openmouthed before saying, "Perfect. Yes, yes, I knew you would be!"

The way he was staring at her gave her the shivers. Before her eyes a subtle change took place in his normally unobtrusive demeanor. He seemed to grow without getting any taller, to take on a mantle of boldness she'd never before seen.

Or had she?

"You are truly a queen among queens. But the outfit is not quite complete. Perhaps Phaedra told you I am a collector of antiquities?"

"I believe she mentioned it," Aurelia said, trying to concentrate on an image that eluded her.

"I have a scarab and a few other pieces that would do you justice and enhance the authenticity." He turned abruptly and ordered, "Follow me."

"I'll change into my clothing while you get the jewelry."

"No, no, you *must* come with me!" he insisted, facing her once more. "I want you to see all my treasures."

In that instant, looking into his eyes that burned with

deep-seated flames, she suddenly knew. The way he was standing, the set of his shoulders. Why, he was the man from Oak Park . . . the man who had watched her from the yard . . . and perhaps even more!

Shocked to her core, she cautiously followed him into his study. But as he fiddled with a panel next to the fireplace, she looked around. Nothing out of the ordinary.

"Where do you keep this collection?" she asked, her pulse threading unevenly.

In answer, the panel creaked open. "Not where a thief could find it, of course. Come."

He indicated she should precede him. Heart beating far too rapidly, Aurelia took a tentative step forward and noted that the short passageway was lit with hanging lanterns. Theo was staring at her in a manner that made the hair on the back of her neck bristle.

Everything came together for her then. If she told anyone, they would think her crazy. But if she had proof . . .

Her breath grew short and she began perspiring under the light cape. Could she go through with this? She was alone in the task. She no longer believed that Phaedra was coming. Theo was lying.

But she could do anything she had to, Aurelia told herself, certain she could learn the truth and still keep herself safe.

Reassuring herself with the fact that she was still armed, Aurelia stepped into the tunnel.

19

Liam hadn't expected Aurelia to clear him. Last night he'd assumed she would let him stew in his own juices to protect her relationship with Carlton. He'd been wrong. Terribly wrong. Mounting his chestnut Coppermine, he left the station house where he'd had another interview with Lieutenant Frigo and turned toward Prairie Avenue.

He had to see her.

What if he'd been wrong about other things, as well? What if Aurelia hadn't meant to marry Carlton at all? If so, he'd been an utter and complete fool!

Would Aurelia ever forgive him?

He was determined to find out.

But the fates were against him. She was not at home, and, going to Mariel's as directed by the housekeeper, he learned from the Sheridans' butler that Aurelia was no longer there either. He cursed with frustration.

What now?

As he untethered his horse, a dray loaded with a grand piano was just leaving the property. The driver stopped the wagon. "I overheard you say you was looking for Miss Kincaid. She left a while ago with a gentleman."

Fearing that perhaps he hadn't been altogether wrong, Liam had to know. "A young man with blond hair?"

"Hair was silvery. An older gentleman, one who looks like he's used to the cushy life. Said he was taking her home."

Mansfield. Strangely uneasy at the knowledge, Liam frowned. "Thank you. I must have just missed them." He flipped the man a Liberty quarter for his trouble.

No sooner had he remounted to return to the Prairie Avenue house, then he saw Phaedra's carriage approaching. Though he was anxious to be after Aurelia, he thought it in his best interests to be polite to her aunt, who was waving him over. He pulled up next to the carriage.

"Liam!" Phaedra gave him an intent look. "Have you seen Aurelia, then?"

"Would that I had. She'd left with Mansfield by the time I arrived."

"Theo? You say Theo took her?"

Liam sensed her immediate agitation and his own unease returned twofold. "What's wrong?"

Phaedra was visibly distressed. "I hate to speculate . . ."

"Please, tell me."

"I have some terrible suspicions. You know someone has been following Aurelia. I've noticed Theo seems . . . well, very enamored of her."

Liam remembered Mansfield's expression the night

before, when it had been pinned to aunt and niece. Then he'd thought the fascination had been for Phaedra.

"I'm not certain a man's having an affection for a woman is a reason to suspect him of wrongdoing, however," he said.

"Last night after the meeting ended, I separately asked both Dr. Rossiter and Dr. Cunningham which of them painted the coffin face that looked like Aurelia. Both men told me it was Theo. And Theo seemed upset when he overheard Aurelia say she was going to clear your name with the police." Phaedra took a deep breath. "Liam, I've been thinking . . . Theo is the only member of the society who knows our house well. What if he had found an opportunity to sneak in to the parlor and abscond with your stud?"

A sick feeling filled Liam. He'd been mulling over the murder, considering who could be acquainted with the specifics of mummification. Not too many people outside of the society. Mansfield understood the procedure in theory. Perhaps somewhere he had learned the practice.

"Liam, please go to Theo's. I have no doubt he's taken her there. Make certain that my darling Aurelia is safe while I go for reinforcements."

Liam needed no urging. "I would give my life for Aurelia," he declared, digging his heels into Coppermine's side.

Though if Mansfield had harmed one hair on his beloved's head, it would be Mansfield who would die.

He was very thorough, she would see that now. He was glad the pretense was nearly over. They reached the secret room at the other end of the tunnel where a table groaned under the weight of a veritable feast and the promised jewelry.

Theo immediately handed Aurelia a chalice and took one for himself. "A toast to authenticity." He looked around. "And to the gods who make it all possible."

Giving him a tentative smile, Aurelia put the cup to her lips for a moment. "The wine is so . . . unusual."

A tiny line marred the perfection of her brow as if something worried her. No more. No worries. No new lines to mar her beauty. He would say so, but not just yet.

"Yes, the scarab will be perfect." He lifted it reverently. "Allow me."

Aurelia seemed uncomfortable moving the mass of dark hair out of the way. Theo couldn't help himself. After the clasp caught, he allowed his fingers to linger on her neck just a moment longer than was necessary. She jumped and pulled away, began moving around the room, boldly inspecting the gods who watched her from their niches.

"You are to sit," he protested, afraid they might take offense. "And partake of the feast."

"I am not hungry."

She stopped at the screen dividing the room and, before he could protest, moved it aside, demanding, "What in the world is this?"

Growing petulant, he said, "A sarcophagus. But you were not to see it yet!"

Though what would it hurt to show Aurelia, while she could still appreciate it? For she would never leave this room. Before sundown, he would move the orphan to some makeshift operation and Aurelia would be ripening for his collection. Besides, he'd waited so long to share his expertise with one who would truly appreciate it. He'd despised the lurid headlines and stories in the tabloids, every one. None of them had given him proper credit.

"I shall show you my newest treasure if you like."

Eyes wide, she nodded.

He drew closer to Aurelia and the familiar scent of fear assaulted his nostrils, adding to his sense of power. He turned the crank, his anticipation multiplying with each squeak.

"You won't recognize her now," he said as the lid lifted enough for her to look inside. "But I'm certain you've been wondering what happened to your sister's maid."

"Gina?" Aurelia gasped, swaying and appearing sick.

Plus, she sounded more horrified than awed. Theo was disappointed. He wanted appreciation now. He would savor the rest later.

"Soon the little orphan will join the others," he told her, taking a lantern and circling the area of the back wall to show her. More than a half dozen of his larger niches were filled with coffins very like the ones the members of the society had built for the temple.

"You killed them all?" she shrilled, her dark eyes blazing accusingly.

Suddenly he felt her fury and he took a step back. Didn't she understand? All of this honored her, his queen. Why, then, did she look so angry, making sweat trickle down the back of his neck?

"I gave them the gift of eternal life, as I will do for you," he promised.

If she weren't already eternal, he thought, his mind growing more muddled. For at the moment, seeing the furious face, dark hair streaming out like dozens of cobras, he could imagine an avenging goddess coming after him.

But no, he reassured himself, she was no avenger. He hadn't done anything wrong. Had he?

Nervously, he went on with his explanation. "Do not worry about suffering. The asp will ensure you won't feel the cut of the knife or the removal of your organs."

She wavered and appeared faint, making him feel much better. More in control.

"The mummy you planted on the midway," she gasped. "Why did you do it?"

"To display my depth of knowledge. I hoped you especially would see her. Equally important, I had to get rid of O'Rourke before he could soil you any further."

"You planted the shirt stud, then," she choked out. "Where did you get it?"

"From your very own parlor. You neglected to bolt the kitchen door. You shouldn't have been doing such distasteful things with him, Aurelia," he chided her. "You are already aging, you know."

"You were watching?" Aurelia seemed to have trouble breathing, but then recovered enough to ask, "And how did you have the skill to do the actual mummification? You're no physician."

"I learned more than art appreciation in Italy. My course studies also included anatomy and dissection."

"But . . . why?"

"To preserve beauty forever—what else? In my youth, I was almost destroyed by my young cousin's death. I loved Lucinda, but she grew ugly with the pox, you see. Of course a gentlewoman like yourself wouldn't know of the disease spread by indiscriminate mating. Disease that mutilates the soul as well as the body."

"You're the one with the diseased soul!" she accused.

He grew furious that she still didn't seem to understand.

Possessed by memories, he went on, seeing Lucinda in his mind's eye. "I once tried mating with Lucinda when I grew to manhood." He sighed. "I was unable to perform and Lucinda laughed at me. I wished then that she would die, and within the year she did. Then I realized I was powerful, not weak. Fondling her corpse and finally spilling my seed on her cold form was the most exciting and rewarding moment in my life." He paused a moment before adding, "Until now."

Suddenly Theo realized Aurelia was no longer standing next to the sarcophagus. She was inching away from it, and from him. This would never do.

As quickly as a cobra, she bolted for the tunnel entrance. He was quicker, catching and enveloping her in his arms. She was a bit unsteady and confusion clouded her gaze. Good, the drug was finally working.

"I was drawn to you because of your dark Mediterranean beauty," he whispered in her ear, as he gingerly helped himself to the fullness of one breast. "You are as fine as the others were coarse. You are an Egyptian queen, while they are but your handmaidens."

"They were human beings!"

"They were common, worth nothing."

She was struggling and he was having trouble keeping hold of her, no matter his strength. He thought to gentle her with ancient verse.

"'The land of the dead beckons on the horizon./ My love makes an offering, her chalice of fruit for the god with the shining face—"

"Theo, you don't really want to do this."

"But I do, oh, how I do." He pressed himself into her bottom so she could feel his erection and know how excited he was. When he became nauseated, however, he quickly drew away. It would be so much more enjoyable later when she was cool and quiet and still. "You will be the centerpiece of my collection. A feast rather than a mere offering for my gods."

"No!" Aurelia shouted, almost breaking free.

But he had her wrist, and before he could think, he struck her across the face. She fell to the floor, finally trembling and doubling over as if trying to protect her body from his.

"Now see what you've made me do!" He, too, was trembling with anger and desire. "You've spoiled it. All I wanted was to stop the torment and to appreciate your beauty forever. Now there will be a mark to mar your lovely face . . . unless I act quickly." Looking around for his tools, he mumbled to himself. "Perhaps I can prevent the bruise from starting."

"And perhaps I will prevent you from ever doing this to another woman again." Aurelia fumbled with the skirt of her shift and unsteadily rose to her feet, arm outstretched, a glint of metal in her hand.

A weapon!

Mesmerized, Theo stepped back, suddenly certain the deities were angry and had sent an avenging goddess after all.

Liam was frantic when no one answered the door. Where the hell was the butler? Mansfield had to be here. The carriage stood in the drive, the harnessed horse still warm and damp with its exertion, so Aurelia must be inside.

Liam circled the house until he found an open window. Launching himself inside, he searched the ground floor quickly though he found no one about.

He almost passed the bedroom on the first floor without actually going in, then stopped and gave it a more thorough look. Articles of women's clothing lay neatly folded across the bed. They belonged to Aurelia, he was certain. Dear God, what had Mansfield done with her?

"Aurelia!" he shouted, but no response came to comfort him.

He took the stairs two at a time, searched the second floor and the attic rooms, but she was nowhere to be found. The place was completely empty.

Then he remembered talk of secret rooms and tunnels that led to them.

Aurelia knew she shouldn't have so much as sipped at the wine. She'd suspected it was drugged as soon as she took the first swallow and had pretended to drink more to fool Theo. Now she was certain. Even that small taste of the stuff left her knees weak and her head muzzy. The pistol in her grip shook.

"I knew you were special!" Theo hissed, coming closer. "A goddess, not a queen!"

His eyes burned with more than desire. He was insane and out of control.

"Stay right there," Aurelia ordered weakly, wondering what to do now.

She had to act fast, but the drugs slowed her mind. When he lunged for her, she told herself to pull the trigger, but as she'd feared, she was having trouble making herself do so. And then it was too late to act. He wrenched her wrist and the gun went spinning out of her hand in the direction of the sarcophagus.

At the same time, the tunnel door flew open and a man's voice grated, "Unhand her, Mansfield!"

"Liam!" she cried, never so grateful to see anyone in her entire life.

Theo didn't bother to hide his fury at the intrusion. "You! How did you get in here?"

Liam ignored him as he flew forward, muscles bunching beneath the fine linen of his white shirt.

Theo pushed Aurelia to the side and rushed to the table where he picked up a heavy candelabra. While Liam was normally the more powerful of the men, Aurelia knew Theo was caught up in the throes of madness, and, as such, had untested strength and an unnatural lack of fear. Liam's gaze was focused on the weapon in Theo's hand as the two men faced off and danced in a circle whose diameter diminished with every step.

Liam got in a punch that made Theo stagger, but the crazed man then swung and let go of the heavy candelabra, which grazed Liam in the forehead and sent him shooting into the table. While Liam was trying to recover from the blow, Theo rushed to a nearby column stand where he picked up what Aurelia assumed was a surgeon's knife. The blade was thin and honed, its fine edge glinting even in the low light.

"My God, Liam, he's got a knife!" Aurelia screamed.

Even so, a weakened Liam lunged for the crazed man, then jumped back when Theo arced the deadly blade near his face.

Dear God, what if Theo killed Liam?

Without considering whether or not she was actually capable of using the pistol this time, Aurelia forced her still woozy mind to steady for a moment. She went in search of the weapon while the men continued to test each other. She *would* use it for Liam. She wouldn't think of Theo as a human being. He wasn't human. He was an animal who vilified women. Now he was threatening not only her life, but that of the man she loved.

A loud *crack* made her turn to see Theo reeling. Liam had hit him again, but still the lunatic held on to the deadly weapon.

"Give up, Mansfield!" Liam ordered. "And promise not to hurt you."

Theo shook his head to clear it. "But I do not make the same promise." His expression grew cunning.

Aurelia picked up the gun.

The pistol felt heavy. The carved hawk's head bit into her palm as she raised and grasped it with both hands the way Bill Cody had taught her. She willed to steady, willed her eyes to focus.

"Theo, stop this madness right now or I sha

shoot!" she yelled, trying to look straight down
the sight. For a moment there seemed to be two of
him.

But either the madman didn't hear or he was
beyond caring, for his upraised weapon was slashing
down toward Liam's chest, a glinting portent of
death. Liam lunged even as Aurelia squeezed, the
pistol firing at the exact moment Liam grabbed Theo,
therefore putting himself in the bullet's path. His
body jerked and bright red blood flared across the
back of his shirt.

"Liam!" Aurelia screamed, horrified at what she
had done.

He slumped to the floor and Theo turned in triumph.
"I knew you would not desert me, not after all I have
done for you! For your love!"

Aurelia wanted to run to Liam, to stanch the life's
blood that even now was draining out of him, but
Theo was approaching her, surgeon's tool in hand.
She had to end this travesty quickly, before Liam
died.

Backing up, she fumbled under her linen shift for
another bullet, almost tripping on the edge of the
cape as she secured the metal bit from her garter.
"Stay away from me!"

"I cannot. You, dear goddess, are my destiny."

She was circling the sarcophagus as she broke
open the gun, popped out the used shell and inserted
the fresh bullet with shaking hands. "A destiny I fear
will not be to your liking."

"Ah, but there you are wrong. I shall enjoy every
moment."

In that instant, Aurelia realized Theo had backed

her into a corner, no way out but past him. *If* her trembling legs would even obey her. She raised the gun once more. "Don't come any closer."

When he ignored her warning, she clenched her teeth and squeezed again.

His shoulder jerked and blood splashed through his fingers as his hand came up to cradle the wounded area. "Ah, lightning from the hand of Isis herself!" He licked his lips and a strange glimmer entered his eyes. "I find myself stimulated beyond my wildest imagination."

He was raving. Unstoppable. For she had no more bullets to use.

Aurelia glanced around searching for another weapon. Other than the statues in their niches, there was only a basket on the floor. She snatched it up and almost jumped when it seemed to jerk from within.

"I exalt the Lady of Heaven!" Theo intoned, holding out a bloody hand as he took a step forward toward her.

"Aurelia!"

Distracted for a second, she looked toward Liam. He was staggering to his feet! Suddenly she realized how close Theo was! Aurelia heaved the basket at his chest with all the force she could muster. The lid flew off and faster than anything she had ever seen, a hooded snake popped up and struck him in the neck. Holding onto the writhing reptile with both hands, Theo faltered, the backs of his knees hitting the edge of the sarcophagus.

"Oh, golden goddess, give me . . . peace." He caved over with a gasp, his flaccid body tumbling atop the remains of what had once been a beautiful, young woman named Gina.

Aurelia didn't stop to see if he were dead or not as she whipped by him to reach Liam who was on his feet now, his shirt front as bloody as the back.

"My God, Liam, I am so sorry. I almost killed you."

But his concern was for her. "Are *you* all right?"

"I shall be, once the drug he gave me is gone."

"You're quite a woman, but I believe I've told you that before."

Aurelia hugged his good side. Still, he muffled a grunt. She loosened her grip, looked back to the sarcophagus.

"How could anyone be so . . . sick?" she whispered, the horror of what Theo had intended for her finally penetrating to her very soul.

"I don't know if there is an explanation for someone like Mansfield." Liam surveyed the room thoroughly, his gaze eventually falling on the coffins lined against the wall. "Those aren't what I think they are?"

"He killed them all," she said in a deliberately controlled voice. She felt like weeping for the victims, but if she began, she feared she would never stop. "Poor, defenseless young things. How could they have been forewarned when no one ever speaks of monsters disguised as human beings?"

A slithering sound made her freeze.

"The cobra," Liam said. "Come. Let's get to safety."

Aurelia caught the movement as the snake slid over the side of the sarcophagus. Liam pulled her close, and together they stumbled into the tunnel and through another door she hadn't noticed earlier. Steps that seemed to move took them up into the carriage house where they were assaulted by a cacophony of approaching sounds.

Horses hooves.

Men's voices.

And was that a war whoop?

Balancing herself against Liam's weight, Aurelia stumbled outside to an amazing sight. Charging down Grand Boulevard were a dozen or so roughriders from the Wild West Exhibition, Buffalo Bill Cody in front. His long hair streamed in the wind. Annie Oakley flanked him on one side and a whooping Indian with a warbonnet on the other. They were followed by several badly suited men on nags and a familiar carriage.

Startled local citizens moved their mounts out of the way or scurried into their houses. Aurelia could see dozens if not hundreds of people peering out of the surrounding windows as Cody reined in his mount merely yards away from where Aurelia and Liam stood.

"Appears my posse arrived in the nick of time." Cody waved back toward the others who followed close behind. "Boys, over here!" He indicated Liam, who was soaked with blood. "This man needs doctoring."

Two men dragged Liam away from Aurelia, who then swayed on her feet. She breathed more easily when Annie followed and she realized they would tend to Liam's wounds.

"Are you all right?" Cody asked, slipping an arm around her. "What happened to Mansfield? If he has dared to harm even one hair on your head, I'll shoot him down like a dog!"

Aurelia leaned against Cody gratefully. "I already shot him," she ground out, her vision going fuzzy for a moment. "I-I killed him." That fact was still sinking in.

The men in plaid suits crowded around the famous man. One of them asked, "Hey, Cody, you gonna tell us what's going on?"

Cody did a theatrical sweep with his free arm. "Boys, I want you to meet a real live heroine. Good thing I taught her to shoot."

Through the muzziness that kept threatening her, Aurelia realized the "boys" were reporters and Cody was in his Buffalo Bill mode, ready for some tall tales that would get his name in the tabloids.

Questions assaulted her.

"How many of them were there?"

"Where did you get that wild costume?"

"How did your friend get shot?"

Suddenly it was all too much for her. She'd been fighting for what seemed like an eternity. She didn't have any fight left in her.

Thankful when she saw Phaedra's dear face, she gladly let go, and for the first time in her life, fainted.

20

HEROINE UNEARTHS MORE MUMMIES
PRICELESS ARTIFACTS FOUND IN
SOUTHSIDE TOMB

Phaedra stared in disgust at the caricature
of Aurelia dressed in the Egyptian costume and
holding a smoking gun that had made the front page
of the Sunday *Chicago Times*. It had been two whole
days after the horrible incident that ended with Theo
Mansfield's death. "Will the tabloids never tire of
printing these lurid stories?"

"Not if they're wanting to turn a profit," Sean said
practically.

Phaedra threw down the paper, unwilling to let it
spoil their day. The sounds of a carriage and team
announced an expected arrival.

"They're here!" She flew to the stairs. "Aurelia!"

"Coming."

As Phaedra went to signal Fred and Mary so the

couple would join them as previously instructed, Sean grumbled, "Where's that son of mine? I told him to be here at noon sharp."

"Now, Sean, be patient with the boy." Phaedra affectionately smoothed the hair from his brow. "He was, after all, severely wounded."

"A mere flesh wound . . . inflicted by your niece."

But Sean was grinning and Phaedra knew he saw the irony in the situation. They were equally relieved that both young people had escaped the fates that Theo had planned for them.

"Women in love do desperate deeds," she warned him with a fleeting kiss. "You would best remember that."

She slipped out of his intended grasp for they had no more time to dally or to ruminate on the situation. The bell was ringing. A glance out the parlor window told her Fiona, Upton, Mariel, and their assorted children were at the door.

"I've got it," Mary said, rushing into the kitchen and through the house with uncustomary speed. "I'm not too old to answer doors yet."

Phaedra was glad to let the housekeeper do so. She was finding it difficult to breathe normally. "I'm so nervous."

Coming up behind her, Sean gave her a reassuring squeeze and then stared out the window, no doubt in vigil for Liam. Phaedra was too distracted by the arrival of her family to worry about it. She hugged each of the little ones as they rushed through the door.

Mariel kissed her cheek. "Aunt, you are looking well."

"You also, my darling."

Actually, Mariel's cheeks were as flushed as her pink afternoon dress trimmed with crisscrossing lace. She did not at all resemble the stricken, beaten-down wife Aurelia had described.

Fiona peeled off her gloves and removed her plumed hat. "I expect your calling us all together like this is of some import. I certainly hope so since I cancelled a very important social—"

"Fiona," growled Upton. "Hush."

Her eldest niece blinked at her husband, mouth agape, then agreeably said, "Yes, dear."

"I rather think this must have something to do with our heroine," Mariel said, staring at Aurelia, who was just coming down the stairs.

Looking lovely in a mauve-and-yellow striped dress that Phaedra had bought for her, Aurelia paused to glance over her shoulder as if looking for this esteemed person.

"I think your sister was speaking of you, darling," Phaedra whispered theatrically.

"I am no heroine."

Phaedra knew Aurelia wasn't feeling settled about the matter. Being responsible for Theo's death would undoubtedly bother her for a very long time.

"What you did took incredible courage," Mariel told her. "Even the tabloids said so."

"I want to thank you personally for being so brave to bring a murderer to justice," Fiona added, her eyes looking suspiciously watery. "Nothing will bring back Gina, but at least the horrid man can't hurt another young woman ever again."

"Of that I am glad," Aurelia said.

Then, still on the lookout, Sean practically shouted, "That son of mine has finally arrived!"

Aurelia rushed to the window and peered out. "Should Liam really be riding Coppermine rather than taking the carriage?"

"Liam is an O'Rourke," Sean said, as if that explained everything.

Phaedra's stomach began to flutter. The time was at hand. "Mary, why don't you bring the children to the sun porch and give them some of your lemonade and orange sponge cake."

"Yes, of course. Children?"

With the promise of the treat, the little ones were herded out of the room easily.

"And hurry," Phaedra called after the housekeeper. "We won't begin without you."

Liam's entrance caused quite a stir. His forehead was bruised and he held his shoulder awkwardly, from the bandages as well as the soreness of the wound itself, Phaedra surmised. Luckily, Aurelia's bullet had gone straight through the flesh below his shoulder without attacking any vital organs.

"Here's our hero," Fiona announced, giving Aurelia a sly look.

Phaedra glanced over to her youngest niece to see what Aurelia would do. She remained standing as if frozen near the window. She was too pale by far. A question filled her eyes, one Phaedra knew only Liam could answer. The young lovers hadn't had a chance to be alone since their nightmare ended. From the way Liam was staring at her niece, Phaedra surmised that the question would not go unanswered for long.

Sean moved to Phaedra's side, and as Mary reentered the room, wiping her plump hands on her apron, he cleared his throat loudly to get everyone's attention. "We have called you here because we're to be making an announcement," he began.

Unable to wait a second longer lest she faint as Aurelia had, Phaedra blurted, "We're to be married."

Fiona couldn't disguise her shock. "You intend to commit bigamy?"

"You'll not be speaking to my wife in such a disrespectful tone," Sean admonished her.

Phaedra placed a soothing hand on his chest. "She has every right to be concerned, darling. That is, she thinks she has." As had every other person in the room but Aurelia, who knew the contents of the telegram from California. "I am pleased to announce that I am no longer married and have not been for more than twelve years."

"What?" Mariel cried. "You mean Fernando divorced you and didn't bother to contact you to let you know?"

"Divorce didn't end our marriage," Phaedra explained. "Death did. I am a widow."

"But not for long," Sean announced. "I plan on making an honest woman of her, next Saturday to be exact. And you'll all be coming to our wedding."

It wasn't an invitation, but an order, one Phaedra knew her darling nieces wouldn't dare refuse. "Mary, Fred, the champagne, please."

Phaedra was near bursting with emotion. Only one thing could add to her happiness at the moment.

If only Aurelia and Liam would admit that they, too, were destined for each other.

* * *

Aware of Liam's every move across the room, Aurelia sipped at her champagne, unbegrudging of her aunt's happiness no matter how much she wished it had been Liam claiming her. Still wondering how they had let things get so impossible between them, she stayed out of his orbit. She had no intentions of ruining Phaedra and Sean's shining moment by exchanging what could easily become angry words with Liam.

"Aura, are you quite all right?" Mariel startled her out of the reverie.

"Quite."

"I'm sure it will take some time to get over what happened to you. If you need someone to talk to—"

"You forget you've been forbidden to speak to me at all."

Mariel heaved a sigh. "You do not know that I have taken the children and moved in with Fiona."

"What? When?"

"Yesterday. Trouble has been escalating between Wesley and me. It started *before* you returned from Italy," Mariel assured her. "While Wesley has always been demanding, he has been rational in the past. All the attention my music began getting stirred up his insecurities. Having my piano removed, ordering me not to see *you* . . . well!"

"But, Mariel, are you certain you want to leave Wesley?"

"Until he comes to his senses."

Fiona joined them. "He will. He's already been to see her twice since Friday."

"Yesterday, he demanded my return. This morning he begged it, promising to find my piano and bring it home."

Aurelia laughed for the first time in days. "That part is easy enough. Your piano is here, in your old music room. I couldn't let those workmen dispose of it."

Mariel gave her an excited hug. "Oh, Aura, how can I ever thank you?"

"By being happy, whatever that takes."

"I have hopes that Wesley and I will work things out. This morning I told him that I've already contacted Albert Drury and committed myself to one guest appearance with the orchestra. That's all I ever really wanted, one single shining moment. Wesley sputtered a bit, made some vague threats about breaking Mr. Drury's neck, then promised to hold off doing anything until he was in a more rational state."

"I hope Wesley does come around for your sake," Aurelia said with sincerity and pride in her sister. How far Mariel had progressed in standing up for herself. The very thought gave Aurelia hope that anything was possible.

She also realized more than ever that relationships between men and women would always be difficult, but also that some women like her sister Fiona were perfectly content within the status quo. It wasn't up to her to say what kind of a life a woman should choose for herself, much as she hoped that the future would allow them a broad range of choices. If her sisters had been judgmental of her, she had been equally so of them.

"And in the meantime," Fiona was saying, "it

would be appropriate for you to play to celebrate Aunt Phaedra's engagement, don't you think?"

Mariel agreed, so the party reconvened to the music room, with Aurelia being the last to follow. As she stepped through the parlor door, however, she came face to face with Liam, who blocked her way.

"I was hoping to talk to you alone."

Aurelia's pulse raced. Gaze glued to his poor, bruised forehead, she backed up. "The parlor *is* free."

"And holds some of my fondest memories."

Hers as well, not that she was ready to admit it. She set down the champagne glass she was still carrying and moved to the sofa. Rather than sitting, however, she circled its length and clung to the wooden peak at its back with all her strength.

"What did you want to talk about?"

"Have you signed on with Frank Lloyd Wright yet?"

Aurelia stared at him as if he were mad. All that had happened to and between them and that was uppermost in his mind? "Not yet," she said stiffly, more disappointed than she could have imagined. Actually, she hadn't given the threat another thought since walking out of the O'Rourke and O'Rourke offices.

"Then will you reconsider your position?"

"You mean my resignation?" she clarified.

"Among other things."

Her pulse skittered with hope. "What other things?"

"Us. Our relationship. Can you ever forgive me for being so . . ."

"Hotheaded?" she supplied for him, her pulse picking up in rapidity.

"Yes."

"Uncompromising," she added.

He was looking decidedly uncomfortable now. "That, too."

"Wrong!"

"Go ahead, make this as difficult as you wish." Liam frowned, though Aurelia could tell the expression was reserved for himself. "I deserve every terrible name you can think of to have believed one word Theodore Mansfield told me."

She shoved away the horror the very name conjured. "Theo said that DeWitt and—"

"Mansfield said that you were to marry, and believed DeWitt was the, uh, other man in your life. And if there's a bigger fool alive than I, you'll have to point him out to me."

Guilt nagged at Aurelia. She couldn't let him take all the blame for the situation. "It's not only your fault, Liam. If I had told you the truth to begin with, you would not have believed Theo so easily."

"Can't we put that behind us now? Start over?"

"No." He looked crestfallen until she qualified her statement. "Not until I tell you everything: why I came back from Italy in the first place." Now she would finally tell him about Rosario.

"If it has to do with a man, I don't need to know the details," Liam insisted. "You owe me no explanations for your past infatuations any more than I do for mine, though one day when we have time, I would like you to know why I was so quick to think the worst of you from the beginning. I was used by one society belle, slighted for my humble origins by others."

"Then they were very stupid women." Aurelia

went on to ask anxiously, "Are you sure you don't want to know about my past?"

"I only want to know that you love me desperately, that you have eyes for no other man than me, and, pray God, that you are willing to at least consider marriage."

His speech took her breath away. She choked out, "Liam O'Rourke, are you proposing to me?"

"That I am."

She whirled around the couch and threw herself against him, ignoring his wince at contact. "I accept."

Happiness shone from his eyes for the moment she could still see them. Then he was claiming her mouth as indelibly as he had already claimed her soul, and her lids fluttered shut as she floated on a promise for the future. As far as Aurelia was concerned, Liam ended the embrace far too quickly.

"So, will you come back to work for me or not?"

"You aren't just marrying me so that you get to keep the best new architect Chicago has seen in your firm?" she asked with mock suspicion.

"You haven't just accepted because you think you'll take over O'Rourke and O'Rourke?" he returned.

"Only one O'Rourke," she promised, kissing him. "And, hopefully, that O'Rourke will want to take me traveling into the desert or mountains sometime."

"An archeological trip?"

Aurelia nodded enthusiastically.

His smile was joyful. "I would be more than delighted."

Aurelia knew that never again would she feel like the common little blackbird after which Mama had named her. She was beautiful in

Liam's eyes and satisfied in her own heart. Fearing
no net or trap, Liam beside her, she could fly high.
Together, they would cherish the wonders of life and
explore the future.

> *Even when the birds rise,*
> *wave upon wave in great flight,*
> *I see nothing but you.*
> *Caught up as I am,*
> *two hearts beating,*
> *My life is joined with yours.*
> *Your love is the binding.*
> —Anonymous
> Egypt, 1200 B.C.

AVAILABLE NOW

ONE GOOD MAN by Terri Herrington

From the author of *Her Father's Daughter*, comes a dramatic story of a woman who sets out to seduce and ruin the one good man she's ever found. Jilted and desperate for money, Clea Sands lets herself be bought by a woman who wants grounds to sue her wealthy husband for adultery. But when Clea falls in love with him, she realizes she can't possibly destroy his life—not for any price.

PRETTY BIRDS OF PASSAGE by Roslynn Griffith

Beautiful Aurelia Kincaid returned to Chicago from Italy nursing a broken heart, and ready to embark on a new career. Soon danger stalked Aurelia at every turn when a vicious murderer, mesmerized by her striking looks, decided she was his next victim—and he would preserve her beauty forever. As the threads of horror tightened, Aurelia reached out for the safety of one man's arms. But had she unwittingly fallen into the murderer's trap? A historical romance filled with intrigue and murder.

FAN THE FLAME by Suzanne Elizabeth

The romantic adventures of a feisty heroine who met her match in a fearless lawman. When Marshal Max Barrett arrived at the Washington Territory ranch to escort Samantha James to her aunt's house in Utah, little did he know what he was getting himself into.

A BED OF SPICES by Barbara Samuel

Set in Europe in 1348, a moving story of star-crossed lovers determined to let nothing come between them. "With her unique and lyrical style, Barbara Samuel touches every emotion. The quiet brilliance of her story lingered in my mind long after the book was closed."—Susan Wiggs, author of *The Mist and the Magic*.

THE WEDDING by Elizabeth Bevarly

A delightful and humorous romance in the tradition of the movie *Father of the Bride*. Emma Hammelmann and Taylor Rowan are getting married. But before wedding bells ring, Emma must confront not only the inevitable clash of their families but her own second thoughts—especially when she discovers that Taylor's best man is in love with her.

SWEET AMITY'S FIRE by Lee Scofield

The wonderful, heartwarming story of a mail-order bride and the husband who didn't order her. "Lee Scofield makes a delightful debut with this winning tale . . . *Sweet Amity's Fire* is sweet indeed."—Mary Jo Putney, bestselling author of *Thunder and Roses*.

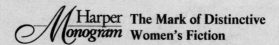

*M*Harper **The Mark of Distinctive**
Monogram **Women's Fiction**

COMING NEXT MONTH

LORD OF THE NIGHT by Susan Wiggs

Much loved historical romance author Susan Wiggs turns to the rich, sensual atmosphere of sixteenth-century Venice for another enthralling, unforgettable romance. "Susan Wiggs is truly magical."—Laura Kinsale, bestselling author of *Flowers from the Storm*.

CHOICES by Marie Ferrarella

The compelling story of a woman from a powerful political family who courageously gives up a loveless marriage and pursues her own dreams, finding romance, heartbreak, and difficult choices along the way.

THE SECRET by Penelope Thomas

A long-buried secret overshadowed the love of an innocent governess and her master. Left with no family, Jessamy Lane agreed to move into Lord Wolfeburne's house and care for his young daughter. But when Jessamy suspected something sinister in his past, whom could she trust?

WILDCAT by Sharon Ihle

A fiery romance that brings the Old West back to life. When prim and proper Ann Marie Cannary went in search of her sister, Martha Jane, what she found instead was a hellion known as "Calamity Jane." Annie was powerless to change her sister's rough ways, but the small Dakota town of Deadwood changed Annie as she adapted to life in the Wild West and fell in love with a man who was full of surprises.

MURPHY'S RAINBOW by Carolyn Lampman

While traveling on the Oregon Trail, newly widowed Kate Murphy found herself stranded in a tiny town in Wyoming Territory. Handsome, enigmatic Jonathan Cantrell needed a housekeeper and nanny for his two sons. But living together in a small cabin on an isolated ranch soon became too close for comfort . . . and falling in love grew difficult to resist. Book I of the Cheyenne Trilogy.

TAME THE WIND by Katherine Kilgore

A sizzling story of forbidden love between a young Cherokee man and a Southern belle in antebellum Georgia. "Katherine Kilgore's passionate lovers and the struggles of the Cherokee nation are spellbinding. Pure enjoyment!"—Katherine Deauxville, bestselling author of *Daggers of Gold*.

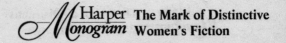